THE ICE STAR

By CHRISTOFFER PETERSEN

Published by Aarluuk Press

Second edition 2018

This book is a work of fiction. The names, characters, places and incidents are products of the writer's imagination or have been used fictitiously and are not to be construed as real. Any resemblance to persons, living or dead, actual events or organisations is entirely coincidental.

ISBN: 978-1-519044-07-5

www.christoffer-petersen.com

Sun has failed me,
Light has bolted,
Polar Night's Darkness,
On Earth folded.

Author's translation from
ISBLINK
by
LUDVIG MYLIUS-ERICHSEN (1872-1907)

Solen har svigtet mig,
Lyset er stængt,
Polarnattens Mørke
paa Jorden sænkt.

AUTHOR'S NOTE

The Sirius Sledge Patrol (Slædepatruljen Sirius) is an elite special forces unit within the Danish military with the primary mission of maintaining Danish sovereignty in Northeast Greenland. Since 1814, Greenland has been recognised as a part of Denmark, with Home Rule established in 1979, and Self Rule since 2009. When Climate Change finally captured the interest of the world's politicians in 2007, the question of who owned Hans Island - a tiny piece of barren land in the Nares Strait between Ellesmere Island (Canada) and Greenland (Denmark) - had already been dramatised with Canada and Denmark both laying claim to the island. Today, the political battle for ownership of Hans Island has been superseded by a far greater goal: ownership of the North Pole itself. In 2017, Canada and Denmark are both allies and players in the great stakes game of Arctic Sovereignty.

The Ice Star is written in British English and makes use of several Danish and Greenlandic words.

The Cabin

NORTHEAST GREENLAND

Chapter 1

ITTOQQORTOORMIIT, EAST GREENLAND

The wheels of the AugustaWestland AW139 slammed onto the gravel helipad of the remote arctic settlement with a bloated squeal of rubber and ice. The rotor chop of the phoenix-red twin-engined helicopter thundered through the fog. As the side door of the aircraft slid open, two men clad in arctic camouflage jumped down onto the gravel. A crewman inside the aircraft fiddled with the gun holstered on his belt as he dragged a woman from the helicopter's functional interior and out of the door. The camouflaged men hauled the woman out of the aircraft and dumped her limp body into the back of a pickup truck, nodding at the crewman and waving at the pilot as he twisted the collective and pulled the aircraft up and into the fog. The walls of the wooden houses dotted about the settlement shook until the aircraft was clear of the long, broad, frozen fjord.

The woman stirred in the bed of the pickup. Thick strands of her matted chestnut hair falling across her wind-bronzed and blood-speckled face in the aircraft's wake. There was more blood clotted between the fibres of her wool sweater, crusted in patches on her windpants, and grooved in the frost fractures of her hands. The shorter of the two men, a Nepalese man similar in height and skin tone to the Greenlanders, jumped into the back of the pickup and pressed his knee into the woman's spine. His breath misted in the cool air as she coughed beneath him. The second man, tall and blond with a build that challenged the seams of his Arctic smock, yanked the passenger door open and slid his muscled frame onto the torn leather seat. He stared out of the cracked window as the Greenlandic driver turned the pickup in a tight circle around the helipad and accelerated along the gravel road.

The driver, wearing the dark overalls of Mittarfeqarfiit, the Greenlandic Airport Authority, jerked through the gears, braking to a stop outside a frost-beaten wooden house at the top of the hill above the fjord. The flaked timbers and paint of the house, once red, was now salmon-coloured, skinned and gutted by Arctic hurricanes. The blond man and his Nepali partner exited the pickup, splashing through the meltwater streaming along the side of the road as they carried the woman up the wooden steps and into the vacant house. The Nepali closed the door as the driver crunched the pickup into gear and drove down the hill, as the last *whop* of the helicopter disappeared. He watched the pickup drop out of sight and turned to nod at his partner.

In the dusty silence of the house, they bound the woman's hands with a length of puppy chain and dragged her across the bruised wooden floor to the wall opposite the door. They gripped her arms and pulled her into a sitting position, wrapped the end of the thin chain around a thick nail in the wall, ripped the boots from her feet and tossed them into the centre of the room.

"Wake her up," said the tall man. He handed his partner a syringe of milky fluid.

The Nepali unscrewed the cap and pressed the needle into the woman's neck. He injected the fluid into her body, tossed the empty syringe into the corner of the room, rocked back onto his heels, and waited.

The woman noticed the chain first as the thin rusted links bit into her pale bloody wrists. She opened one eye and blinked until the room stopped spinning. In the dim interior of the house the woman tugged at the chain and closed her eyes. Images of dogs in harness, blood-spattered snow, the smell of burning wood and cordite fumes chattered through her mind. The memories jolted to a stop with a chain rattle as she tried to wrap her arms around her knees.

The first backhand slap across her face split her lip. Her head rebounded off the wall. She licked the blood from her lips, opened her eyes and stared at the short Nepalese man leaning over her. He hit her again. She snorted blood out of her nose and wiped it from her face with her sleeve. The Nepali took a step back; the floorboards creaked beneath his stubby polar boots.

Soft polar light persevered through the salt-grimed windows, edged with tired wood, flecked with fly shit. The woman winced as she stretched her legs, one eye on the Nepali man with the brutal backhand, the other on a glass of water on the floor. She jerked her head backwards as the blond man stepped into view and his large military boot connected with the glass, kicking it against the wooden wall where it smashed, showering her in jagged shards and splinters.

"Konstabel Fenna Brongaard, my name is Burwardsley. We met on the ice."

The man crouched in front of Fenna. He picked a shard of glass from her knee, studied it in the light. "You probably don't recognise me," he said. "I was wearing a ski mask. However, you might remember my friend, Bahadur." Fenna shrank into the wall as the short Nepali stepped forward, the wicked curve of his kukri knife in its black scabbard prominent upon his white camouflage fatigues. "Ah, yes," Burwardsley said with a grin. He flicked the glass onto the floor. "You *do* remember Sergeant Bahadur. I call him *Bad*, for obvious reasons," he laughed. "Sergeant?"

"Yes, Saheb?" Bahadur said and smoothed the wrinkles of his combat smock.

"Piss off outside and check on the neighbours."

"Yes, Saheb," Bahadur nodded and left the room. He pulled the door closed with a quiet snick of the lock.

"You are here so we can have a little chat," Burwardsley said. The floorboards creaked as he stood. "There are some things that need clearing up."

Fenna stared up at Burwardsley, the ceiling of the room less than half a metre above his head. His thick northern accent irritated her. *He's definitely English*, she thought. *And that name, something upper class, way back in the family tree.* She pushed her observation to the back of her mind, focused instead on the physical, more immediate details, and threats.

Burwardsley tucked his hands into the broad webbing belt around his waist, a Browning *Hi Power* 9mm fighting pistol hung in a canvas holster at his right hip. "Bahadur," Burwardsley said and nodded toward the far window, "found your partner." Fenna shivered. "Gregersen, wasn't it?"

Fenna focused on a patch of dried blood on her trousers, covering her right knee, she tried not to think of Mikael.

"Oversergent, I think his rank was. It doesn't really matter; he died by a bullet from *your* Glock." Burwardsley walked over to the wall and leaned against it. "Did you hear what I said, Konstabel? He was killed with *your* personal weapon. You killed him with a bullet to the head."

"No," Fenna thrust her chin forward. *That's not right.* "I didn't kill him."

"Back of the head," Burwardsley rubbed his palm through his blond hair just above his neck. "Execution style. Then you pulled his body into the cabin and set fire to it."

"No," Fenna said with a shake of her head. "I didn't kill Mikael." That doubt again, lurking in the splintered memories of the past twenty-four hours.

"You didn't?" Burwardsley pushed his body away from the wall with his shoulder. Dust puffed from beneath his boots as he clumped around the room. "Somebody did. It took four hours for me and Bad to get to the cabin. That damned storm, the one that grounded your unit, I've never seen anything like it." He stopped in front of Fenna. "Convenient, eh?"

"Mikael was alive when you and your gun-thug stepped out of that helicopter."

"Really?" Burwardsley shook his head. "I don't know about the Danes, but in my navy we don't kill our mates, no matter how big the pay off."

"I didn't kill him."

"You just keep telling yourself that, love."

"I'm not your *love*," Fenna spat.

Burwardsley pulled his hands free of his belt and crushed Fenna's stocking feet beneath his boot. He gripped the chain and pulled her arms straight above her head. Fenna choked for air as Burwardsley punched her in the stomach with his free hand.

"You, *my love*, will be anything I want you to be." Burwardsley released the chain and Fenna slumped to the floor. He strode out of the room, ducked into the tiny kitchen and returned with a wooden chair. Burwardsley herded Fenna into the corner, slamming the legs of the chair onto the floor, pinning her shins beneath the cross bar. He sat astride the chair, his long legs bent higher than the seat, the back facing Fenna. "It's time for a more intimate chat, Konstabel."

Fenna's knees pressed tight against her chest, her elbows caught in the gap between the slats of the chair back. She stared around her forearms, wiped sticky strands of hair away from her cheeks and stuck out her chin. *I will not be afraid.* Her eyes flickered across Burwardsley's face. "I did not kill Mikael."

Burwardsley leaned forward, his breath tickled the ragged cuffs of Fenna's greasy, wool sweater. "The evidence suggests otherwise. Do you have another version of events? A witness perhaps?" Fenna pulled her head back behind her arms, strands of her hair caught in the chain pressing into her wrists. "Tell me, Konstabel." Burwardsley gripped Fenna's metal leash between thick fingers. "Where is the Greenlander?"

"What Greenlander?"

Burwardsley yanked the chain. "Don't get smart, *love*. Where is the fucking girl?"

"I don't know," Fenna shook at the end of the chain.

"She was there. At the cabin. I saw her," Burwardsley pointed to the door as Bahadur walked in. "*He* saw her. Where the fuck is she?" Burwardsley pulled at the chain, the nail ripped out of the wall. Fenna smacked her forehead on the back of the chair. "Come on, Konstabel. Where is she?" Burwardsley stood. He threw the chair against the wall and pulled Fenna onto her chest. "Grab her feet, Bad."

"But, *Saheb*," Bahadur took a step forward.

"Just fucking do it." Burwardsley dragged Fenna across the floor to the opposite wall. He wrapped the chain around the radiator and reached for the kukri at the Nepali's waist. He ripped it free of the scabbard and gripped Fenna's sweater. He pressed rough, frost-chapped knuckles into the small of her back. "Where's the fucking girl, Fenna?"

"*Saheb*," Bahadur gripped Burwardsley's arm.

"Shut up and hold her legs, Sergeant."

"Yes, Saheb," Bahadur said and lowered his eyes.

"No." *Not like this*, she thought. Fenna screamed as the Nepali Sergeant gripped her legs, one on each side of his waist. He stretched her, pulling her legs tight against his body. The chain rattled around the radiator. Burwardsley nicked a strip of Fenna's skin from her back with the tip of the kukri as he pared the sweater in two. It hung from her shoulders like a matted fleece.

"It's your thermal top next, love. How about that?"

"No," Fenna cried as tears stung her chapped lips.

"Then your bra."

"Please, God, no," she mouthed. She twisted her head to stare at Burwardsley, glaring at him through her tears.

"Then tell me, Konstabel, where is the girl?"

"I don't know where she is." Stretched taut, Fenna squirmed within Bahadur's grip.

"I warned you, love," Burwardsley said with a renewed grip on Fenna's leash. "Now I'm just getting started." Fenna screamed as Burwardsley pressed the tip of the kukri into the tear in her thermal layer.

She wasn't trained for this. *But he is*, Fenna realised as Burwardsley gripped the chain and Bahadur stretched her legs.

Chapter 2

Fenna screamed one more time. She bit back another and forced herself to stare straight ahead. She looked out of the window and caught the eye of a young Greenlandic girl standing astride the iron pipes insulating the water supply between the houses. The girl held a toy dog whip in her hand. Sledge dog puppies tugged at the frayed plastic rope curled on the dirt-speckled snow at her feet. The girl's deep, brown eyes widened as her mouth opened. Fenna shook her head. The girl turned, disappearing into the fog rolling in from the sea, trailing a wake of fat puppies in front of a dark blue police Toyota that slewed to a stop in the gravel outside the house.

"*Saheb*. Police," Bahadur said and dropped Fenna's legs to the floor. She crumpled onto her knees and elbows.

"Fuck," Burwardsley said and slapped the handle of the curved blade into the Nepali's palm. "Unchain her." He strode to the door, slamming it shut behind him.

Bahadur sheathed the kukri and unwound the chain from the pipes. Fenna collapsed against the radiator. "Put on clothes," he roughed Fenna's sweater around her shoulders. She flinched at his clipped English – sharp like the kukri. "If can't put on, hold in place. Now stand up." Bahadur stood behind Fenna. He pulled her to her feet. The sweater fell from her shoulders. He kicked it into the corner of the room, turning Fenna to face the door as the men entered the house. The Toyota's engine growled outside.

"Here she is," Burwardsley said and gestured at

Fenna as he opened the door, standing to one side to allow three men to enter the room – two Danes, both wearing naval uniform, and a Greenlander. The Greenlander, a policeman, slipped in past Burwardsley. He leaned against the wall and cast a glance at Fenna, taking in the room. "We held her here until you could take her into custody." Burwardsley addressed the Danish officer, the senior of the two Navy men entering after the policeman.

Fenna watched the Danes strut into the room. *Not Sirius*, she thought, *but my own people at least.*

The officer, his uniform partly hidden beneath a bulky Canada Goose parka, turned his head toward Burwardsley, wiped his glasses and pointed at Fenna. "You said something about evidence?"

Burwardsley walked into the kitchen, unwrapping an oil cloth as he returned. He presented the officer with a *Glock 20* pistol, the magazine lying next to the pistol grip.

"Petersen will take care of that," said the officer. He watched as Burwardsley wrapped the pistol in the cloth and handed it to the Danish Sergent standing at the door. Petersen carried the pistol out of the house, the echo of his footsteps rumbling through the floor as he left.

"Konstabel Brongaard," the officer said and stepped forward. "My name is Premierløjtnant Vestergaard. I'm the investigating officer for your case and you are now in my custody," Vestergaard said and waved the policeman forward. "Cuff her, Maratse."

Fenna watched the Greenlander as he walked towards her. About the same height as Fenna, he wore the classic Greenlandic look of casual indifference together with a matching swagger. Fenna studied him as he approached. She glanced at Vestergaard and then flicked her eyes back to the policeman. *He is Greenlandic. He understands this place.* She allowed herself a breath as Bahadur let go of her arm. *He might understand me.*

Maratse unclipped a pair of handcuffs from the leather pouch on his belt as he approached Fenna. He circled the metal around her wrists, pausing to examine the red marks on her skin, the blood on her face. Fenna sagged under his scrutiny as her body shivered from the memory of the Nepali's backhand and Burwardsley's interrogation technique. He nodded at Vestergaard and locked the handcuffs, tightening them with a click.

"Premierløjtnant," Fenna said.

Vestergaard wagged his finger. "Don't speak, Konstabel," he said and nodded at Maratse. "Take her out to the car."

Fenna stood firm as the policeman guided her towards the door. "What about my boots?" she said and pointed to the middle of the room with her foot.

"Get her boots, Maratse," Vestergaard said with a sigh.

Fenna stumbled forward. Struggling with the handcuffs, she whispered to Maratse. "Can you help me?" The policeman nodded and crouched on one knee. He squeezed Fenna's left foot into her worn boot. He fumbled with the right one. Fenna tried a smile, but the Greenlander ignored her.

"Don't leave town, Lieutenant," Vestergaard said and shook hands with Burwardsley.

"I can't," he said. "Our ride flew out just ahead of the fog."

"Yes, the helicopter. Is your pilot going back for the body?"

"Yes. Until your lot get back in the air, we'll continue to help."

"Good," said Vestergaard. "And I'll need a copy of your report."

"I'll have Bad bring it over later."

Vestergaard gave a quick nod and followed Fenna as Maratse steered her out of the house. At the steps, Burwardsley waved to Fenna as the policeman helped her into the back seat of the Toyota. Dirty fumes from the exhaust mixed with the fog, staining the melting snow. The fog chilled the air, the peaks of unclimbed bergs of ice locked in the frozen surface of the sea poked through the gaps in the huge fjord below the village.

"See you soon, *love*," Burwardsley called as Maratse closed the car door.

Fenna slumped onto the cushioned car seat. Her hands in her lap, she sank into the soft fabric and sighed. She closed her eyes and rested her head on the dog guard separating the back seat from the rear compartment. She tried to block Burwardsley from her thoughts.

"Konstabel Brongaard?" said the Sergent in the front passenger seat. "My name is Petersen. I'm with the naval legal bureau. I will be helping the Premierløjtnant with the investigation."

Fenna squinted at the Sergent through dirty lashes, her eyes drifting to her *Glock* bundled in leather on the dash. "When do we go to Daneborg?" she said.

Petersen shook his head and tapped the window. "The fog is too thick. We were lucky to get in yesterday on the Air Greenland flight. There are no naval ships in the area," he said with a shrug. "We are at the mercy of the Scoresbysund police."

The low growl of the engine rocked the Toyota with a gentle vibration. Fenna stared past Petersen to look through the windscreen at Burwardsley joking with his Nepali Sergeant. He turned to look at her and she stiffened at Burwardsley's predatory looks. Fenna looked away as the rear passenger door opposite her was opened.

"Stop talking to the prisoner, Sergent Petersen," Vestergaard said as he ducked inside the car and sat next to Fenna. His shoulder pressed into hers as he struggled with the bulk of his parka, cursing as he closed the door. Maratse climbed in behind the steering wheel, slamming the driver door shut three times before it caught. Vestergaard leaned forward to tap the policeman on the shoulder. "Take us back to the station."

The Toyota spat gravel from beneath its wheels as Maratse backed the car onto the dirt street and set off down the hill.

"Listen closely, Konstabel." Fenna stared out of the window as Vestergaard talked. "You are to be detained here in Scoresbysund," he said and raised his voice above the click of gravel missiles raking the underside of the Toyota. "What is the Greenlandic name?"

"Ittoqqortoormiit," Maratse said as he braked to avoid a string of puppies crossing the road. The larger of the puppies, Fenna observed, its tail beginning to sag, would soon be put on a chain.

"This is a Danish military investigation," Vestergaard continued. "Whereas the Greenlandic police are structurally Danish, Maratse will not be questioning you."

Fenna stared out of the window as they passed a hunter pushing an outboard motor on a weathered wooden sledge behind a dog team. The runners grating up the dirt road reminded Fenna of training her team on the beaches near Daneborg - jagged mountains on the land, behemoths of ice dogging the shore. There was more flex in the hunter's sledge, she noted, watching the roll of the hunter's gait and the wobble of the uprights in his hands. She leaned forward to look at the bindings. The sledges preferred by the Sirius patrol were broader and longer, more like the sledges of the west coast than the raised runners designed to cope with the deep snow of Greenland's east coast.

"Konstabel, are you listening?"

Fenna turned in her seat as they passed the hunter. He stopped to adjust his trousers, sewn from the skin of the ice bear. He winked at Fenna.

"Konstabel?" Vestergaard said and tapped the policeman on the shoulder. Maratse glanced at the Dane's fingers. "Stop the car." The Toyota slowed to a stop outside the bright red wooden walls of the *Pilersuisoq* supermarket and Vestergaard turned to look at Fenna. "I don't wish for this to be a difficult investigation, Konstabel Brongaard." He waved at the children playing on top of the RAL shipping containers outside the supermarket. "This is the first time since the Second World War that a Sirius Patrolman has been shot and killed on patrol. What's more, this is the first time that a fellow patrolman has been accused of doing the shooting, *and* the very first time that a Sirius patrol has included a woman."

Vestergaard turned away from the window and looked at Fenna. "All these facts make for a very interesting and unique case." He paused to clear his throat. "Am I making myself clear, Konstabel?"

Fenna turned to look at Vestergaard. "My partner was killed, Premierløjtnant," she said and stabbed her fingers in the direction they had driven. "You should be talking to that British bastard and his Sergeant. They are the ones who..." Fenna fell back into the chair.

"Who *what*?" Vestergaard said. He waited for Fenna to look at him. He took a long breath before resuming. "Unfortunately for you, the British have a solid alibi with plenty of witnesses."

"Witnesses?"

Vestergaard leaned forward between the driver and passenger seats. "Excuse us, gentlemen." He waited until Petersen and Maratse were out of the car and the policeman had succeeded in closing his door. "Your mission was classified, Konstabel. You were tasked to retrieve a sensitive piece of hardware."

"It was a satellite," Fenna said. She looked out of the window as Petersen bummed a cigarette from Maratse. "Canadian. But then you must know that already."

"Yes," he said with a sigh. "Yes I do." He paused. "Konstabel Brongaard, you must understand. We are cut off from the world. The fog has seen to that. If you want a shot at clearing your name, you have to tell me everything before the weather lifts, before the helicopters and ships start to arrive." He paused once more. "Before any journalists get hold of the story."

Fenna flinched at the mention of the press. "And

Burwardsley? What about him?"

"You are in my custody now," Vestergaard said. He pointed at Maratse. The Greenlander stood, hands in his pockets. His cigarette, tucked in the gap of a missing tooth, smouldered between his lips. "And his."

Fenna watched the Greenlander. She noted the way he nodded to the people passing on the street, the way he kicked stones at the packs of sledge dog puppies, and the way he ignored the Dane.

"The weather report says we have two days before the fog lifts. Maratse says three."

Fenna watched Maratse, holding his gaze as he turned and caught her eye. "Premierløjtnant?"

"Yes?"

"Can I trust you?"

Vestergaard fluffed at the tails of his jacket. "This is Denmark," he said. "Not America, Konstabel. We are very far from Hollywood, and happen to be on the same side."

"Actually," said Fenna as she bit at a flake of skin on her chapped lips. "It's Greenland," she said and the corners of her mouth twitched with the faint suggestion of a smile.

Chapter 3

Maratse unlocked the door to the tiny police station. Vestergaard followed him inside, leaving Petersen and Fenna on the steps, sheltered from the breeze but exposed to the inquisitive nature of the children scrabbling toward them over the rusted pipes between the houses. Wearing little more than thin sweatshirts and an assortment of scruffy trousers, the children were impervious to the chill fog draped around the buildings.

"They're curious," Petersen said as a squirm of four children and a toddler approached them.

"They're children," Fenna said and waved at them. She looked at Petersen. *Why did they leave me outside*, she wondered.

"What about you? Any family plans?" Petersen glanced at Fenna. Behind the bruises, the matted fringe, the spots of dried blood and grime, Fenna's hair framed a pretty face with steel blue eyes like ice.

"I'm with the Sirius Patrol," she said and smiled at the children who were teasing them with cheeky faces. "That will have to do for now."

She looked up as ravens scratched along the bitumen roof of the house opposite the police station. The birds dropped down to the rocky foundations and assailed the rows of halibut heads, impaled on nails through the lower jaw and hanging from wooden racks on the balcony to dry. Fenna watched as two sledge dog puppies and three ravens tussled for possession of a fish head that had ripped from its nail and fallen to the ground. Too heavy to carry away, the ravens croaked and cowed the puppies away from their prize.

Maratse joined them on the steps. "*Iserniaa,*" he said and nodded at the door, turned and went back inside.

Petersen shrugged at Fenna before gesturing at the door. "After you." They followed the policeman. The children swarmed after them, beating the door with small, grubby fists and poorly shod feet, before scrambling over the pipes to play in the street.

"I've put you in here," Vestergaard said and guided Fenna into a small room with a cot and a washbasin the size of a football.

"It's a cell," Fenna said as she stopped at the heavy door. She spun the flap on the peephole. "Do you want my belt and laces?"

"That's cute, Konstabel." Vestergaard motioned to Maratse to remove Fenna's cuffs. She rubbed her wrists where the cuffs had irritated the rusty lacerations from Burwardsley's chain.

"We'll start in here," he said and led the way out of the cell and into the kitchenette next to Maratse's office. Fenna glanced at the picture of the Danish Queen Margrethe hanging on the wall above the policeman's desk. Vestergaard wrinkled his nose as he picked up the ashtray from the table squeezed between the wall and the refrigerator in the corner of the kitchen. He handed it Petersen. "Do something with this." Maratse lit a cigarette, took the ashtray from Petersen's hands and retreated into his office. He smoked quietly in the corner beneath the queen.

"Cosy," Fenna said as she squeezed past Vestergaard into the kitchen.

"Sit at the table, Konstabel. Petersen will stand over there," Vestergaard pointed at the kitchen counters.

"What is he going to do?"

"He will record our conversation. When the *Knud Rasmussen* arrives, he will get to work on your service pistol aboard the ship." Vestergaard paused, one eye on Fenna's face. "He'll do a ballistics check, to make sure it was your bullet. Once we retrieve the body."

Fenna looked around the small kitchen, avoiding Vestergaard's scrutiny. She suppressed the image of Mikael's body inside the burning cabin, and the smell of roasting flesh. She focused instead on the proximity of one of the Danish Navy's two offshore patrol vessels patrolling fishing grounds and enforcing sovereignty in the Arctic. *The Knud Rasmussen is close. More of my people.* She looked up. "Okay," she said.

Vestergaard steered Fenna into the chair by the wall, returning with a second chair from Maratse's office. He pushed the chair up close to the table to give Petersen room to make coffee. Vestergaard removed his jacket. He draped it over the back of the chair and sat down.

"Is Maratse the only policeman?" Fenna asked.

"No, there is a Dane, a summer replacement, but he is stuck in one of the other settlements. The fog is notorious on the east coast."

"It doesn't get much better further north," Fenna said and placed her hands on the table. "How far north have you been?"

"This is my first visit to Greenland."

"Oh," Fenna said.

"Greenland was never on my career map, Konstabel." Vestergaard turned at the sound of fresh coffee percolating through the filter. "How long have you been with the navy?"

Fenna tapped the table with an idle rhythm. She

stopped to study her hands. The fingernails were worn and chipped, the skin scratched and scabbed through the rigours of sledging, the pores were stained dark with the blood of her partner. "Can this wait? I could really use a shower."

"We'll see about that." Vestergaard took two mugs of coffee from Petersen and placed one in front of Fenna. "You were telling me about your service?"

Fenna lifted the coffee to her mouth and winced as the hot liquid singed her dried lips. She put her mug on the table. "I was twenty-two when I tried out for Sirius. It was in the spring of 2014. I shipped out to Greenland in the summer and completed my first patrol as a *fup*, a first-year-man, last November."

"So this patrol, with Oversergent Gregersen, was your second patrol?"

"My third. We had a training run in November, a short spring patrol early this year. And then another spring patrol - the mission - following that. Mikael," Fenna swallowed. "Mikael was the second year man."

"He is quite the Sirius legend, getting separated from his team during *his* first spring patrol."

"Yes."

"I read an article about his experience, how he survived. You were lucky to have him as a mentor."

Fenna bit her lip. "He was a good man. He..."

"Yes?"

"He saved my life."

"Really?" Vestergaard said. The chair creaked as he leaned back and sipped his coffee. "Tell me."

"You wanted to hear about my service record?"

Vestergaard looked out of the window at the fog. "I need to understand your relationship to Gregersen, Konstabel. If it's relevant then we have the time."

"All right," Fenna said. She took a breath. Mikael's death was still so close. "It was my first spring patrol, and I had just fallen through the ice."

NORTHEAST GREENLAND NAT. PARK

Mikael kicked off his skis, his breath smoking in the glare of his headlamp. The light caught the icicles tugging at his full red beard. The black wind jacket merged with and was lost in the black polar night. He pulled the wrist-thick brake rope from his shoulders and slipped along the length of the patrol sledge to where Fenna struggled to keep her head above the black water. A sledge dog gripped in each hand by the wet ruff of its neck, Fenna felt as though her lungs were being hammered on an anvil. She kicked at the water, kicked to stay alive.

"Keep kicking," Mikael shouted. He pushed past the sledge dogs closest to the hole, slipped onto his stomach and crawled forward, the loop of rope gripped in his right hand, the light from his lamp reflecting on the surface of the ice. "Let go of the dogs."

"No," Fenna said through trembling teeth.

"Let go of the dogs, Fenna."

The two dogs behind the leaders clawed at the fractured ice. They whined as they slipped. Mikael gripped the gangline in his left hand. Tossing one end of the braided rope to Fenna, he held onto the other with his right hand.

"Fenna. Let go of the dogs. Grab the loop," Mikael shouted as Fenna floundered in the freezing water. The dogs in her grasp started to sink. "Forget the fucking dogs and grab the line."

Fenna let go of the dogs. She struggled to circle

her fingers around the thick braid.

"Put your arm through it," said Mikael. "Get the loop in the crook of your arm. That's it. Now hold on." Mikael pulled Fenna towards the edge of the hole. He squinted in the beam from Fenna's headlamp as her body ploughed a wedge in the ice until it thickened. "That's it. I've got you." Mikael held the rope tight. He released the gangline with his left hand and grabbed Fenna's jacket in his fist. He pulled her out of the water and onto the ice. "Kick you bastard. Kick."

Fenna kicked, generating feeble splashes of frigid seawater with barely a ripple on the surface.

"I've got you. Fucking hell, I've got you." Mikael slid onto his backside and dragged Fenna onto his legs. "Got you." He slipped onto his feet. What little heat she had left steamed out of Fenna's body in the lamplight. Mikael dragged Fenna alongside the sledge towards the rear. "Take hold of the uprights. Pull yourself up. Stamp your feet."

He left Fenna at the rear of the sledge and worked his way along the gangline. He pulled the dogs away from the hole. The line bit into the edge of the ice and stopped as the two lead dogs, sodden and near-drowned, anchored the team at the water's edge. Mikael drew his pistol. With one hand on the line, holding the team in place, he shot the first and the second lead dog in the head. Mikael holstered his pistol and cut the line with his knife. He hurried along the length of the sledge to where Fenna shivered at the uprights.

"Come on Fenna. Strip for fuck's sake." Mikael pulled a grab bag from beneath the cord binding the equipment to the sledge. He opened the canvas bag, pulled out dry thermal underwear, socks, and a wool sweater. He looked at Fenna. "Come on. Keep moving."

"Trying," said Fenna as her body shivered, her fingers rigid and useless.

Mikael hung the clothes on the back of the sledge. "Arms up." He tugged Fenna's sodden sweater over her head. Fenna's eyes locked on Mikael's as he tossed the sweater onto the ice. He grinned.

"What?" Fenna said with a slur of blue lips.

"The boys placed bets as to when I would see you naked." The beads of ice in his beard sparkled as Mikael's mouth twitched into a smile. He tugged Fenna's thermal top over her head, and pulled her trousers, long johns and panties to her ankles. "These aren't regulation underwear," he said and lifted her feet to remove her sodden panties.

"Bastard," Fenna said. She smiled though stiffened cheeks.

Mikael towelled his partner with brisk and rough movements, before helping her into dry clothes. "Get your socks on." The Oversergent tugged a chocolate bar from the cargo pocket of his trousers and pushed a piece into Fenna's mouth. As Fenna crawled onto the sledge, he pulled a sleeping bag out of a stuff sack. "Wrap this around you."

"Okay."

Mikael poured Fenna a cup of coffee from the patrol flask. "It's cold. I'll make more." Fenna shivered the coffee to her lips, splashing brown spots upon her knuckles.

"Where's Hidalgo?"

"Dead," Mikael said as he fiddled with the MSR

stove. "I shot him. Pyro too. You didn't hear the shots?"

Fenna shook her head. "They were gone?"

"Yep." The stove spat, Mikael adjusted the fuel regulator. "Drink up. I'll have a fresh brew for you in a minute."

"Who's our lead dog? Betty?"

"Worry about that when your teeth have stopped chattering."

Fenna twisted on top of the sledge. "Mikael?"

"Yes?" he said and looked up.

"Thanks."

"Don't mention it." Mikael smiled. "Bad ice. We'll get going once you've warmed up." Mikael reached for Fenna's empty cup as steam drifted out of the pan on the stove. He dropped a teabag into the mug and poured hot water over it, handing Fenna the mug as he turned his head to save her from the glare of his headlamp.

"Thanks," Fenna said as she reached out from inside the folds of the sleeping bag and cupped the mug between her hands.

Mikael turned off the stove and made a coffee with the remaining water. He looked up as Fenna pulled the dry thermal top over her head, covering her breasts. The white light of the headlamp flickered across her stiff nipples.

He looked at Fenna and his eyes softened. "You had me worried for a minute."

"Me too," she said and tugged the sleeping bag around her shoulders.

Mikael packed away the stove. "You ready to move on?"

"Yes," Fenna said.

"Good. Get dressed. I'll stow the rest of the gear."

At the rear of the sledge, Mikael collected his skis before checking the dogs. Fenna watched as he walked the length of the gangline, stopping to make a fuss of each dog as he passed them. She looked beyond Mikael and stared at the hole in the ice. Fenna shivered as the moonlight danced upon the tiny floes bobbing in the black water.

Chapter 4

ITTOQQORTOORMIIT, EAST GREENLAND

Fenna's mug burred the tabletop as she turned it between her fingers. The thought of Mikael being reduced to a memory angered her. She stopped turning the mug and looked up, the memory of the chill of the Greenland Sea goose-bumping her skin. The men were silent and Petersen looked away as Fenna caught his eye. Vestergaard coughed and gestured to Petersen for more coffee.

"So," Vestergaard said as Petersen refilled his mug. "The Oversergent saved your life?"

"Yes," Fenna said. She shook her head as Petersen leaned over with the coffee jug. "I'm fine."

"You're fine?" Vestergaard looked up.

"I mean I don't want more coffee."

"Right." Vestergaard shuffled through the pages of his notebook and pulled a pen from his shirt pocket. He scribbled a note in the margin. "Oversergent Gregersen had an outstanding service record," he said as he wrote. "I had not heard, however, of him plucking you from an icy death." He looked up. "Your record, Konstabel, is a tad less notable."

"This is my first year of patrol."

"Yes. First," Vestergaard said and scribbled another note. "You are the first woman to ever pass selection for Sirius?"

"Several have tried, but the physical selection is where they drop out."

"You didn't."

"I was a biathlete at Esbjerg Gymnasium. I competed in the under 21s for Denmark."

"That explains your physical abilities, shooting and skiing," he said and circled something on the page of his notepad. "What drew you to Sirius?"

Fenna paused. "What about that shower?"

"Later," Vestergaard said with a wave of his hand. "The water tank needs refilling, so I hear. In the meantime, you can continue, Konstabel."

"All right," Fenna said and straightened her shoulders. "It was the challenge. Competing in a biathlon is one thing, but I always wanted something more. Maybe it's my father's fault?"

"Ah, yes," Vestergaard nodded. "He was military too, wasn't he?"

"Yes. Special Forces, Jægerkorps. He was killed in Afghanistan in 2006." *Dad*, she thought. *How come everything always comes back to you?*

"You were..."

"Fourteen," Fenna picked at the blood and grime beneath her fingernails. "All the men in my life seem to die young." Fenna looked up but Vestergaard ignored her.

"You were fond of your father?"

"Most of the time."

"He raised you?"

"In his own way." Fenna shivered as she recalled the early morning exercises and discipline he enforced to push her to excel in sports. *And I was only fourteen. What was the bastard thinking?*

"He was a bit of a character, so I've heard."

"Try living with him."

Vestergaard snickered as he made a note in his pad. "What about your mother?" he said and stopped writing with a click of the pen.

Fenna turned her attention to her nails and

picked at the blood beneath them. *My mother*, she thought. Fenna could almost smell the alcohol on her mother's breath as she remembered her goodnight kisses. *With a mother like her, there's no wonder I choose to live in a world surrounded by men.* She was silent until Vestergaard got the message.

"Mikael then. What about him? You had feelings for him?"

"Yes." Fenna looked up and caught the quizzical look on Vestergaard's face. "No, not like that. There was no time for that."

"You have a boyfriend back in Denmark, I presume," Vestergaard said with a smile.

"I did have. Ravn and I split up a few months after I was posted to Greenland." Fenna paused as Vestergaard sipped at his coffee. "It seems some men aren't cut out to be sailors' wives." She laughed as Vestergaard spluttered coffee over his jacket. It felt good to laugh.

"But Mikael," Vestergaard said as he dabbed at his jacket with a handkerchief. "There really was nothing between you?"

"I've answered that," Fenna said with a sigh. "Mikael was my patrol partner. My mentor. He taught me everything I needed to know."

"And then you killed him?"

"What? No," Fenna slammed her palms on the tabletop. The table rocked as she pushed herself up, the coffee spilling onto the floor.

Vestergaard leaned back in his chair, his palms open in front of his chest. "You didn't kill him, Konstabel?"

"What is this? An ambush? You ambushed me, with all this..." she waved her hands at the table.

"This coffee and small talk bullshit."

"Calm down, Konstabel," Vestergaard said. He nodded to Petersen to stand down.

"You asked me to tell you about the time Mikael saved my life. Then you accuse me of taking his. What kind of officer are you *Premierløjtnant*?" Fenna spat Vestergaard's title through clenched teeth.

Vestergaard raised his eyebrows and waited. Maratse, a cigarette between his lips, appeared in the doorway.

"Sit down, Konstabel," Vestergaard said and gestured at the chair. "Finish your coffee." He lifted her mug from where it lay on the table. "Petersen, can you get the Konstabel some more coffee?"

"I don't want more coffee."

"Okay," Vestergaard said and lowered the mug. He turned around to look at the policeman. "Is there enough water in the tank for one shower?"

"*Iiji*," said Maratse with a nod.

Vestergaard scuffed his chair away from the table. "I think we can take a short break while I get set up here. Petersen will show you to the shower. Can we trust you not to jump out of the window?"

"Where the fuck would I go?" Fenna said. The skin of her left cheek flickered, just below her eye.

"Funny," he said and slipped his notebook into the pocket of his jacket. "One more thing before you go. The English Lieutenant, Burwardsley." Vestergaard paused as Fenna's body stiffened. "He mentioned something about a witness. A young woman? A Greenlander? Perhaps Maratse can locate her while you shower?"

Fenna turned from Vestergaard and looked at the police officer. Maratse pulled another cigarette from a crumpled packet of *Prince*.

"I'm sure I don't have to remind you, Konstabel, that a witness in your favour could make all the difference."

Fenna watched as Maratse lit his cigarette. "Her name is Dina."

"*Iiji*," Maratse said and puffed a cloud of smoke from between his lips. He rolled the cigarette into the gap between his teeth. With a nod towards Fenna he turned and left the room. The door to the police station swung shut behind him as Maratse clumped down the steps to the Toyota.

"Good," Vestergaard said as he scribbled a note onto a fresh page in his notebook. He tore it out and gave it to Petersen as the Sergent pushed past him.

"There is soap in the shower," Petersen said as he led Fenna out of the kitchen. He stopped to pick up a pile of clothes from the cupboard in Maratse's office. He pressed them into Fenna's arms. "There are towels upstairs. Used ones."

"I'll be fine. I just need a shower." Fenna looked around Petersen's shoulder as Vestergaard tore another page from his notebook. He folded the note into his jacket pocket, followed them to the doorway, and leaned against a filing cabinet at the entrance to the kitchen. "Do you require medical attention, Konstabel?"

"No," Fenna glanced at her wrists.

"Nothing," Vestergaard said and paused, "internal?"

"They didn't rape me, Premierløjtnant. If that is what you mean."

Vestergaard nodded. "That's just as well. The doctor is stranded in Kulusuk."

"The fog," Petersen said and shook his head.

"Twenty minutes, Konstabel. Petersen will wait outside the door."

"It's this way." Petersen led Fenna up the stairs to the first floor. "It really is just a shower. If you need the toilet, it's one of those bucket jobs downstairs." Petersen ducked his head and leaned against the window as Fenna squeezed past. "It's right in there. I'll wait here."

"It's not necessary, Sergent. I'm really not going to run away."

"I'll wait here," Petersen said and leaned against the wall.

Fenna entered the bathroom and shut the door behind her. Attached to the wall with clips and screws, the water pipes served as shelves with a blunt razor tucked behind one pipe, a dirty sponge behind another. Fenna turned on the water, peeled off her clothes and stepped beneath the shower head. She tugged the shower curtain around a rusty rail and distanced herself from the outside world. She twitched as the hot water sluiced the cuts and grazes on her skin and rinsed the blood and grime from her hair. Fenna worked up a lather of soap between her hands and smoothed it into her body, the Arctic ichor of blood, grit and grime streamed down her skin and pooled at her feet. She ran a soapy hand over her body, tracing the bruises around her ribs and stomach with a finger. Her thighs were untouched but her shins bore yellow shields of old haematomas from the prod and stab of sledge runners and the trials of sledging around boulders, across the ice. She lingered over the dog bite healing on her forearm and smiled.

"Lucifer," she said and traced the bite with her

fingers. She pushed her face under the shower head and let the water rinse the slow well of tears from her eyes. "Where the hell are you, Lucifer?"

"Fenna?" Petersen knocked on the door. "Vestergaard says it's time."

"Two minutes," Fenna said and turned off the water. "I'll be down in two minutes."

She stepped out of the shower and wiped the mirror above the clothes hook and looked at herself with tired eyes. Her gaze lingered over her bruised cheek until the steam disguised her face as the mirror was obscured. She towelled her body with brisk movements, then stepped into Maratse's police trousers, securing them as tightly as possible at the waist with the draw cord she removed from his hooded sweatshirt. She pulled on the sweatshirt and socks and stepped into her boots, tying most of her hair into a ponytail, letting the wayward strands cling to her face. Petersen stood up as she opened the door to the bathroom.

"Better?" he said as his eyes lingered over Fenna's hair clinging to her cheeks.

"Much," Fenna said and nodded at the stairs. "Shall I go first?"

"Yes, I'll follow you."

Fenna descended the narrow staircase. She waited at the bottom as Petersen clumped down the stairs behind her.

"Handball?" Fenna said and pointed at the Sergent's left leg.

"Yes, I ripped a ligament in my knee."

"Same thing happened to my mother. That's why I chose skiing and shooting."

"Smart move," Petersen said and pointed over

Fenna's shoulder. "He's ready."

Vestergaard stood to one side as Fenna entered the kitchen. As she sat down Petersen set up a microphone in the middle of the table.

"This is the formal part of our conversation. It will be recorded in full. You are encouraged to tell me everything. It might feel informal, given our surroundings, but anything you say may of course be used for the purposes of your prosecution and defence. I'm not your lawyer. I do, however, represent the navy in this case. Do you understand what I have said so far?"

"Yes," Fenna said. She poked at the tripod beneath the microphone.

"Then you will also understand that it's in your best interests to tell the truth," Vestergaard said and waited as Petersen placed a Thermos of coffee on the table. "As regards the sensitive nature of your mission, Petersen has full clearance and you can speak freely."

"How do I know that?"

"What?"

"That he has clearance?"

Vestergaard turned to Petersen. "We'll need the letter from the Admiral's office. It's in my briefcase."

"Actually," Petersen said and folded his hands behind his back, "I think it's in your overnight bag, in Maratse's car."

"It's okay," Fenna said and shrugged. "You said it was formal. I just wanted to be sure."

"We can show you the letter later. As for now, if we are to get this done before the fog lifts, we must begin."

"I'm ready."

"Coffee?"

"Yes," Fenna held the mug as Vestergaard unscrewed the Thermos and poured. Petersen reached around Vestergaard and switched on the microphone. He returned to the sink, rested against the kitchen units and waited.

"Start from the beginning of your patrol, when you were first tasked with the mission." The Thermos lid squealed as Vestergaard screwed it closed and placed it on the table.

"Well," Fenna said as she warmed her hands around the mug. "There was a storm coming, but we had a window to get as far north as possible. Hauksson was the pilot's name."

Chapter 5

NORTHEAST GREENLAND NAT. PARK

The tundra tires of the Twin Otter bounced along the gravel landing strip at Daneborg. As the pilot pulled back on the control stick Lucifer sank his canine teeth into Fenna's arm. She smacked the dog between the eyes once, twice before it let go. In the confines of the cabin, squeezed between the long, broad, wooden sledge, patrol gear and twelve sledge dogs, Fenna watched the blood stream between her fingers. After a brief halt between the fibres of her cargo trousers the blood dripped on the packing cases, traced the scratched surface of the aluminium deck and ran beneath crates and sledging boxes towards the rear compartment of the aircraft. Fenna clamped her hand on the wound, leaning back as the aircraft peeled from the earth into the polar sky. The wind whistled through the airframe. Lucifer squirmed and received another clout on the head.

At the front of the cargo area, closest to the open cockpit, Oversergent Mikael Gregersen tugged at the pilot's trouser leg, twisting an invisible dial back and forth with his hand in the air between them. The pilot nodded, reached forward to the console and turned the heat up to full. Mikael unclipped the first aid kit and a bottle of saline from the bulkhead. He squirmed his feet for the deck between the dogs and worked his way towards Fenna, bracing himself halfway. His knuckles bruised the plastic veneer of the ceiling as the aircraft bounced in a patch of turbulence. The two Sirius Sledge Patrollers grinned. Mikael pointed at Fenna's arm. She lifted a bloody palm from the puncture wound with a shrug. Several sledge dogs yawned as Mikael pushed off from the ceiling and stumbled over to kneel beside her.

"We forgot to turn up the heat," he shouted.

"What?"

"Heat, to make them drowsy," Mikael repeated, his mouth but a finger's width from Fenna's ear. "How bad?"

"It's okay," Fenna said and drew the ragged sleeve of her sweater and thermal top above the wound. Mikael passed her the saline with a squirting motion and Fenna diluted the blood seeping out of her punctured skin.

"More," he shouted.

With one squeeze Fenna emptied the bottle, cleaning the bite and loosening the clumps of blood within the wool fibres. Mikael dried the wound with a square of lint from the first aid kit. The two patrollers butted heads during another bout of turbulence. Mikael fell onto Lucifer and the dog squirmed beneath the Oversergent's body before flopping back onto all fours on the deck. Mikael pushed himself off the dog. He pulled a packet from the kit, tore off the top and dumped the white powder contents onto the open wound. He pressed his mouth to Fenna's ear as he dressed the wound.

"Antibiotics," he shouted. "Keep an eye on it. I'll give you a shot when we land."

"What?"

Mikael pressed two fingers and a thumb together in front of Fenna's face.

"Okay," she said and flashed the thumbs-up sign.

Mikael slapped Fenna on the shoulder and picked his way through the dogs to his seat by the cockpit. He clipped the first aid kit in place and nodded to the pilot before picking up the spare headset.

"Everything's okay," he said. Mikael leaned into the cockpit and pulled a pen from the pilot's chest pocket below his name tag. He tugged a laminated section of the aerial chart for northeast Greenland from under a bungee screwed into the dashboard. With the pilot's pen he traced their route with the nib.

"About an hour," said the pilot. "See that?" Hauksson pointed at the anvil of clouds in the vast, moonlit distance.

"We'll be all right," Mikael said and stowed the map.

"*You* might be. Make sure you have your shit together when we land."

"Not a problem," Mikael said and slipped the pen into Hauksson's pocket. He pulled off the headset and lurched onto the sledging box by the door. Mikael steadied himself with a hand on the sledge and grinned through his beard at Fenna. He tickled the ears of Betty, the lead dog at his feet, closed his eyes and listened to the drone of the engines.

Hauksson slid the Twin Otter to a halt. The engines idling, he teased the aircraft within a tight arc pointing the nose of the aircraft north. Fenna and Mikael extricated themselves from the dogs, the sledging boxes, and the webbing straps securing everything inside the cargo area. They pulled ragg wool mittens over thin thermal gloves and popped open the door, coughing with the first intake of dry polar air. The thermometer on the inside of the door began its steady contraction to minus thirty-nine degrees Celsius. Fenna jumped after Mikael through the fog of their breath onto the ice. The dogs' eyes flashed green and blue in the torchlight from their headlamps as they reached into the cargo area, grabbed an ice axe each, and a length of travelling chain and cord.

Mikael dug the first loophole in the ice closest to the aircraft. He removed his mittens and fished the cord through the arch in the ice, tying a bowline knot through the last link of chain, securing it. Fenna pulled the chain into one long length, digging loopholes at intervals, threading a cord through the closest link at each before stretching the chain taut at the final loophole. Her breath frosted on the chain and beaded the cord. The freezing metal burned through the thin fingers of her thermal gloves as she tied the last knot and slipped her hands into her mittens. Mikael worked behind Fenna, untangling the short lengths of chain branching out of the main line. As Hauksson killed the propellers, the hush of fur inside the Twin Otter leaked out of the aircraft with silent anticipation.

As Fenna trotted back toward the aircraft Mikael stopped her.

"All set?"

"Yep."

"How's your arm?"

Fenna rolled up her sleeve, her arm pale in the lamplight, shrouded in the fog of the patroller's breath. Mikael gripped Fenna's wrist and smoothed his thumb across the bandage.

"Sore?"

"It's okay. It wasn't too deep, more a panic-bite than anything else."

"All right," he said as he tugged Fenna's sleeve over the bandage. "We'll have a look at it in camp tonight and I'll give you a quick jab in the arse."

"You'll try," said Fenna.

"You'll love it," Mikael said and grinned behind a mask of mist. He nodded at the aircraft. "Let's get to work. Hauksson gets twitchy the longer we stay on the ice."

As Fenna clambered into the cargo hold the dogs erupted in flashes of bared teeth, whimpers and growls. Too closely related to the wolf to bark, the dogs half-barked and whined with abandon.

"Shut your noise," Hauksson shouted from the cockpit. Fenna grinned back at him, ignoring the finger the pilot flashed in return.

Fenna found Betty and wrestled her out of the canine mass. She tripped on the dog's tail and stumbled the lead dog out of the aircraft. Mikael caught Betty by the collar as Fenna tossed her out of the cargo door. Betty bounced on the balls of her hind feet as Mikael crunched the air from the surface snow in massive strides along the full length of the chain. He reached the end of the anchor line, fumbled for the karabiner clip and secured the team's lead dog at the collar. Betty stood rigid on the ice as Mikael returned for the next dog. One by one, Fenna bundled the dogs out of the aircraft and Mikael danced them into position. With a rap on the nose here and there, the Oversergent avoided the territorial arcs of piss marking the boundaries of each dog. Lacking trees, the dogs pissed on each another.

Fenna slid onto the floor of the Twin Otter, her legs, weighed down by the boots on her feet, dangled out of the doorway. Strands of fur floated in the light of her headlamp, twisting in the frigid breeze as Mikael joined her.

"How's Hauksson?" he said.

"Crotchety."

"Have you told him about the whisky?"

"I thought I'd leave that to you."

"I heard that," said Hauksson from the cockpit.

Mikael cuffed Fenna to one side as he leaned in through the doorway. "Are you going to earn it?"

"I'm not shifting boxes for one lousy bottle of *Jack*," said Hauksson. "How many have you got?"

"Two bottles," said Mikael. "They're yours as soon as you get off your arse and help us."

The wrench of worn springs masked another round of cursing as Hauksson carped out of the pilot's seat and staggered into the cargo bay.

"You're a sucker for a drink," said Mikael.

"There's fuck all else to do up here," said Hauksson. "Which box?"

"The last one."

"Bastards." Hauksson straightened up and pushed past Fenna. He picked up a rectangular wooden box and hefted it onto his knee. "Come on then, dog-fuckers." Hauksson shoved the box at Fenna, forcing her out of the door as he dumped the first sledging box of patrol equipment out of the aircraft and onto the ice. Fenna arranged it on the ice a few metres from the aircraft. Mikael checked each box and item on a list tucked behind a flap of canvas in the sleeve of the patrol document wallet. It took all three of them to get the sledge out of the aircraft. They slid it out of the door and onto the ice alongside the equipment. Mikael fastened the canvas sledging bag between the uprights of the sledge with a webbing loop over the left and right wooden handles. The frosted links of chain rattled as the dogs shifted within the limits of their tethers.

As Hauksson and Fenna swept the aircraft interior for forgotten items, Mikael performed a thorough check of the sledge, scrutinising each of the bindings with his fingertips and eyes. He smiled when his fingers smoothed into the well of a cosmetic dent on the third cross-thwart.

"Found it," he said as Fenna hopped out of the aircraft.

"My dent?" she said and laughed at the memory of Mikael's exasperation at her carpentry skills. "Hey, I never said building a sledge was my forte."

Mikael cuffed Fenna on the shoulder. "She's going to have more than a dented cross-thwart when we've finished with her." He turned to wave at Hauksson.

"We've got two minutes before he starts prepping the Otter," said Fenna.

"Did you give him the whisky?"

"Just the one. See for yourself."

Back in the cockpit, Hauksson waved the bottle of *Jack Daniels* in the window.

Mikael pulled a pipe from his jacket pocket and tamped a twist of tobacco into the bowl. He thrust the pipe into his mouth. Fenna lifted the sledge boxes onto the sledge and Mikael shuffled them into position. He slid the first box between the wooden uprights at the rear of the sledge. Sanded and smoothed in the shape of a woman's breast and firm belly, the nipple on each upright made for a quick tease when cupping the tit on downward slopes and through gullies. In the harsh light of the Twin Otter the shadow of the sledge swelled on the ice. Fenna turned away from the aircraft to read the call-sign *Fever Dog* stencilled the length of each sledge runner.

The mission, she realised, was just about to begin.

Chapter 6

The cough of a propeller hurried the two patrollers as they fixed the sleeping mats and tent on top of the load, securing the canvas tarpaulin with trucker's hitches, passing the cord through heavy eyelets and around the thwarts sticking clear of the sledge runners. Mikael slid the padded rifle holster between the cord and the load, Fenna organised the skis. The second propeller coughed – a hoarse bark that caught their attention. Hauksson waved from the cockpit window and the patrollers continued their work. Mikael hung thick rope, woven into coils, over each of the uprights. The coils, the only piece of equipment designed to slow the sledge's progress, would be slipped over the runners when going downhill. Fenna and Mikael would wear them across their chests once they started the patrol. Like the sledge and almost everything else the patrol carried, they were easily repaired.

As the engines of the Twin Otter spun into an idle rhythm, Mikael and Fenna dug out the second bottle of *Jack Daniel's* tucked into the heavy canvas sledge bag hanging at the back of the sledge. Hauksson blotted the interior light of the aircraft as he filled the doorway.

"Hmm," he said. "Sledge bag, eh?"

Mikael shrugged. "You're getting old."

Hauksson nodded. "Too old for that," he said with a nod toward the sledge. "You want to get back on board?"

Fenna shook her head and grinned.

"She's eager, Gregersen. You want to watch her."

"She'll be all right. How about you?"

"Weather's holding for the moment. It's you who should be worried. I don't know why you couldn't wait a day." Hauksson turned in the doorway. "You've got my frequency?"

Mikael nodded.

"Fine then," Hauksson said and took the bottle. He yanked the door closed, clapping his last visible breath in half. Hauksson grinned through the window and flipped his middle finger. Mikael and Fenna returned the gesture.

They stepped back to the sledge as Hauksson revved the Twin Otter's engines in a tight circle, the arc from the wing lights blinding the patrol. The aircraft lurched to a stop as Hauksson applied the brakes, holding them firm as the engines whined, releasing them at fever pitch to roar down the short stretch of smooth ice before leaping into the black air. Fenna and Mikael watched as the Twin Otter traced a low and lazy circle in the sky returning to buzz the patrol with a waggle of wings. They waved and watched the aircraft disappear in the night sky. All was still. The polar air sank around them, they switched off their headlamps and the dark enveloped them.

ITTOQQORTOORMIIT, EAST GREENLAND

Vestergaard looked up as Petersen walked into the kitchen waving his mobile.

"All telecommunications are still down, sir. But I'll keep trying."

"The fog?" Vestergaard said and reached into his jacket pocket for his mobile.

"No, sir. The *TELE Greenland* guy at the store says it's a fault and they're working on it."

"How long?"

"They're working on it, sir. I have no idea."

"Very well," Vestergaard said and checked his mobile once more before slipping it back into his pocket. "Konstabel, did you have any experience of working with dogs before Sirius?"

Fenna smoothed the fabric of the sweatshirt over the dog bite. "No. Not so much."

"So, tell me the nature of your mission. What was it you were tasked to do?" Fenna glanced at Petersen. "It's all right, Konstabel. I assure you Petersen *is* cleared for this."

Fenna looked at Petersen. She watched as Vestergaard clicked the button on his ballpoint pen back and forth. "You'll show me the letter when Maratse returns?"

"As soon as he gets back," Vestergaard said and smiled. "Okay?"

Fenna took a deep breath. "At our second briefing, when the location of the satellite was confirmed, we were told to retrieve certain parts of the satellite, if we couldn't get it all."

"Just parts of it?" He looked up from his notes. "The satellite is called *Sapphire*. Correct?"

"Yes."

"I understand the Canadians launched it back on the 25th of February, 2013." Vestergaard closed his notepad and took a breath. "*Sapphire* is a surveillance satellite."

"I know," said Fenna.

Vestergaard frowned and continued. "It's part of the Canadians' programme to improve their ability to patrol their Arctic territory, something that I understand is becoming increasingly important as the ice retreats and shipping lanes are freed."

"Kjersing told us that *Sapphire* is the first spy satellite the Canadians have ever launched," Fenna looked up. "Since we've been flirting with the Canadians over Hans Island, and not forgetting the *Xue Long* incident..."

"*Xue Long*?"

"A Chinese icebreaker that arrived in Tuktoyaktuk, in the far north of Canada, without them noticing," Fenna said and paused. "The Canadians have been having sovereignty issues in the Arctic for quite some time now."

Fenna remembered the briefing, with details about the Canadians and their snow machines getting stuck in bad ice in the far north. It had been a good joke at the time. Something for Sirius to feel proud about, proving once again, that as long as the sea continued to freeze, dogs were the only way to patrol the Arctic. That might change, Fenna realised, if the ice continues to retreat to the pole. *Who will have the last laugh*, she wondered.

"The Chinese," Vestergaard said and looked up from his notepad. "I assume you were also briefed on the Chinese cargo plane that flew over the area around the same time the satellite was reported lost?"

"Yes," Fenna said. "Kommandør Kjersing was quite concerned."

"It strikes me as strange they would only task you to bring back a piece of it."

"I think they were worried about the storm and the Chinese," Fenna said. "And our ability to get in and out with the entire satellite."

"*They*?"

"Kommandør Kjersing's seniors, sir."

Fenna paused as she thought about the briefing at Daneborg, when they were first tasked with the mission. Mikael, she remembered, had been as close to insubordination as a second year man could get. He'd made it crystal clear that picking up a piece of space junk was the last thing he wanted to do, especially when it shortened the patrol. *He lived for the wild*, she thought and sniffed to ward off a round of tears. *Shit, Mikael, what the hell did we get ourselves into? And,* she added as an afterthought*, did Kjersing know?*

"Tell me again why did they not just send a helicopter?"

"Okay," Fenna said and flexed her shoulders. She shifted her position on the chair. "All aircraft were about to be grounded due to a storm rolling in from the east. Hurricane strength. What the East Greenlanders call a *piteraq*."

"But you can operate in that kind of weather?"

"The dogs can cope with temperatures in the minus fifties."

"And the men?"

"That's the challenge," Fenna said. "Yes, we can do it. We *do* do it."

"And your mission?"

Fenna paused for a sip of coffee. She let her eyes drift across the tabletop, letting her mind wander as the coffee stains grew into lichen clustered outcrops of rock, pits in the surface of the table became ravines, scratches transformed into contour lines on the map, and the edge of the table became the ice foot rising and falling with the tide as the table rose and fell with Fenna's breaths.

"Konstabel?" Vestergaard said and tapped his pen on the table. "The mission?"

Fenna shook her head before answering. "We planned to sledge from our insertion point – where Hauksson dropped us off. Locate the satellite and retrieve the components before they were lost in the storm or buried in the snow." She looked up. "Total mission time: three to five days to reach the area. At which point we anticipated being contacted by helicopter."

Petersen shuffled for a better seat on the kitchen counter as Fenna waited for Vestergaard's next question. She took another sip of coffee and recalled the *shush* of sledge runners in the snow compared to the grating noise they produced when the dogs pulled them smartly across pure sea ice. Not the inland ice sheet that people thought they patrolled, but the sea ice along the coast of Northeast Greenland. Wild and untamed – polar bear territory.

"Was there any indication of a credible threat?"

"What?" Fenna said and looked up.

"Were you informed of any hostile groups interested in the satellite?"

"No," Fenna shook her head. "Perhaps that was our biggest mistake."

Fenna closed her eyes tight as the picture of Burwardsley, striding across the snow with the Browning pistol in his hand, invaded her mind. As the image focused, the details flooded back. As he'd approached the hut, he had pulled down the hood of his white camouflage jacket. He wore a green beret on his head and a low-cut mask that hid most of his face bar the blond hair flicking out from under the beret. Fenna recognised it now from a photo she had seen in one of her father's books. It was a British Royal Marines uniform. The shorter man with a machine gun, the one he called *Bad*, also wore a beret, green or black, it didn't matter. Fenna focused her memory on the eighteen inch sword at the man's waist, a kukri, a Gurkha blade. *A credible threat?* She opened her eyes and breathed out with a long breath as she focused on Vestergaard. *A Royal Marine and a Gurkha. I'd say that was a pretty fucking credible threat.*

"You seem a little preoccupied," Vestergaard said.

"It's just the questions. It brings everything back," she said. "They drugged me, you know?"

"Who? Burwardsley?"

"Who else. I think I'm still working the effects out of my body. The coffee helps," Fenna said and nodded at Petersen.

"There's plenty more," he said.

"Please continue, Konstabel," Vestergaard said with a click of his pen.

Chapter 7

NORTHEAST GREENLAND NAT. PARK

The constant shush of the sledge running across the crusty surface of the snow, hardened by the evaporating effect of the wind, thrilled Fenna. The dogs had found their rhythm, the patrol had established a routine and, with their fourth camp looming, they were making good progress despite the cold, despite the long hours of darkness. The rhythm of life in the far north, Fenna mused, came down to discipline, experience, and common sense.

They skied with short methodical strides, Mikael and Fenna each on opposite sides of the sledge, one hand on the uprights, the nipples already forgotten. Fenna breathed through the ice-laden fleece looped around her neck. She glanced at the yeti skiing beside her and grinned.

"One more laugh out of you and I swear," said Mikael.

Fenna smirked and picked at the ice beading on her eyebrows. She studied the line of dogs before them and picked out the rump of each, noting the position of its tail and gait. Lucifer at the front, just behind Betty.

"Lucifer is a little lazy today," she said. "I'll check his pads tonight."

"I checked them this morning, clipped a little more of the fur between his toes. He had a few marble-sized balls of ice at the end of yesterday. We might try him with socks tomorrow." Mikael's breath misted before him adding another layer of ice to his weighty beard.

The sledge slowed, causing Fenna and Mikael to

look up and around. Each of the dogs in the team ran with a light-hearted lift of their feet. Tails wagging the dogs stopped pulling and the sledge ground to a languid stop. Betty sniffed and glanced back at Mikael.

"Go on girl," said Mikael. "Go on."

Fenna scanned the horizon as Mikael slipped his hold of the uprights and skied to the front of the line. His hands unhindered by sledge poles he slid to a stop and took hold of Betty by the ruff of fur around her neck. Mikael glanced back at Fenna.

Fenna lifted a hand and rested her finger on her nose. "There," she pointed, arm straight. "Eleven o'clock. A wolf?"

Mikael stood and looked in the direction Fenna indicated. The sledge shuddered as the dogs tugged. "Hold them, Fenna."

Fenna slipped the anchor coil from around her chest and looped it over the left-hand runner. On her return, halfway along the length of the sledge, the sledge shrugged and slipped past her. Fenna caught the left hand upright and slipped her skis in line behind the sledge. To the right, Mikael hopped towards the sledge as it turned away from him. The anchor coil ploughed the light coating of snow into a shallow furrow, lifting the upright and creating more drag on the surface. Not enough, Fenna realised as the sledge picked up speed when the dogs caught the wolf's scent, their erratic course dragging the sledge further from Mikael.

With both hands on the uprights, Fenna braked her broad-bladed skis in a V-shape, the dead man's rope trailing from the sledge between her legs. The rope tightened as Mikael took hold. It slid along the ice layered within his woollen-gloved palm. He pressed his cold hand into a fist and wrapped the rope twice around it.

Fenna felt the rope press against the inside of her right boot, travelling up the inside of her leg. She lifted one ski from the ice to free her leg. The rear of the ski caught in the rope, the binding opened and Fenna's ski cart-wheeled onto the ice.

"What are you doing?" said Mikael.

"Nothing. Fuck."

Fenna turned her left ski to follow the sledge and pushed the toe of her right boot onto the thwart between the uprights. The sledge increased speed as the dogs pursued the wolf down a slight hill. The wolf loped towards the ice foot and Fenna knew the sledge had to be stopped before it reached the smooth black ice. *If they get on the ice, we'll never stop them.*

"Roll the sledge, Fenna," Mikael shouted. "Roll it."

As the sledge crested the hill, Fenna pulled on the right upright facing downhill. The sledge tipped onto its side and she threw herself clear. Like an anchor the sledge slowed the team, frustrating the dogs to a halt. Mikael skied up to Fenna and offered her a hand.

"Fucking dogs," she said.

"It's not every day they meet a wolf."

"Where is it?"

"Somewhere beyond that mound – close to the ice foot. Thirty metres, maybe." Mikael clapped the snow from Fenna's back. "We'll see it again."

"I thought it would be frightened off."

"No chance. We're the most interesting thing out here. Come on; let's get the sledge turned around. We'll be ready next time."

Mikael loosened the sledge boxes while Fenna anchored the sledge. The dogs took turns to yawn and curl into a ball, watching Fenna and Mikael through the thick brush of their tails. The wolf lay down and watched from afar. When the sledge was ready, the boxes lashed, the gangline checked, Mikael skied to the end of the line and held Betty by the collar.

"We'll try again, shall we?" he said and brushed beads of ice from the lead dog's eyes.

"Wait a minute," Fenna said. "I need my ski."

Mikael shook his head. Betty nudged into his legs and he tugged gently at the dog's ears while they waited.

"Got it."

Mikael roused the dogs with a shout and pulled Betty in an arc, back up the hill. As the dogs turned the sledge, Fenna glanced back at the wolf. It lay with its head down on its front legs stretched flat on the ice. As Fenna kicked off and guided the sledge back on course, the wolf stretched and loped after the team.

The stars picked at the black canopy, the moon purged the ice of shadow. Fenna fed the dogs in a mist of breath. She pulled her hat firmly onto her head and looked at the tent, smiling as the glow of the tent light painted Mikael's movements on the dirty canvas walls. Fenna could hear the stove; she could almost smell the evening meal. It was the same routine every night. Tasks were completed in the same order, regardless of the weather. Anchoring the dogs and pitching the tent together before taking it in turns to work outside or inside. Tonight it was her turn to be outside and feed the dogs, while Mikael organised the tent and the evening meal. She smiled as she approached Lucifer. After just four days, despite the wolf, the team was beginning to gel.

Lucifer whined as she clumped towards him. The other dogs became restless. They had eaten particularly quickly, she had noticed. Faster than usual. Fenna whirled at a glimpse of white as the wolf circled the dogs and the camp. Betty, the bitch, whimpered, jogging in circles at the very limit of her chain. It was not long before the team began to howl. Sporadic and broken at first as the dogs found their voices in the frigid polar air, it became stronger and plaintive as the team found their rhythm. Fenna, her moon shadow cast on the ice before her, threw back her head and howled with the dogs. They stopped; Fenna howled alone for a few moments before the team took up the howl once more. In another unforeseen lull, she heard the answering howl of the wolf. In the far distance, the wolf sat upright between the lines carved by the sledge runners.

"How's dinner?" Fenna said as Mikael poked his head out of the tent baffle.

"Close. Was that the wolf?"

"Yep. Over there." Fenna pointed at their tracks in the snow.

"Got it." With one last look, Mikael crawled back inside. Fenna gave Lucifer a last hug, secured the dog food on the sledge and made her way to the tent.

"Bloody hell," she said as she closed the baffle behind her. "What died?"

"Your socks. My thermals," said Mikael. "You decide."

"Dinner ready yet? I'm starving."

"Salt needed, and then we're good."

Fenna pulled off her boots and hung them upside down from the tent loft. She crawled onto her sledge bag and looked around the tent. "I like what you've done with the place."

Mikael grinned and stirred the pot one more time. Steam evaporated in damp clouds, the vapours clung to the ceiling to form beads of ice.

"I thought I saw some blood on the trail today," said Fenna.

Mikael picked at his beard. "I can't believe Betty is coming into season. When the hell was she last in heat?"

Fenna shook her head. "I'll check the diary." She reached over to the wooden sledging chest that doubled as both bedside table and office space. While she flipped through the pages, Mikael melted snow for their coffee.

"Here we go," she paused for a moment. "Yep, she was last in heat in December. Just before Christmas." She looked up. "So, we have a problem."

"No more than usual," Mikael shrugged. "We should have thought about it but…"

"What?"

"The wolf," said Mikael.

"She must be just starting. You want to bring her in the tent tonight?"

"Not tonight. Give it one night and see what happens." A wicked grin parted Mikael's red beard. "Of course, it's only a myth, but Greenlanders used to tie their bitches out on the ice when they wanted new blood."

"Wolf blood," said Fenna.

"Not sure what the boys back at Daneborg would

have to say about that."

"Would they know?"

"Ever seen a hybrid?"

Fenna shook her head.

"Me neither. But it would be interesting to see what we got out of it."

"We're leaving her outside tonight then?"

"I think so," Mikael said and handed Fenna her food. He paused at the first howl of the wolf.

ITTOQQORTOORMIIT, EAST GREENLAND

Vestergaard closed his notebook and tapped his pen on the tabletop. He wiped his hand over his face. "This is all very interesting, Konstabel," he said and inspected his fingers. "But what does it have to do with the mission?"

"The dogs *are* the mission," Fenna said. "Without them we won't get anywhere, we won't survive." She paused and said, "You don't understand, do you?"

"I need facts, not an encyclopaedic knowledge of the ins and outs of sledge dog breeding."

"That's funny, because that is exactly what Sirius needs. But, hey," she said and shrugged. "You're asking the questions. You wanted to know about the patrol."

"Have you forgotten, Konstabel, that you're being investigated for murder?"

Fenna slumped into the chair and fidgeted. "No," she said. "How could I forget?"

"Then why don't we get back to the mission, and away from this stuff about wolves and puppies."

"Sure, but if I leave something out, you'll only wonder at it later."

"Cut to the chase, Konstabel. Before the fog lifts

and you are out of time."

Fenna leaned forward and slapped her hand on the table. "When the fog lifts, I expect someone from Sirius to arrive." She lifted her head and stared at Vestergaard, searching his face for the root of his impatience. "Is that it? You want the details in a hurry before the fog lifts?"

"I want the facts as they are fresh, so that I can compare them with the British version of events."

"Burwardsley," Fenna said. She struggled to stop her bottom lip from curling. "Who is he anyway?"

"We'll get to that," Vestergaard said and picked up his notebook. He turned to a fresh page and nodded for Fenna to continue. "The wolf then. If we must."

Chapter 8

NORTHEAST GREENLAND NAT. PARK

Stars of ice fractured from the canvas loft and whispered onto the sleeping bags, showering Fenna and Mikael with intricate crystals. Fenna turned several times in the night. During the coldest hour she woke to see Mikael sitting up straight on his camp bed. He placed a grubby finger upon his lips and nodded toward the wall of the tent. Fenna sat up, shedding the top portion of her sleeping bag and sending a light avalanche of ice onto the tent floor. They listened to the sound of dogs coupling outside the tent.

"He's stuck," Mikael said. "Hear that?"

Fenna nodded. "Betty's whimpering."

"Now the fun stuff begins. He has to keep the others at bay while they are joined. We should get a photo."

Fenna nodded and fumbled inside her sleeping bag for the camera battery. She unzipped it from a pocket within the down hood of the bag. Mikael listened to the dogs as the team began to challenge the wolf. The anchor chains rattled as the wolf turned to face the excited males. The dogs' complaints increased as Fenna thrust her feet into her boots, glanced at Mikael and untied the tunnel entrance.

Under the glow of the moon, the white arctic wolf shone greater than its shadow. The wheel dogs anchored next in line to Betty tugged at their chains in frustration and lupine energy. The wolf snapped, incisors bared, nostrils flared and gums pulled so far back its red maw burned in the moonlight. As Betty and the wolf danced to the limit of her chain, Fenna crept closer and exposed the pair. In the sudden glare of the flash, the wolf pulled at the bitch, their hindquarters lapping and overlapping in his frenzy. The team howled and the wolf, maddened with flight instincts, finally ripped its penis from the team's lead dog and cut a path across the ice, its black shadow three feet to the left of a blur of white.

Fenna slipped the camera in-between the thermal upper layers of her clothes. As she approached Betty she reached down and stroked a thumb over her nose and between her eyes. Betty nuzzled into Fenna's legs. She knelt down in the snow and Betty buried her head in the crook of her arm. As Fenna stroked the dog's fur, cold and dry, encrusted with snow and the wild scents of feral sex, she glimpsed the wolf in the distance, sitting on its haunches, silent, waiting. Fenna slipped free of Betty and retreated to the tent. The smell of coffee drifted through the tunnel entrance as she wormed her way inside.

"Everything alright?" said Mikael as he handed Fenna a mug of coffee, steaming in the lamplight.

"They were locked tight," said Fenna. "You didn't look?"

"I stuck my head out of the tent for a bit. Came back in to make another coffee. He was a big fella. His paws must have been the size of my hands," Mikael said and held them up in the light. "A little scrawny though."

"He was," Fenna said and took a sip from the mug. "Are we getting up?"

"I thought so. Seeing as we're all awake." Mikael collected the ingredients for breakfast. "Besides, I didn't like the look of the clouds in the east, yesterday. I want to crack on. Let's get this satellite and get home."

"Sure." Fenna placed her mug on top of a sledging box. "Pass me the diary. I'll make a note of the day. It's going to be pretty interesting to see what we've got seven weeks from now."

Mikael stabbed a spoon in the air between them. "I've yet to meet a single fire-breathing hairy bastard that didn't go week at the knees at the sight of a puppy. You, my friend, are going to be just one more gooey mess of glee when Betty whelps. There, I said it."

"And you won't?"

"We're not talking about me, rookie."

"Fine," she said and blew on the surface of the coffee. With her first sip she caught sight of Mikael's prized Webley revolver, hanging in its holster by the side of his sledging bag. "Shouldn't that be outside?"

"What?" Mikael turned in the direction Fenna was pointing. "Oh, the Webley." Mikael pulled it onto his lap, set his coffee mug down on the box and drew the revolver. "Yeah," he said. "It might freeze a little, but it's not as critical as the rifle." The Enfield lay underneath the right side of the tent, close at hand, but far removed from the condensation within the tent that might freeze the working parts and block the barrel. While the rifle was necessary to protect the patrol from chance encounters with bears, the patrol's service pistols were used as a last resort to put down a dog that could not complete the patrol.

"I thought the Glock 20 was our only sidearm?" Fenna commented. Her pistol was secure within a metal sledging chest still fastened to the sledge as ballast in the event of an unexpected arctic storm.

"It is," Mikael said and presented the Webley to

Fenna, "This is more of an heirloom. A little bit of unnecessary weight passed down from one patrolman to the next." He smiled as Fenna tested the weight of the pistol. "It's yours when we're done with this patrol."

"Mine?"

"Yours to pass on to your first-year patrolman, next year, if you think he deserves it."

"If *he* deserves it, eh?" said Fenna. "*He* might be a *she*, you know?"

"You're the first woman ever to make it through selection. I won't hold my breath."

"We'll see. Got any ammunition?"

"Plenty," said Mikael. "Well, enough anyway. Never had to use it. And I don't remember it ever being used for more than target practice. It's a museum piece you know? Some collectors out there would pay a lot of money for a Webley."

"eBay?" said Fenna.

"eBay? Sod that," Mikael scoffed. "Anyone selling this would want to put it into the classifieds of an international gun magazine or sell it at auction." Mikael snatched the revolver out of Fenna's hands. "It's not yours yet, mate. And you're not bloody selling it."

Fenna held out her hands in apology as Mikael tucked the revolver back in its holster and hung it out of reach. As silence settled once more within the tent they grinned at each other over their mugs.

"eBay?" Mikael said and shook his head.

ITTOQQORTOORMIIT, EAST GREENLAND

Petersen tugged at the doors of the sticky cupboards in the tiny kitchen, searching for more coffee as

Vestergaard read through the last page of his notes. Fenna glanced from the microphone to Vestergaard and back again. She pursed her lips and tapped a finger on the table.

"I'll be with you in just one moment, Konstabel," Vestergaard said without looking up.

"I was just wondering," Fenna said as she pointed at the microphone. "Why are you making such thorough notes when you are recording the whole thing?"

Petersen paused mid-search and turned to glance at the microphone. Vestergaard raised his eyes and peered at Fenna.

"Actually," Fenna said. "I'm not even sure it's switched on."

"Petersen," Vestergaard said.

Fenna watched as Petersen leaned around Vestergaard to fiddle with the microphone. She turned to look at Vestergaard as he closed his notebook. Petersen nodded and removed the battery cover. He showed it to Fenna.

"Needs a new battery," he said with a shrug. "Must have forgot to replace it after the last time we used it."

"When was that?" Fenna asked.

Petersen closed the battery compartment. He looked up. "When was what?"

"The last time you used the microphone?"

"Last month," Vestergaard said. He leaned back in his chair and crossed his legs. "I was recording notes for my memoir. I must have left it on." He shrugged. "I'm not the most proficient with technology as any of my daughters will tell you."

Fenna folded her hands on the table and waited.

Petersen removed the microphone and placed it on the counter. There was the sound of raven claws on the roof of the police station as Fenna waited for Vestergaard to continue.

"It's still official," he said with a wave of his notebook.

"But with no guarantees for me," Fenna said.

"Very well." Vestergaard nodded at Petersen. "How is your shorthand, Sergent?"

"Rusty, I'm afraid, sir."

"Well, do your best, for the benefit of the Konstabel." Vestergaard said and folded his hands upon the notebook in his lap. "Is that acceptable?"

Fenna bit at the inside of her lip and waited. She glanced at the wall, pressing her thumbnail into her fingertips as she thought.

"Can we continue, Konstabel?" Vestergaard said. He clicked the top of his pen.

"Yes," Fenna said with a nod. "Let's get on with it."

NORTHEAST GREENLAND NAT. PARK

Call-sign *Fever Dog* ran ahead of the storm for three days before it drove them onto the ice. Fenna cursed stubby digits as the wind chilled the blood from her fingers. The fascination of skin freezing on metal was short lived as they concentrated on routine in the flurry of snow, the ferocity of ice splinters and the fury of an arctic storm. As the dogs curled deeper and deeper into the snow at night the temperatures dropped below fifty. Mikael risked more fuel and they added more fat to their diet. The dogs devoured frozen chunks of seal blubber, waiting out the storm, insulated with every layer of snow that buried them.

Inside the tent, Fenna prodded her finger at the tumours of snow bulging at the canvas walls. The wind shrieked as it wrestled with the tunnel baffle and whipped loose guy lines into blind flails of icy cord. The patrol was grounded, buried and alone.

Fenna woke to a rumbling spatter of bowels. The stale air moved around the inside of the tent as the walls buffeted in the arctic gale. She shifted onto her back and retrieved her headlamp from inside her sleeping bag.

"Don't turn on the light," said Mikael.

"Are you all right?"

"It's messy but I'll live. Just so long as it's just the shits, we can't afford to get sick out here."

"Something we ate?"

"Yeah, that curry you ordered, I think we can get our money back."

Fenna chuckled.

"Laugh it up, mate. It'll be your turn later."

Fenna listened as Mikael tied a knot in the plastic bag. "Are you going to throw it outside?"

"No. I thought I would use it as a pillow. Stupid fuck," said Mikael.

"Well, see you in the morning."

"Yeah," said Mikael.

Fenna listened as Mikael finished pulling up his thermals and crawled into his sleeping bag as gusts of wind buffeted a fetid combination of coriander and herbs around the tent.

ITTOQQORTOORMIIT, EAST GREENLAND

"Very descriptive, Konstabel. Thank you."

"You're welcome," Fenna said and grinned at the

memory.

"So that was the storm? The *piteraq*, I think you called it," Vestergaard said as he checked his notes.

"That night and the following day were the worst. The storm just made everything that bit more difficult."

"So, how heavy is a typical patrol sledge?" Vestergaard asked as he checked his mobile. He frowned and returned it to his jacket pocket. Fenna watched him.

"About 350 to 400 kilos." Fenna pushed the base of her mug with her fingertips. "Maratse has been gone a long time."

"Yes," Vestergaard said and turned in his chair. "Petersen?"

"I'll see if I can find him," Petersen said with a quick drum of fingers on the kitchen counter. "If I can't, I'll be back within the hour."

"Bring something for dinner," said Vestergaard.

"I'll see what I can find. Although I don't imagine there'll be much before the first supply ship breaks through the ice." Petersen left the kitchen, pausing at the entrance to Maratse's office to lift his jacket from the hook.

"Lucifer pulled well the next day."

"Lucifer?"

"We put Betty in a canvas bag on the sledge. Less of a distraction."

"And Lucifer was the new lead dog?"

"Yes. That was the day the storm really hit us. Mikael and I took it in turns to lead the way, the dogs following, Lucifer always on our heels."

"It sounds tough," Vestergaard poured more coffee.

"It was."

Chapter 9

NORTHEAST GREENLAND NAT. PARK

Fenna lifted her foot, a sudden gust of wind pushed her off balance. She fell onto her side and broke her fall with a splayed hand. Lucifer licked her cheek. Fenna pushed herself up, wiped her goggles and brushed swathes of snow from her arms and thighs. The wind whipped snow darts at her body. She pushed on, breaking the trail, one mulish metre after the other. Fenna led the team as Mikael struggled to guide the sledge from the rear.

At the top of a steep gully she braced her hand, palm up, against the wind. She took hold of Lucifer's collar and halted the team's progress. Mikael clumped through the snow. He slipped one hand along the sledge, all the way to the gangline, and then followed that all the way to Fenna's side.

"What do you think?" Fenna shouted and pointed at the slope.

"Steep." Mikael looked back at the team, the wind snapping at his collar. "The sledge will take them out on the way down. We'll have to tip it." He cracked a smile through his beard of ice. "I'm having fun now. How about you?"

"What?" Fenna leaned in towards Mikael.

"Having fun?" he shouted in her ear.

"If I had bollocks they'd be sweating."

Mikael grinned, his teeth flashing between the icicles hanging from his beard. "Then let's keep going before you cool down. I'll go back and anchor the sledge, hold the team until you work your way back to me. We'll tip the sledge on its side and let the dogs pull it over the lip. We can hang onto the dead man's rope."

"Say again. That last bit?"

Mikael stumbled into Fenna, fighting the wind. "Rope."

"Okay," Fenna shouted. "I'll get ready." Lucifer jumped up, tugging at his harness. Fenna clicked a foot out of her skis and stamped down on the gangline. "He's pretty keyed up."

"They all are."

"Let's do it then."

Fenna watched Mikael work his way back along the sledge. She waited as he lifted Betty from the holdall securing her to the sledge. He slipped her free to let her run beside the team. Fenna clicked her heel back into her skis and skied the length of the team. She tugged at the gangline, pulling the dogs back, holding them in check. When she reached Mikael, she made ready to help tip the sledge on its side. The sledge sloped down to the right, its left runner knifed into a snow bank. The gear shifted ever so slightly within the ropes securing it to the thwarts.

"Get on the downward side," Mikael shouted. "Pull it over. I'll lift it as it comes up."

Fenna moved behind and around the sledge. She gripped one of the ropes securing the equipment to the sledge in a criss-cross pattern, and leaned back.

"Come on, Fenna." Mikael squatted on the opposite side of the sledge, fingers under the runner.

The wind snapped at her jacket. Fenna swore. She tugged harder. *I'm about twenty kilos too light for this*, she cursed. She threw her weight away from the sledge and felt it move. "It's coming."

Mikael grunted as the sledge started to tip. "Clear," he yelled. The left hand runner started to slip out of the patrolman's hands. "Fenna? You clear?"

"Let it go," Fenna scrabbled out of the way. She worked her way back to the rear of the sledge, and picked up the trailing line. The sledge slumped onto its side in the snow. Fenna looked along the gangline at the dogs.

Mikael joined her at the rear of the sledge and pulled the rifle out of its holster. He slung the rifle over his chest, positioning it so it hung comfortably from his shoulder to the opposite hip. The spare sling after the buckle cracked like a whip in the wind. "Don't want to damage it," he said.

"Are we ready?"

"Yes," Mikael said and adjusted his goggles. "Let's get started."

"Come on now, boys," Fenna shouted to the dogs. "Let's go." Lucifer tugged at the line, his harness taut, the traces vibrating along the length of the team as each dog pulled. "Let's go." Fenna and Mikael gripped the upright angled horizontally before them, pushing as the dogs pulled. The sledge inched forward.

"Come on, boys," Mikael said. His breath frosted another layer of ice in his beard.

The dogs dragged the sledge through the snow. It inched towards the lip of the slope. Fenna lifted her head, watching as first Lucifer then Piska and the team bully, Ninja, dropped over the lip and out of sight. The wind blasted a fresh salvo of ice into her face.

"Here we go," Mikael said and took a bight of the dead man's rope. "You ready?"

"We'll try and turn it? Maximum drag?" Fenna shouted.

"We don't want it to roll. Keep it straight. Kick off your skis. Slide them under the rifle bag."

As the last of the dogs crested the lip, Fenna and Mikael slipped their skis under the ropes on the sledge. One hand on the upright, the other on the rope, they prepared to guide the sledge down the slope.

"Keep an eye on the dogs. I'll look out for boulders." Mikael leaned into the wind. "When the slope starts to level off, we'll stop the team and pull her back onto her runners."

"Got it," Fenna said and moved out to the left of the sledge, the front of her jacket pressed flat in the wind. She watched the wheel dogs, Cisko and Nansen, closest to the tips of the runners. Mikael leaned out to the right. The runners of the sledge crested the slope as the dogs pulled. The sledge slid free until, see-sawing in the wind, it crashed down onto the slope, picking up speed as the dogs jogged down the thick layer of frost-packed snow on the surface. "She's going." One hand on the upright, Fenna staggered around the side.

"I got it," Mikael shouted and lengthened his strides, crunching air from the snow with his heels as he broke the surface. "Boulder to the right."

"What?" Fenna kicked snow into the wind as she descended the slope. "Mikael?"

"We missed it," Mikael shouted over the sledge. "We're clear until the..."

"What?"

"Let go of the rope," Mikael yelled. He yanked the rope out of Fenna's hand and bounded the length of the sledge. Mikael ducked in front of it and pulled the rope taut around the runners. He waited the second it took for Fenna to join him. "Pull," he said and thrust the rope into Fenna's hands. With snow pillowing under their heels, they hauled on the rope as the sledge pendulumed around the human anchor. The sledge quivered onto both runners as gravity clawed at it. "Keep hold of the rope," Mikael said and leaped after the sledge. He reached for the runners, stumbling as his feet broke the surface crust of snow, pinning him to the spot. "Fenna?"

She tossed the rope at Mikael and took off after the sledge as it slid into position, streamlining behind the string of dogs running before it. As Fenna caught the sledge the tip of the left-hand runner slid up and over Cisko, crushing the wheel dog. Fenna dug her heels into the snow, and hung low from the uprights. With the seat of her trousers dragging like an anchor, she stalled the sledge. Mikael pulled the trailing line over one shoulder and under the opposite arm, belaying the sledge to a stop as Fenna sat down in the deep snow.

"Whoa," Mikael called to the dogs. "Whoa, now." The sledge stopped. The right-hand runner less than a dog's width from Nansen. "Fenna? You okay?"

"I'm fine," she said, both hands gripping the uprights. *Barely okay*, she thought and worked hard to control her breathing, coughing icy air into her lungs.

"Have a look at Cisko," Mikael said as he fed the rope around his body. He worked his way down to the sledge, snow flurrying from his shoulders in the wind. He watched Fenna move along the left-hand side of the sledge. She stopped halfway. "How is he?"

"Not good," Fenna said as she crouched next to the wheel dog. Cisko lay panting beneath the runner. "At least one of his back legs is broken." She pulled the frozen fleece neckie below her chin and stood up. "A few ribs."

"Shit," Mikael said as he reached the sledge and gripped the uprights.

"Shall I do it?" Fenna shouted into the wind.

"I can if you want," Mikael said and tossed the trailing line behind him.

"No. I can do it." Fenna crouched down in the snow beside Cisko and stroked the dog's fur, smoothing his ears flat along the side of his head. "It's okay, fella." Fenna popped the flap of her holster, pulled out the Glock. "It's okay." She stepped back, holding the pistol in a firm two-handed grip. The team shuddered in their traces as she put a bullet through the wheel dog's skull. The crack of the shot pierced the wind, rebounding between the indifferent granite walls of the gully. She took a breath. *It needed to be done.* Fenna holstered the Glock and unclipped Cisko's lines from his harness and collar. She stood up. "We'll have to let the sledge run forward before I can pull him out."

"All right. Come back here and help me." The sledge slid forward as they pushed from the rear. The dogs tugged until they called them to a stop. Fenna stooped to remove Cisko's harness.

"Fenna, you okay?" Mikael said. He held Cisko's body as she tugged the harness over the wheel dog's head. Free of the dog's body it snapped in the wind.

"I'm okay," she said with a weak nod of the head. "He was a good dog." She patted the dog's side and stood up. Fenna looped the harness and Cisko's collar over the upright. "What shall we do with him?"

"Leave him for the foxes and ravens," Mikael said and fiddled with his goggles. He cast a glance over the team at the way ahead. "See where it flattens out?" he said and pointed. "It's only a few kilometres to the ice. We'll make camp just off the ice foot. We can skirt around the next headland on the sea ice and make better time."

"Okay." Fenna reached down and smoothed her fingers over Cisko's eyes.

"Let's go then." Mikael slipped the rifle from his shoulder and returned it to the holster as Fenna clicked her heels into her skis. He put his own skis on and nodded to Fenna that he was ready.

"Come on, boys," Fenna shouted into the wind. The dogs pulled the sledge down the slope, snow from the runners spinning into Arctic dervishes in the wind all the way to the sea ice.

Chapter 10

ITTOQQORTOORMIIT, EAST GREENLAND

The tiny kitchen was cramped and stuffy with stale smoke and old coffee. Fenna longed for the fresh air and open skies of the sledge patrol. She stared at the tabletop until Vestergaard spoke.

"That was the third dog killed during your first year with Sirius," Vestergaard said. He paused to write a note. "There was nothing you could do?"

"Cisko was in pain," Fenna said and drummed her fingers on the surface of the table. "We have an intensive veterinarian course during training. We can pull teeth and stitch bites and that kind of thing. But you can't fix a broken leg on patrol, and a dog can't pull with broken ribs."

"So you killed Cisko."

"I put him down. There's a difference," Fenna said and took a breath. "You need to understand these are 'working dogs'. The Greenlanders understand it better than anyone. We love our dogs. We talk to them, and confide in them on patrol when our partners are driving us nuts. But they're still working dogs."

"I don't know," Vestergaard said and shrugged. "I'm pretty sure my wife would disagree."

"I'm sure she would." Fenna stood up. "I need to pee."

"Okay." Vestergaard pushed back his chair and leaned back as Fenna squeezed past.

She locked herself in the toilet next to the cell, lifted the lid and stared at two days' worth of human ablutions. Fenna sat on the toilet, a plastic bag lining the bucket beneath the seat, rested her elbows on her knees and held her head in her hands.

"Damn, Mikael. I'm sorry," she said and wiped a tear from her cheek. She sat in silence on the toilet and thought about the camp they had made that night near the ice foot, how the tidal creaks and groans in the ice vibrated through the tent as the wind *whumped* at the tent sides and wrenched at the guy lines.

NORTHEAST GREENLAND NAT. PARK

"Fenna? Are you done?" Mikael shouted, slapping his hand on the outside wall of the canvas tunnel tent. "I'm finished with the dogs. Ready to come in."

"Yeah, I'm done."

Mikael crawled through the baffle at the entrance to the tent, rolled onto his backside and removed his boots. "I like what you've done with the place," he said as the ice from his beard began to melt in the heat of the tent. Fenna gave him the finger and stirred the evening meal over the gas burner.

"How are the kids?" she said and leaned to one side as Mikael crawled onto his camp bed.

"They're fine. I gave them your regards," he said and checked his watch. "Is the radio ready?"

"All set. It's tuned to the normal patrol frequency. We don't have to use any of the code words before we get to the cabin." *It's a real shame*, she thought, a smile on her lips. "It'll be nice to get the news from base, hear what's going on with the other teams." Fenna passed Mikael a bowl of beef stew.

"This is good," he said as he wiped his thawing beard and spooned stew into his mouth.

"I know." Fenna leaned back against her camp bed. She checked her watch and turned on the radio, a robust relic from a decommissioned submarine, increasing the volume to compete with the wind.

"Calling all Sirius teams, this is Daneborg," the radio hissed. "We start with a storm warning. Easterly winds increasing from thirty to forty-five metres per second in the course of the night, reaching forty-seven metres per second in the early hours of the morning. Temperatures increasing to minus sixteen. Heavy snow forecast along the coast south of Mestersvig."

"That's us," Mikael said. He held his spoon poised over his bowl.

"It's going to be a hell of a day tomorrow."

Mikael shrugged and took another spoonful of stew as the radio operator in Daneborg read aloud letters and emails from home. He tilted his bowl and spooned the remaining stew into his mouth. "This is really good."

"You've said that already."

"I have," Mikael said and nodded. He tapped the back of the spoon on his chin. "And, considering your cheeky response to your senior..."

"Cheeky response?"

"To a senior officer, yes," Mikael continued. "I think it only fair that it's you who crawls out into the abyss and gives the dogs a cube of blubber."

"Because you forgot?"

"Because I forgot."

"I was the inside man today."

"You were, that is correct. Now you are making amends for hinting that your senior officer has a touch of senility."

"A touch?" Fenna tossed her empty bowl into Mikael's lap. "Seeing as we just switched roles, you're on dishes, coffee and dessert."

"I think I can manage that." Mikael paused at the smile creeping across Fenna's chapped lips. "What?"

"I don't know," she said and shrugged. "It's just..."

"Spit it out, Fenna."

"All right," she said and took a quick breath. "I didn't expect our relationship to work like this."

"Like what?"

"Like two guys on patrol. I thought the weak woman thing would get in the way." Fenna studied Mikael's face as he returned her look. She felt a slight tremor of embarrassment as he opened his mouth to speak.

"You've seen the movie?"

"God," Fenna said and rolled her eyes. "*G.I. Jane*? They called me that during training. Are you saying I'm Demi Moore?"

"Hardly," Mikael said with a cheeky grin. "She is far better looking." He flinched as Fenna looked around the tent for something to throw at him. "And I'm better looking than Viggo," he said and caught the spoon Fenna threw at his head. "I'm just saying that there's a reason you're here. I don't give a shit what they called you in training. We took two new men last year – and one of them was a woman. If you couldn't do the job, you wouldn't be here. But I'm not going to dwell on the woman-in-a-man's-world, crap. Honestly, I haven't got time for that. Sure, we had the meeting..."

"There was a meeting?"

"Don't be naive – of course there was a meeting. You're the first woman to join the patrol. I volunteered to have you on my team, mostly because I was curious. How would the dogs respond to a female patroller? How would I?"

"And?"

"Hah," Mikael said and threw the spoon at Fenna. "Not so fast, rookie. You'll get my evaluation when we're done, and not before. Now, get outside and see to the kids."

Fenna turned to study the walls of the tent, composing her smile as they bowed and flattened with each gust of wind curling in across the frozen surface of the Greenland Sea. She pulled on her outer layers and crawled past Mikael.

"Thanks," she said and squeezed his shoulder on her way out.

"You're welcome," he said and watched as she crawled out through the tent baffle and into the storm.

Fenna staggered among the dogs, treading on those she couldn't see as they lay, all but buried, beneath a thick layer of wind-blown snow. Fléchettes of snow bored into the pores of her jacket, stinging her face in gusts of tiny needles as she bent over each dog, slipping a large cube of seal fat between eager jaws. She made her way back to the tent, kicking the worst of the snow from her boots, clapping great clumps from her mittens, before burrowing into the baffle and pulling the stiff fleece neckie away from her face to breathe. She tied the baffle closed behind her and crawled into the living space of the tent.

"Hot drink," Mikael said and pushed a mug of tea into Fenna's mittened hands.

"It's tea," she said as she sniffed the contents of the mug.

"And?"

"We have plenty of coffee."

"And too much tea," Mikael tossed the teaspoon into an empty bowl. "I'm doing my best to get rid of it."

Fenna leaned forward. She sniffed Mikael's mug. "You have coffee."

"Yes," he said and leaned back on his camp bed. "I didn't pack the tea."

Fenna sat on her heels, placed her mug on the floor and removed her mittens, pearls of ice frozen within the wool fibres rattled as she tossed them onto the floor.

"We made good time today, despite the weather. We are relatively close to the crash site," Mikael said and sipped his coffee. "If we push on through the storm to the cabin, we can dump the gear and be at the site by midday tomorrow. Weather depending."

"Should we push on in this?" Fenna baulked at the thought.

"That's why they sent us. Because we can."

"But should we?"

Another gust of wind buffeted the tent, with a shower of ice grating over the cotton like a swathe of sandpaper.

Mikael swung his legs over the side of the bed. "I think it's implied."

ITTOQQORTOORMIIT, EAST GREENLAND

When did we start calling them kids? Fenna brushed her hair from her eyes as the hollow clump of boots on the stairs roused Fenna from her thoughts. She washed her hands and left the bathroom. Petersen and Vestergaard stood close to one another in Maratse's office, talking quietly. They stopped as Fenna closed the door to the toilet.

"Ah, Fenna," Vestergaard said with a nod to Petersen. He left the younger man in the office. "Something has come up." He gripped her elbow and guided her to the kitchen.

"What?"

"It seems that Maratse has been busy, and his search has been productive." He gestured to the chair. "Sit down, Konstabel."

"Has he found Dina?"

"Not exactly."

"So what is the problem?"

"Petersen found Maratse talking with an older hunter down by the ice. From what he can make out, it would appear that Dina is missing. We presume she is dead."

"Dead?" Fenna said and sank into her chair.

"The details are sketchy," Vestergaard said and put on his most sympathetic look. "This information does put us in a bit of a bind."

"What kind of bind?"

"Well," he said and sat down, "If Dina was the only witness who would be willing or able to corroborate your side of the story..."

"My side of the..."

"You understand? Until we know anything for certain," he paused. "Perhaps you would continue from where you left off?"

Fenna stared at the floor beneath her chair. Her hair fell over her cheeks, hiding her eyes. *She can't be dead, or I may as well be.*

"The fog is clearing, Fenna," Vestergaard prompted.

Chapter 11

NORTHEAST GREENLAND NAT. PARK

The descent to Loch Fyne cabin was uneventful, despite the wind peeling layers of exposed skin from their faces. Mikael helped Fenna to anchor the dogs to the travelling chain before grabbing the shovel and digging the snow from the cabin door. A testament to the determination of the pre-war Danish hunters, the cabin had lasted well, and was a favourite of many of the Sirius patrolmen. The name was carved into a broken ski, the tip tapering above the red wooden door. A muskox skull kept watch from its mount beneath the apex of the roof. The teams repaired the cabins during the summers, caching supplies in preparation for the spring and autumn patrols. Once the door was dug out, Mikael stepped onto the bench to remove the shutters from the window to the right of the door and made a quick inspection for signs of polar bears. Fenna joined him.

"Are we going inside?" she said, her words whipped from her mouth by the wind.

"We'll move the gear inside. Then I'll feed the dogs while you cook dinner." Mikael punched Fenna on the arm. "You get to sleep in a real bed tonight." Fenna grinned, took a breath and turned back into the wind.

The dogs were already half-buried in the snow by the time they had moved all but the essential survival equipment inside the cabin. Fenna closed the door behind Mikael as he returned to feed the dogs. She pulled off her outer layers and left her boots by the door, hanging her clothes on the nails behind it. She turned to explore the interior of the cabin, following the strings and pegs hung from the simple rafters to the map of Greenland pinned to the back wall of the cabin. The dark and aged wood panels framed a long thick mattress dressed with coarse sacking. She ran her hand along the cold metal surface of the Morsø wood-burning stove and smiled at the box of matches by the side of the kindling. Three matches stood proud of the box. Easy to grip and strike, she realised. Even with numb fingers. The stove was ready to be lit, just as the teams had left it the previous summer.

Fenna lit the stove and took a moment to explore the tiny bookshelf as the fire crackled into life, light from the flames licking at the nudes pinned to the walls. The bookshelf wedged a selection of literature between the bruised wooden sides. The titles ranged from airport thrillers to polar texts, some of which belonged in a museum, but it was the cabin diary that caught Fenna's attention. She cracked the spine and let her finger drift over the first few lines, and then slipped it back onto the shelf to read after dinner.

She returned to the stove and closed the glass door before hunting through the supplies piled in the centre of the cabin. She found what she was looking for and lit the propane gas cooking stove the teams had fixed the previous summer. An hour passed before Mikael was finished feeding the dogs and checking their feet for ice. Fenna beamed as he opened the door and sniffed.

"Bread?" he said.

"We have a stove."

Mikael organised his clothes and flopped into one of two armchairs. He picked at the battered leather padding on the arms, crossed his feet and nodded.

"Best place in the park," he said and closed his

eyes.

ITTOQQORTOORMIIT, EAST GREENLAND

Fenna clasped her hands together and rested her elbows on the table. She hid her mouth behind her hands and stared at Vestergaard over her fingers. He looked up as he finished making a note. Petersen had long since given up on his shorthand, and Fenna was beginning to wonder if it was even necessary.

"Loch Fyne," Vestergaard said as he closed his notebook. "Is this *the* cabin?"

Fenna dipped her head and blinked slowly, affirmatively.

"*Best place in the park*," Vestergaard read from his notes. "It's a shame there's nothing left. Of course," he said as Fenna let her hair fall in front of her eyes, "We won't actually know the extent of the damage before the helicopter returns with Oversergent Gregersen's body, will we?"

Fenna took a few measured breaths. If there was pity in Vestergaard's eyes, she couldn't see it, and then her vision was clouded with tears.

NORTHEAST GREENLAND NAT. PARK

An hour had passed since they tethered Betty outside the cabin and sledged in the direction of the satellite. Fenna could still hear the bitch's howl of protest. It echoed in her ears as she studied the compass clasped in the palm of her mitten.

"Use the GPS, Fenna. Forget the bloody compass," Mikael shouted. With both hands on the uprights of the lightly-laden sledge, he leaned into the wind. "Did you hear what I said?"

Fenna staggered back from the front of the team

and placed one knee on the sledge, sheltering the GPS between her back and the sledge bag.

"How far are we?" Mikael said as he joined her. He licked at the ice hanging like candy canes from the hairs above his lip.

"We should be within a few kilometres. I'm using the waypoints to box the coordinates," Fenna said and tugged her neckie down under her chin. "I plotted them last night, but the temperature is playing hell with the batteries. That's why I'm using this," she said and held up the compass secured around her wrist on a thick spectra lanyard.

"Okay, but we need to keep moving."

"I know, but..." She blinked at the stark white landscape. The team had been sheltered from the wind when ascending the gully. On top of the plateau, nearing the crash site, there was no escaping the needle-sharp wind and the freezing temperatures.

"The wind is ripping through us here," Mikael said. "So long as we have reasonable visibility we have to keep moving."

"I know. We should keep going." Fenna pulled her neckie over her nose and cheeks and walked back to the front of the team. She leaned into the wind. With her skis bound to the sledge, Fenna led the team on foot. Mikael pushed the sledge from the rear. After ten minutes of slow progress, a lull in the wind allowed the team to secure their position with the GPS and begin boxing the location of the crash site.

"There," Mikael said and slowed the sledge to a stop. Fenna turned, looked in the direction he was pointing and took a bearing on a black object half a kilometre away on the plateau. She waved at Mikael and jogged back to the sledge. "Do you want to ride?"

"Sure," Fenna said and sat down on the thwarts. She swung her legs into the centre of the sledge.

"Haw," Mikael called and guided the sledge to the left as Lucifer pulled the team around. Sunlight splintered the clouds and the wind brushed little more than a light layer of snow along the surface. The dogs picked up the pace, enjoying the break in the weather and the lighter sledge.

"Finally," Fenna said and leaned back against the sledge boxes containing the tent and basic provisions they would need if they were caught out on the ice. Mikael jogged around the left side of the sledge and leaped on. He squirmed his right foot between the boxes and the upright, standing at the rear of the sledge, like a buccaneer at the wheel of a corvette escaping the doldrums. Fenna fished a compact digital camera out of her jacket and took a shot of her partner, pearls of ice shining in his beard, the light reflecting in his eyes. "Now you're smiling," she said and took another photo. *That's one for Facebook*, she thought.

"Now we're sledging," Mikael said. He grinned and struck a pose worthy of a teenage selfie, framing his ice-matted beard within the apex of his finger and thumb. "Look," he said and pointed. "Lucifer has it now." The traces between each dog pinged tight as Lucifer picked up speed, homing in on the satellite half-buried in the snow before them.

"We should probably slow down," Fenna said and repositioned to a crouch on the sledge, ready to leap off and restrain the dogs.

"Wait until we get a bit closer." Mikael turned his body through a slow arc, searching the terrain in front of and behind the sledge. "I think we've got the place to ourselves."

"We're the only ones stupid enough to sledge through that storm," Fenna said and grinned. "Worth it."

"Yeah, okay rookie," Mikael said and shook his head at her teenage euphemism. "Get ready to get off." Mikael called out to the dogs to slow. He stepped off the sledge and jogged alongside until the team slowed to a stop. Fenna hopped off the sledge and walked the length of the team, securing Lucifer at the lead while Mikael organised the anchor line. He drove three ice anchors into the snow and secured a thin chain in a line between the metal plates. Fenna unclipped one dog at a time from the sledge traces and attached them by the collar to a length of chain branching out from the anchor line. Once the team was settled, Mikael and Fenna pushed the sledge closer to the satellite. Flurries of snow settled as the wind dropped. Beyond the satellite, and stretching across Greenland, ancient tongues of ice licked out from the Greenland Ice Sheet.

"I never thought to ask," Fenna started.

"What?"

"If it was radioactive."

"They probably wouldn't tell us if it was," Mikael said and walked around the satellite, noting the impact rings forming a circular perimeter in the snow interspersed with fragments of shrapnel. "It's relatively intact. What we can see of it." He took a step closer.

"I thought it would be round, like Sputnik," Fenna joined Mikael as he lifted the square panel out of the snow. It came off in his hands.

"Okay, not so intact."

"We'll need a sack, not a net, eh?"

"Looks that way."

"That looks important," Fenna said and reached into the shell of the satellite. She wiped a layer of snow from a panel of chips and circuitry. "No idea what it is, but it has a whole load of serial numbers." She turned it in the light, "and a name: Humble Technologies, Inc."

"That's the one Kjersing highlighted in the mission briefing."

"We'll need the screwdrivers to remove it," Fenna said and stood up. "I'll go get them."

ITTOQQORTOORMIIT, EAST GREENLAND

Fenna stopped speaking and waited as Petersen and Vestergaard exchanged a look. Vestergaard closed his notebook, pushed back his chair and stood up. He leaned against the cracked kitchen counter next to Petersen. The look they gave Fenna reminded her of wolves she had seen in a documentary on television, at the moment when they had run their quarry ragged and were regrouping to finish it off.

"Maybe I should see that letter," Fenna said. "The official one."

Fenna caught the faint smile teasing Petersen's lips before he looked away. She stared at Vestergaard. He took a long breath before reaching into his pocket and removing a packet of cigarettes.

"Do you smoke, Konstabel?" Vestergaard said as he tapped a cigarette into his hand.

"No, and I didn't think you did."

"That thing with the ashtray?" Vestergaard laughed. "I thought it would make you more comfortable to remove it."

"Comfortable?" Fenna looked around the kitchen and smirked.

"Yes," Vestergaard said and paused to light his cigarette. "It's cosy in here isn't it." He took a long drag. The tip of the cigarette glowed as he stared at Fenna. "Leave us for a moment, Sergent."

"All right," Petersen said. He shrugged and walked out of the kitchen. "I'll wait outside for Maratse."

"And go and find out if Burwardsley is done with his report," Vestergaard called after him. He turned to face Fenna, took another drag on the cigarette and then extinguished it with water from the tap above the kitchen sink. "Foul things," he said and tossed the cigarette into a bag of rubbish in the corner of the kitchen.

"Mikael preferred pipes," Fenna said. She watched Vestergaard as he washed his hands and returned to his seat at the table. "Although, I think it was a comfort thing considering the little he actually smoked."

"Yes." Vestergaard nodded. "Comfort." He opened his notebook and flipped through the pages from the beginning. "I can't imagine it was very comfortable on patrol."

"It had its moments."

"Like at the cabin?"

"Yes. Loch Fyne was a..."

"Was that the first time you heard the name Humble Technologies?"

Fenna frowned. "At the mission briefing? Yes."

"Have you heard of Richard Humble? In the media perhaps?"

"No." Fenna paused. *This is taking a new direction,*

she thought. "Is he the owner of Humble Technologies?"

"A relation," Vestergaard said and continued. "What did you do with the component?" he said and pressed the nib of his pen on a fresh page in his notebook. "Where did you put it?"

"In the sledge bag that hangs from the uprights, we put all kinds of crap in there," she said and gauged the reaction on Vestergaard's face. To his credit, she mused, he practically ignored her, but for the smug dimples of satisfaction at the corners of his mouth.

Chapter 12

NORTHEAST GREENLAND NAT. PARK

Fenna unscrewed the part labelled Humble Technologies Inc. and gave it to Mikael.

"Put it in the sledge bag, together with any of the other smaller bits," Mikael said and laid the panel flat on the snow beside him. "We'll put the larger pieces in the net. Should be okay."

Fenna carried the circuit panel to the sledge, opened the flap of the canvas sledge bag looped between the uprights and dropped it inside. She walked to the rear of the sledge, gripped the uprights and pushed it over to Mikael. She teased the cargo net out from where it was wedged under the lengths of cord tied between the sledge thwarts and spread it out on the free area at the front of the sledge. Mikael pulled large sections of the satellite across the ice and laid them on top of the net.

"We'll have to dig the last part out. I'll do that while you box the area and see if we have everything. Better do that now, while the wind is favourable." He looked at Fenna and paused. "Better call it in on the satphone."

"I'll do that," she said and pulled the satellite phone from the sledge bag. Fenna called Daneborg while boxing the crash site. She scanned the ground three times in ever increasing boxes, finding nothing of interest. She walked back to Mikael as he placed the last parts of the satellite on the cargo net. "The guys at Daneborg say 'hi'."

"Okay. Thanks." Mikael pointed at the sledge. "I found the lens. That's probably the most important part."

"The most expensive," Fenna stared at the scrap metal lying on the sledge. "Not quite so glamorous anymore. Not worth Cisko."

Mikael walked to her side and let the shovel fall into the snow at his feet. "Somebody thinks so," he said and shrugged. "I think we have everything. If we leave now we can be back at the cabin in a couple of hours," he said and glanced up at the clouds. "The weather is holding. If all goes well, we can arrange a pick-up for tomorrow morning and save what's left of our patrol."

"Even without Cisko?"

"Yeah, I think so. We'll hit the books tonight in the cabin. Make a new plan."

"Sounds good." Fenna reached for the shovel. She slid it between the lines securing the boxes at the rear of the sledge. They worked from both sides, secured the cargo net, and added the smaller chunks of space debris to the bag before lashing the net tight to the sledge.

The mid-morning light burned through the clouds as the sun shone down on call-sign *Fever Dog*. Mikael and Fenna pulled off their outer layers and hooked the team up to the sledge. They stowed the anchor line and clicked their heels into their skis for the return journey. Picked clean of debris, the crash site disappeared with a fine dusting of snow blowing gently across the surface. With a last look to check they had everything, Mikael nodded to Fenna and gave the command for Lucifer to lead the team back along the tracks they had made.

They slowed at the crest of the long, shallow slope leading down to the cabin. Situated on the exposed shore fifty metres above the ice foot, the cabin overlooked the smooth sea ice covering the fjord. A thin, grey drift of smoke from the chimney twisted in the breeze. Fenna rubbed Lucifer's ears as she crouched in the snow by the side of the lead dog. She pinched the ice beading her eyelashes and turned as Mikael clumped through the snow to join her.

"What's up?" he said. The air creaked out of the snow as Mikael dropped to his knees.

"Smoke coming out of the chimney," Fenna said and pointed at the cabin.

"Who? I haven't heard any helicopters." He took a moment and scanned the snow around the cabin. "No dogs. We're way too far north of the Greenlanders' hunting grounds."

Fenna stroked Lucifer's nose as he wormed his head underneath her arm. "How do you want to play it?"

"If it wasn't for the satellite," Mikael glanced back at the sledge, "we would have been down there already."

"And now?"

"I don't know."

Fenna looked to the east across the flat expanse of ice covering the Greenland Sea. A shiver trembled across her shoulders. *This is it then*, she thought. *This is when life gets interesting.*

ITTOQQORTOORMIIT, EAST GREENLAND

Richard Humble. Fenna considered the name in her head. She remembered the manufacturer's name stencilled onto the satellite component, although she had no idea how it functioned or how secret it was, only that she and Mikael had been tasked to retrieve it. *During a hurricane.* She recalled the prick of ice on her cheeks and rubbed her fingers over the skin on either side of her nose. The sun had brought her freckles out, and the wind had burned her skin to a shade lighter than her hair. A sigh from Vestergaard brought her out of her thoughts and back into the close confines of the police kitchenette. Fenna decided to take a chance.

"Who is Humble?"

"We've already established that you don't know who he is," Vestergaard said and checked his mobile. "Still no signal."

"So, humour me," Fenna said.

"To what purpose?"

"Curiosity. We pushed through a storm for a piece of satellite with his name on it..."

"The name of his father's company," Vestergaard corrected her.

"Mikael died for it."

"Yes," Vestergaard said.

"Then people will kill for it, or him."

Vestergaard leaned back in his chair and studied Fenna's face. She felt his scrutiny pick at the peeled skin on her cheeks, peeling it back further and deeper as if he was searching for something. *If I'm lucky*, she thought, *he will think I'm just a dumb pawn in this game, and let something slip. Mikael died for something. I'm in the shit because of the same thing, and this guy Humble, he must...*

"Richard Humble is the third in a line of Richard Humbles. His father and his grandfather before him have run Humble Technologies Inc. successfully for the past forty years, under one name or another. The current Richard Humble maintains a more advisory role within the company – he became a lawyer. Humble and Lunk is a well-established law firm with a main office in Toronto. I read this in *Variety* magazine."

"The entertainment magazine?" Fenna said and frowned. "What does satellite technology have to do with entertainment?"

"Absolutely nothing, but the money," Vestergaard said and smiled, enjoying the topic. "Money and entertainment go hand in hand, and Richard Humble enjoys plenty of both."

"So we sledged after a piece of kit to save some millionaire's reputation?"

"No. You retrieved a sensitive component to stop it falling into the wrong hands."

"Whose?" Fenna said. "This is Greenland. There are fewer people in the entire country than there are in a small town in England. In the National Park, there is only a handful."

"And one of them is dead, Konstabel. I would say the *wrong hands* are obviously in this up to their necks. As are you," Vestergaard said and picked up his pen.

Bastard, Fenna thought. *And yet*, she realised, he had been relatively forthcoming with the information.

Fenna flicked her head towards the door as Petersen walked into the station. She noticed the sheet of paper in his hands, focusing on it as the Sergent handed it to Vestergaard. The light from the window highlighted a watermark in the centre of each of the two pages of printed writing. Fenna tilted her head and studied what looked like an image of a large ship sailing past an iceberg.

"What is *The Ice Star*?" she asked as she read the words around the logo. Vestergaard folded the papers to his chest and stared at Fenna. "It's written on the paper," she said.

"It's not important."

"No? Nothing I could read in a magazine?"

"Actually," Vestergaard said, and tucked the papers inside his jacket. "*The Ice Star* has been the subject of several articles."

"It's a ship?"

"A ship?" Vestergaard said and laughed. He turned to Petersen and gave the Sergent a look that made Fenna feel stupid. "Yes, Konstabel, you could say it was a ship."

"And Burwardsley works on it," she said and held her breath. It was a gamble.

Vestergaard's laugh died on his lips. "More coffee?" he said and waited for Petersen to take his mug.

"He wrote his notes on headed paper from the ship. Didn't he?" Fenna said and nodded towards the papers Vestergaard had inside his jacket. "His version of the story, written on the only paper he had available."

"You're quite the detective all of a sudden."

Petersen stopped pretending to make coffee and turned to listen. Fenna pressed her hands together beneath the table and steeled herself to meet the Premierløjtnant's scrutiny.

"Yes," she said. "I have nothing to lose."

"All the same," Vestergaard said and pulled his mobile from his pocket. He thumbed the screen and then put it away, a slight fleck of irritation flickered in his eyes. "You shouldn't ask too many questions, Konstabel. It's not your place."

"So I can't ask about his side of the story? Burwardsley's?"

"No."

"Then I have nothing to go on."

"You suggested you were drugged..."

"Yes," Fenna said and stabbed her finger at the corner of the paper sticking out of Vestergaard's jacket pocket. "By him."

"Which he maintains was necessary, given your heightened level of anxiety. You were," he said and paused to remove the papers, "*...a danger to yourself and others.* Lieutenant Burwardsley administered a sedative as a precautionary measure prior to transporting you here, to Scoresbysund, where you could be both *treated and questioned regarding the death of your partner.*"

"Bullshit."

"And yet, that's what it says," said Vestergaard as he pocketed Burwardsley's report.

"This is a setup," Fenna said. She clasped her fingers together as they began to shake.

"Perhaps so. But if we don't get to the bottom of it, then the Lieutenant's report will be the only report that matters."

"What about my statement? Don't I get to write my version of what happened?"

Vestergaard tapped his notebook. "I have my notes. Petersen has... Well, he started making a shorthand reference. Perhaps you can resume once we have the proper facilities at our disposal?"

"Yes, Premierløjtnant," Petersen said and glanced at Fenna. "As soon as the *Knud Rasmussen* gets in."

"This is a sham."

"I beg your pardon, Konstabel? A sham?" Vestergaard said. "Whatever it might be, it only exists because of you. So, call it what you will."

Fenna pressed her palms to her eyes to shut out

the light. *Think, Fenna, think.* The logo of the ship, *The Ice Star*, floated in her mind. A big ship. One Burwardsley works for – Vestergaard didn't deny that. But what was the connection? If *The Ice Star* was in the area, and it had to be for Burwardsley to be here, then it must have an ice class certification. It had to be able to operate without the need for an icebreaker to be this far north. *And it has to have a helipad*, she realised.

"You're doing a lot of thinking, Konstabel. Please, don't wear yourself out," Vestergaard said and tapped the nib of the pen on his notebook. "We need to continue."

Fenna rubbed her eyes one last time and lowered her hands. She blinked in the light. She took a long breath, lifted her heels and let her knees rock up and down as she bounced on her toes.

"I'm lost," she whispered.

"Then stick to the facts," Vestergaard said. "And let me help you."

"Okay," she said and nodded. "Okay."

"What happened next, Konstabel?"

Chapter 13

NORTHEAST GREENLAND NAT. PARK

Lucifer bit at the balls of ice frozen in the hairs between the pads of his feet. The rest of the team lay curled in the snow or flat on their bellies, their long forelegs stretched out before them. Fenna glanced at the team and then crawled back into position beside Mikael, the snow crunching beneath her elbows and knees.

"Well," he said, "Whoever they are, they have all our gear and supplies."

"I'll get on the phone." Fenna pushed Lucifer away and stood up. Mikael gripped her arm as she turned toward the sledge.

"This could be nothing. We might even have left something on the stove."

"You know we didn't."

"I know." Mikael glanced at the Glock holstered to Fenna's waist. "You ready to use that?"

"You have to ask?"

"This is different, Fenna. Euthanising dogs is one thing..."

"And when was the last time you pulled a gun on someone?"

"I haven't."

"So don't suggest this is any different for you than it is for me."

"I'm just saying we don't know what to expect and I want you to be ready for anything." He turned to glance at the satellite and Fenna caught a flash of concern in his eyes. "Okay?" he asked.

"Yes, okay," said Fenna.

Mikael pulled Lucifer by the harness and turned

the team away from the crest of the slope, drawing them down below the lip and out of sight. The dogs waited as he secured the travelling anchor line in the snow. Fenna stood a few metres behind the sledge, trailing the antenna for the satellite telephone from the handheld unit. She pressed the buttons on the phone and dialled the Sirius base at Daneborg.

"Hello? Noa? This is Fenna. I need to speak to Kjersing," she said and waited for Noa's response. She shook her head at Mikael. "Kjersing's not in the office. He has to go look for him."

"Just give him the message and we can get down to the cabin," Mikael said. Fenna noticed the rifle slung on his shoulder. She nodded.

"Hey, Noa. Wait. Just give him this message." Fenna paused to look at Mikael.

"Tell him," Mikael stopped and held out his hand for the phone. "Hey, Noa, it's Mikael. Tell Kjersing that we think we have a guest at the cabin." He paused. "No, no-one we know and no sign of helicopters or dogs. A bit of a mystery really." Mikael paused again, nodding as Noa repeated his message. "Yep, we're going to go and take a look. We'll call you when we know more."

Mikael ended the call and handed the satphone to Fenna. She packed the antenna away and tucked the unit inside her jacket.

"You ready?" Mikael said with a flash of teeth beneath his beard.

"As much as I'll ever be," Fenna said. "Nothing like a bit of smoke from the chimney to get the heart racing, eh?"

"Yeah," Mikael laughed. "But remember," he said, "We're Special Forces."

"Oh, we're special all right."

"So very special." Mikael nodded. He took a breath and slipped the rifle from his shoulder and into his hands. "Be careful, Fenna."

"I will," she said and tugged her pistol from its holster. "I'll come in from the south."

"Sounds good." Mikael took a last look at the dogs and nodded. "I'll cover you from above as you go inside the cabin." He cuffed Fenna on the arm, turned and slipped over the crest of the slope.

Fenna watched Mikael as he boxed the cabin from the east, stretching out on the snow, the Lee Enfield rifle balanced on a smooth rock covering the cabin entrance. He waved at Fenna to advance. She held the Glock 20 in a double-handed grip and slid through the powder snow until the slope flattened on the southern, window-less side of the cabin. She reached the wooden wall and leaned on it. The wind whipped a polar devil of snow around her boots, the snow stuck to the ice clogging her laces. Fenna bit her lip.

"Okay," she breathed. "I'm going in."

The squeak of the door of the Morsø wood-burning stove broke the polar quiet surrounding the cabin. Fenna glanced in Mikael's direction. With her back against the wall, she shushed through the snow until she was leaning against the hinges of the door. She reached for the handle with her left hand, and, remembering it was designed with polar bears in mind, she turned it upwards. The stove door clanged shut. Fenna slammed the door against the wall, left palm flat against the wood, the Glock shaking slightly in her right hand, the iron sight wavering over the face of a young Greenlandic woman, her hazel eyes startled, darker, stronger than the coffee-cream skin of her face framed by long jet-black lengths of hair. The woman trembled but didn't move.

Fenna stared at the Greenlander. "You're wearing my jacket," she said, and lowered her pistol. Fenna stepped inside the cabin. "Are you alone?"

The woman squeezed her lips shut.

"Do you speak Danish?"

The woman nodded.

"Are you alone?"

Fenna caught the hint of a nod as Mikael called from the snow beyond the cabin.

"Fenna?"

She turned to wave to her partner. "It's a woman. A Greenlander." Fenna beckoned for Mikael to approach. "Sit down on the floor," she nodded at the space between the door and the stove. As the woman lowered herself to the stained floorboards, Fenna holstered her pistol. "I'm going to put this away. See?" She snapped the holster flap over the grip of the Glock and leaned back against the door. Mikael crunched through the snow to the cabin, the rifle slung over his shoulder,

"Is she alone?"

"I think so. We can ask her again."

The woman pointed at her lips. Opening her mouth she clucked guttural noises until Fenna stepped closer, crouched in front of her.

"Jesus Christ. She's missing her tongue."

"What?" he said and stepped into the room. He closed the cabin door behind him. "Let me see." The woman glanced at Mikael, opened her mouth wider. "Jesus." Mikael slipped the rifle from his shoulder and leaned it against the table by the side of the stove.

"That's not from birth."

"No," Fenna stood up. "It looks recent." The woman tilted her head, glancing from one Dane to the other as they talked. "We still don't know if she is alone. I guess a hunter left her here while he went out on the ice."

"Then why is she wearing your jacket?"

Fenna turned back to the woman. She held out her hand and helped her to her feet. "What are you wearing?" Fenna pulled at the woman's arm, turning her to one side. "You're wearing a cocktail dress?"

"Plus your extra jacket and my spare socks," Mikael said and wiped at the ice thawing in his beard. "I don't think she is with a hunter."

The woman made a sound in the back of her throat.

"What was that?" Fenna said and studied the woman's face.

The woman moved to crouch by the ragged mouth of the oil barrel, cut down to store wood, and traced letters in the dust with her finger.

"Dina," Fenna read aloud. "Your name is Dina?"

Dina nodded. Smoothing the dust into a new pile, she wrote the number two with her finger.

Mikael stepped closer. "Two people? You and one more?"

She shook her head and pointed at her chest, held up one finger.

"One person," Mikael said and waited as Dina nodded. She held up two fingers and pointed to the door of the cabin. "Two people outside?" Dina nodded. "Okay," he said and reached for the rifle. "I'll go and have a look outside."

"Take my Glock," Fenna pulled her pistol out of

her holster and pressed it into Mikael's hand. "I'll take yours from the gear."

"All right." Mikael tucked Fenna's pistol into his belt. "You'll stay with her?"

"I'll find out what I can."

"See if she is injured, besides her mouth." Mikael looked at Dina. "And try to find out why the hell she is wearing a cocktail dress." He shook his head and walked to the door. "I'll have a look around. Be back in ten minutes."

"Fire off a shot if you need help."

Mikael paused in the doorway. "If it's all clear, I might just bring the dogs down with the sledge."

"I can help you."

"You could," Mikael said. "But I think one of us should keep an eye on our new friend. She's already been in our things, and she could use some help."

"I'll keep an eye on her. You be careful."

"Always." Mikael pulled the door handle up and pushed the door open. He stepped out into the snow and the eerie pink light of the polar evening.

ITTOQQORTOORMIIT, EAST GREENLAND

"And you never spoke to him again?" Vestergaard said as he leaned against the refrigerator, his pen poised over a fresh page in his notebook. Fenna shook her head. "Why did you give him your pistol?"

"It was colder. We try to keep one pistol inside and the other outside when on patrol. Stops them freezing up."

"But you had your Glock and Mikael the rifle, both of you were inside the cabin."

"Not for long, it was only a few minutes before Mikael left. I stayed with Dina."

"We will come to that," Vestergaard said and waved his pen at Fenna. "But you left Mikael's Glock in the cabin with the rest of your gear when you departed that morning."

"Yes."

"How many rounds did you fire from your Glock, Konstabel?"

"One, when I put Cisko down."

"Just the one?"

"Yes." Fenna watched Vestergaard make a note in his book.

"Do you know how many rounds were fired in total from your Glock?"

"No," Fenna shook her head. "There was a lot of shooting. I lost track of how many shots were fired, from any weapon."

"There was more than one weapon?"

"Yes."

Fenna looked up as Maratse appeared in the doorway. He plucked the cigarette out from the gap between his teeth and blew smoke into the kitchen. The policeman caught Fenna's eye and flicked his head towards Vestergaard and back again. She frowned at him as Vestergaard waved his hand at the smoke and moved to sit down at the table.

"So, let me check. Your unit had two pistols and a rifle."

"And the Webley," Fenna said.

"And where was that?"

"In Mikael's personal kit."

"Inside the cabin?"

"No. He had a satchel he carried inside the sledge bag. The Glock won't stop a polar bear."

"But a handgun from World War II will?"

"Yes. It was the same age as the rifle."

"I suppose there are things I will never understand about the Arctic," Vestergaard said as he made another note. Fenna saw the elongated W at the beginning of the word Webley.

"Clearly," she said and glanced again at Maratse, but the policeman withdrew from the kitchen without another word.

Chapter 14

NORTHEAST GREENLAND NAT. PARK

Fenna pulled a spare pair of heavy cotton trousers and thermals from her pack. She pointed at the clothes as she pulled the satellite telephone from the cargo pocket of her trousers.

"You had better get more clothes on, and then we can talk," she said and turned on the satphone. Fenna paced around the room as she searched for a signal. Dina pulled the thermal bottoms over Mikael's thick socks. She shrugged off Fenna's jacket and pulled off her dress. Fenna stared at the lacerations on Dina's back. "What happened to you?"

Dina reached for the thermal top. She pulled it over her head and tugged it down her back, hiding the thin raised lines and welts. Fenna placed a hand on Dina's arm as she reached for the jacket.

"Are you hurt, Dina?" Dina shook her head and then pointed at her mouth. "Your mouth hurts?" Dina shook her head, no. She raised her hand and pinched a few centimetres of air between them. "A little then?" Dina nodded. "Okay, I'll see what we have in the medkit." Dina pulled on the jacket.

The report of the first shot echoed about the rock walls surrounding the cabin. Fenna looked up at the howl of a sledge dog and the *crack*, *crack* of two more shots.

"Wait here," Fenna said and tugged the sledge box containing Mikael's personal kit from beneath the pile of gear. She opened the lid, pulled out Mikael's pistol and stuffed it into her holster. A wave of adrenalin trembled through Fenna's body. Her hands shook as she picked up the spare magazine and slipped it into her jacket pocket. Fenna held her palm flat in front of her face, clenching her fist to stop it shaking. Dina grabbed Fenna's arm as she walked to the door. "It's okay," she said. "Just wait here while I go and look."

Dina pulled at Fenna's arm and shook her head; low guttural mewls fleeing from her mouth. She pointed at the cabin door, shook her hand and then pointed at the window in the rear wall of the cabin. Fenna jerked her arm free of Dina's grasp as three more shots echoed around the cabin. Dina crawled away from the door and hid behind the table and extra clothes and equipment littering the floor.

"That's good, just stay there," Fenna said and held up her palm. She stopped at the sound of her name drifting on the polar breeze across the snow, breaking on the walls of the cabin.

"Konstabel Brongaard? We have your partner. Come on out and we can talk."

Fenna flicked her head towards the door. *English? And how do they know my name?*

Dina stamped her feet. Fenna glanced at the Greenlander before reaching for the door handle. Another round of stamping caught Fenna's attention and she paused.

"It'll be okay. I'm just going outside."

Dina shook her head, her black hair whipping from one side of her face to the other. Tears caught the occasional strand, gluing them to her cheeks.

"You know them, don't you?"

Dina nodded.

"I'll see what they want. We'll be all right." Fenna turned her back on Dina's cries, unsnapped her holster and placed her hand on the grip of her pistol.

She took a breath and opened the door.

Fenna had the door half open when Mikael was pushed onto his knees about twenty metres from the cabin entrance. She let go of the door handle as the man holding Mikael by the shoulder, pulled a pistol from his belt and shot her partner through the back of his skull. Fenna's breath caught in her throat as Mikael's body twisted, slumping into the snow in slow motion. She slammed the door shut and slid to the floor. With exaggerated gasps she fought to breathe.

"Konstabel? Fenna? Are you ready to come out?"

Fenna tugged the Glock from her holster and forced herself onto her knees. She shook as she slid over to the window and peered over the sill. Fenna watched as the taller of the two men kicked at Mikael's body. Her partner didn't move. The man adjusted the white ski mask, smoothed his hands down his Arctic camouflage smock and nodded at the second man. Fenna watched as the smaller man opened the tripod legs beneath the barrel of his weapon and slid into a prone position in the snow. She ducked as the man leaned into the weapon and shredded the door with three measured bursts of lead.

Fenna leaned over to the splintered door frame, pushed the muzzle of the Glock around the wood and loosed two 10mm rounds into the space in front of the cabin. Dina choked a long scream from where she hid at the back of the room. A fourth burst from the machine gun forced Fenna away from the door.

"Dina. Can you hear me?" she said and ducked beneath the window. Dina stared from behind the sledge boxes. "I need to know if you can drive a dog team." Dina stared at Fenna, waiting. "Can you drive dogs?" Dina nodded. Fenna took a breath. "Thank

God for hunters' daughters," she said and bit her lip. "Okay. I'm going to get you out of here. Are you listening?" Fenna watched as Dina opened the box nearest to her, the Greenlander began stuffing snack bars into the pockets of Fenna's spare jacket. "Okay then. When you're ready, I want you to go out that window and wait until it's clear. When these guys come in here, you run for the top of the slope," Fenna pointed the Glock in the direction of the dog team. "There's a team of dogs and a sledge. You can get away," she said and slid the satellite phone across the floor to Dina, "far enough to use this. Have you used one of these before?" Dina nodded. "Good," Fenna let her head rest against the wall of the cabin. "This might just work." She turned back to Dina. "When you get a signal, dial the last number and just leave it on. Someone will come for you."

Dina searched among Mikael's personal items. Pulling a floppy mad bomber hat from the box, she held it out to Fenna.

"Take it," Fenna said as another bout of adrenalin shivered through her body.

Dina pulled the hat over her head, tucking loose strands of black hair beneath the rabbit fur. She looked at Fenna and stuck out her thumb.

"How old are you, Dina?" Dina flashed both palms twice, a single palm once. "Twenty-five, eh? Same age as me." Fenna shook her head. "What the hell are we doing?"

Dina stomped stocking feet on the floorboards. She pointed at her toes.

"In the box at the back," Fenna said and pointed.

"What's going on in there, Fenna?" The Englishman called from outside the cabin.

"No. The other one." Fenna waited until Dina found her spare boots. As Dina tugged them onto her feet, Fenna fired another round out of the cabin door. Dina stopped. "Keep going. Get them tied and get out of the window."

"Come on, Konstabel. That's no way to treat friends. We just want to talk."

Fenna pressed her head closer to the doorframe, listening as the men outside trampled the snow to either side of Mikael's body. "Dina, you ready?" Fenna pointed at the window. Dina moved to the window, opened it and unlocked the bolt holding the bear shutters in place. They swung open when she pushed them. Fenna blinked in the pink glow of the polar sky as Dina lifted one leg up and out of the window. Fenna nodded. "Go."

Dina climbed out of the window as Fenna fired three rounds out of the door, to the right of the cabin. She fired three more to the left. Two bursts of 5.56mm blistered the cabin walls. Fenna fired again. She looked back at the open window, a reflection in the square-framed glass revealed Dina moving away from the cabin. Fenna reached around the door and fired another two rounds. When she looked back, Dina was gone.

ITTOQQORTOORMIIT, EAST GREENLAND

The smoke from Maratse's cigarette still clouded the kitchen. Vestergaard coughed.

"I don't understand," he said and sighed. "How the hell does a twenty-five year old woman, wearing a…" Vestergaard checked his notes, "cocktail dress, escape from a remote cabin during a gunfight." He shook his head. "You expect us to believe this crap,

Konstabel?"

"I'm sure Maratse does," Fenna said and nodded towards the policeman's office. She pictured him there, smoking beneath the portrait of the queen.

"Wearing a cocktail dress."

"She was wearing my spare clothes, Premierløjtnant."

"Sorry, yes of course. That makes it all the more plausible that a young woman leaps out the back of a cabin and makes her getaway on a sledge loaded with a top secret Canadian spy satellite," Vestergaard tossed his notebook onto the table. "Your words, Konstabel," he said and pointed the tip of his pen at her.

"You don't believe me?"

"I'm struggling, Konstabel, believe me."

"I'm the same age as Dina," Fenna said and crossed her arms over her chest.

"You've been trained by the military."

"And I grew up in a flat in Esbjerg. The most adventurous thing I did before Sirius was competing on groomed biathlon courses in Sweden and Norway. I cycled to school every day. When it was windy, my dad drove me. This was my life until I was finished with school and gymnasium." Fenna paused and gestured towards the tiny kitchen window. "Dina grew up here, wrangling sledge dog puppies as a toddler, she learned to throw stones at the big ones to keep them away. She grew up with dogs and ice and temperatures below forty. Do you hear what I'm saying?"

"Konstabel. Fenna," Vestergaard said and lifted his hand from his notes. "It's not that I don't believe she could get away. It's just highly improbable."

"For a Danish girl, sure. And yet here I am. But if we don't find her, before Burwardsley does, if we just sit on our arses, then Mikael..." Fenna gripped the table edge. "Mikael will have died for nothing."

"I understand that, Fenna."

"Then..."

"Wait a second. Let's agree that I believe you. Then you're right, we need to find Dina and retrieve the satellite, or what is left of it. But first," Vestergaard pulled out the chair. "I need to finish your debriefing. Petersen needs to get these recordings sent to the navy legal office and..."

"We're wasting time with all this protocol."

"Be that as it may, Konstabel. This protocol might just save your life. Now, continue, if you will, and tell me what happened next. Then, afterwards, we will find out what happened to Dina and get you to a safe place."

"A safe place?"

"Well, not here," Vestergaard looked out of the tiny kitchen window. "The fog is lifting. It's just a matter of time before helicopters can resume flying. The *Knud Rasmussen* is en route and as soon as we have communications again, I can hand the operation over to the navy."

"I thought you were the navy."

"I am," Vestergaard said with a look that Fenna couldn't interpret. "Now let's get this finished."

Chapter 15

NORTHEAST GREENLAND NAT. PARK

Fenna ejected the magazine from the Glock. She weighed the magazine in her hand and slid it back inside the pistol grip, flicking her head to the left at the sound of footsteps in the snow.

"Don't do anything stupid, Konstabel," said the Englishman as the short, black barrel of a bullpup rifle wormed its way around the door frame. Fenna squeezed her hand around the grip as the Glock shivered in her grasp. "Just drop the pistol."

"And if I don't?"

"It's your choice. Doesn't bother me either way. Although..." the barrel slid down the bruised wood as the man dropped to his knee. "You might want to look out the rear window." Fenna turned her head toward the back of the cabin. She grimaced as the Nepali waved from behind his rifle. "You understand now, eh? Just toss your Glock out through the doorway." Fenna turned the pistol in her hand and threw it outside. "Now get on your knees. Slowly. That's it. Place your hands behind your head..."

Fenna shuddered forward as a gloved hand gripped her fingers. She watched the shorter man climb through the window as her wrists were bound with a plastic tie. The tie snapped as it was pulled tight.

"Damn this fucking cold," the man said and gripped her fingers tighter. "Bad, come over here and help me."

The shorter man crossed the floor, slung his rifle and pulled a length of paracord from his pocket. He stood behind Fenna and wrapped the cord tight around her left wrist, pulled her arms behind her back and tied both wrists together.

"That'll do it. Now then," the tall man said and kicked Fenna onto the floor. "Let's have a little chat."

"Who are you?" Fenna turned her head to one side. The man with the ski mask shook his head.

"You're obviously new to this," he said and kicked Fenna in the stomach. "That isn't how this works." He squatted by Fenna's side, his breath misting out of the pores in his mask. "Where is the girl?"

"What girl?" Fenna said and coughed a spat of blood onto the floor.

"Seriously? You want to play rough? Bad," the man said and looked up at his partner. "Do you have any advice for this gal?"

"Yes, Saheb," Bad said and punched Fenna in the kidneys. Fenna grunted as she doubled over and swore in Danish.

"Speak English, love, or my friend will have to do that again and you will be pissing blood for a week, if you live that long." The masked man sat on the floor. "We'll try again, shall we? Where is the girl?"

"The Greenlander?"

"Yes, the fucking Greenlander. How many other girls have you seen wandering around this shithole?"

"She came with you?"

"More questions? Wait a minute, Bad," he said and held up his hand. "We'll give her that one. Yes, she came with us. A loose end, needing tidied up."

"Like my partner?"

"The Oversergent? Yes, you could say he was a loose end. If I had to choose between interrogating him or playing with you, well... it was a no-brainer, really."

"So you just killed him?" Fenna said and took a ragged breath.

"That's right, love. But it's a little more complicated than that," the man drew Fenna's Glock from his belt. "You killed him, actually. This is your Glock. This one is Gregersen's," the man pulled a second Glock from the belt at his back. He slid it over to his partner. "Wouldn't want to get them mixed up."

"Do you want the satellite? Is that what this is about?"

"You're a quick girl," he said and nodded. "Good guess. Where is it?"

"On the sledge."

"And the girl? The Greenlander?"

"Dina."

"Yes," the skin around at the corners of the man's eyes creased. "Dina."

"She escaped."

"Escaped? What, like she was your prisoner?"

"No. She escaped from you."

"No one escapes from us. Where is she going to go?"

"She has a sledge with a fully-rested team of Sirius dogs. She is going to get help."

Fenna watched the man's eyes flick to look at his partner before they turned back to her. He shook his head and laughed. "Damn, you are funny. You think your new friend is just going to disappear. Just like that."

"Yes."

The man lifted his head at the sound of rotor blades chopping the air from the east, nearing the cabin.

"I hope for your sake that she doesn't, or this is going to be a really long day for you. Get her up, Bad." He stuffed the Glock back into his belt and pushed himself to his feet. "That's our ride."

Snow blasted in through the cabin door as the AugustaWestland thundered into a hover, landing fifty metres away from Mikael's body. The men held Fenna inside the cabin as two crewmen from the aircraft dragged Mikael's body inside and began dousing the equipment and wood floors with aviation fuel.

"Get her on the chopper, Bad," Burwardsley said and handed him a syringe.

Fenna stumbled through the snow, the barrel of the man's rifle prodding her toward the aircraft. She turned as a wave of heat washed over her back. The masked man slipped a Zippo lighter into her jacket pocket as he passed. Fenna watched the cabin ignite, ducking as the rounds from Mikael's Glock started cooking off in the heat.

ITTOQQORTOORMIIT, EAST GREENLAND

"Well," Vestergaard leaned back in his chair. "That is quite a turn of events."

"That is what happened."

"Burwardsley paints a rather different picture, Konstabel."

"And you believe him?"

"He has a witness."

"Who shot my partner."

Vestergaard picked at a loose thread on his trousers. "So you say."

"Did I miss something? Have you switched sides

all of a sudden?"

"I think you misunderstand, Konstabel. I was sent to debrief you, to discover the truth behind Oversergent Gregersen's death. I was never on your side."

"And Burwardsley?"

"The Lieutenant has been helping us with our enquiries. Burwardsley and his Nepalese friend have been very cooperative."

"And I haven't?"

"Fenna," Vestergaard said and stood. "I'm sure you are tired. Perhaps it's best if we take a break and you take the opportunity to get some rest. Maratse? Please escort Konstabel Brongaard to her quarters."

Maratse smoothed the creases from the front of his uniform sweater. He nodded at Fenna, beckoned her to follow with a wave of his hand.

"My quarters, Premierløjtnant? I take it you mean my cell?" Fenna said. She pushed back her chair and stood up. "I guess I now know just how far the navy will go to protect its own."

"It's for your own good, Konstabel." Vestergaard picked the empty coffee mugs from the table and carried them to the sink. He turned around, leaned against the unit, and drummed his fingers on the work surface.

"You're not interested in what happened in the house, before you turned up?"

"It's not relevant to this stage of the investigation."

"And the satellite? Is that no longer relevant either?"

"I'm sure it's just a matter of time before your sledge and the satellite is retrieved. I'll be sure to wake you if I require any further assistance."

Fenna glared at Vestergaard. She resisted the urge to spit in his face, and followed Maratse into the cell.

"Shoes," Maratse held out his hands. "Belt," he pointed at the draw cord tied around Fenna's waist. Fenna kicked off her boots and slid them out through the door. She pulled the cord through the belt loops of her trousers, with one hand, holding her trousers up with the other. Maratse took the length of cord, wrapped it around the palm of his hand. Glancing over his shoulder toward the kitchen, the policeman leaned in close to Fenna. "*TELE* has repaired the connection. Mobiles are working." Maratse pulled his smartphone out of his pocket, swiped the screen with his thumb and presented an image of a man to Fenna.

"Who is he?" she whispered.

Maratse thumbed forward to the next photograph.

Fenna shook her head. "Who are they?"

"Dead. Danish," Maratse slipped the phone back into his pocket. "In Kulusuk."

"Where the airport is?"

"*Iiji*."

"Is everything all right?" Vestergaard said from the kitchen. "I thought I heard you talking."

Maratse lifted his hand with Fenna's makeshift belt. "She can keep this?"

"I don't think that is wise. No, you should probably keep that."

"Okay," Maratse said and leaned close to Fenna. "I'll be back soon," he whispered. The policeman stepped out of the cell and locked the door.

Fenna walked the short distance to the metal cot. She sat on the floor of the cell and leaned against it.

She wrinkled her nose at the smell of urine drifting in from the toilet bucket next door, turned her head at the cries of children scrambling about the insulated pipes on the rocks outside the police station. Outside the cell, the sound of someone kicking sand and gravel from their shoes, reverberated from the wooden steps through the floorboards. Fenna shuffled closer to the door.

"Ah, Lieutenant," Vestergaard said. Fenna felt her stomach tighten. She tried to ignore it and pressed her ear to the door.

"She's still here?" Burwardsley's English accent slurred through the walls.

"Yes. In there," Vestergaard said and dragged a chair from the kitchen. "We can sit out here."

"She can hear us out here."

"That's the point. Isn't it?"

"Where's the policeman?" The chair creaked as Burwardsley sat on it.

"Maratse? He went out for a moment. He'll be back soon."

"Has he got any jurisdiction?"

"In this village? Yes. On this case? Absolutely none."

"I think we need to remind him of that."

"We?"

"It would be better coming from you. He seems to have taken a little too much interest in our girl in there," Burwardsley raised his voice and turned toward the door of the cell. "Can you hear me, love?"

Fenna pulled her knees to her chest. "Yes."

"Good." The legs of Burwardsley's chair scraped along the floor as the big lieutenant stood. He walked across the office floor and leaned against the cell door. "I hope you've been cooperative with your friend the Premierløjtnant."

"I think," Fenna said and took a breath, "he is more your friend than mine."

"Well, *love*. You have smartened up since we last met. Any more revelations you want to share?"

Fenna pushed herself to her feet and leaned into the door. "I think you had this planned from the start."

"That is possible," Burwardsley laughed. "More than you know."

"And you've covered your tracks well, getting rid of Mikael. Cutting out Dina's tongue…" Fenna waited. "You did cut out her tongue, didn't you Burwardsley?"

"Careful, Fenna," Vestergaard called out. "Don't say anything that can implicate you further."

"It's all right, Vestergaard," Burwardsley tapped the door with his knuckle. "Our little Sirius girl is hardly going to change anything from inside a cell."

Fenna tipped her head forward until it rested on the door. "What would Mikael do?"

"What's that, love? Couldn't hear you," Burwardsley said and laughed. "How about I come in there and keep you company?"

Fenna felt her heart begin to hammer inside her chest.

"We were so rudely interrupted last time we had a little chat." Burwardsley rapped the door again with his knuckles. "How about it, *love*? Shall we have a cosy chat? I'm sure Vestergaard won't mind."

"By all means, Lieutenant. Be my guest."

Fenna whirled around the cell, looking for a weapon as Burwardsley grasped the handle of the cell door. She held her breath as it rattled in his grasp.

"The key, Vestergaard?" Burwardsley said and kicked the door.

"I haven't got it. The policemen must have it."

Burwardsley swore and kicked the door a second time.

"Thank you, Maratse," Fenna breathed.

Chapter 16

Maratse's Toyota churned to a stop in the gravel outside. Fenna waited for the sound of the door closing once, twice, catching on the third go.

"There's one thing I want to ask you," Fenna said and took a step back from the door. She heard Maratse's footsteps as he kicked the grit from his boots at the door to the station.

"And that is?" Burwardsley said.

The door hinge squealed. Fenna leaned close to the gap between the cell door and the wooden frame. "Who are the dead Danes in Kulusuk?" she said and stepped back.

"Damn it, Vestergaard. I have to get in there," Burwardsley said and slammed his fist on the door.

"Not now, Mike," Vestergaard said and stepped closer to the lieutenant. "Not now." He paused as Maratse opened the door. "Officer Maratse. You remember the British lieutenant?"

"*Iiji*," Maratse said and tucked his hands into his gun belt.

"He was just helping with the investigation. Thank you, Lieutenant Burwardsley. I know where to find you if I have anything further."

"Sure. No problem." Burwardsley rapped the cell door on his way out. "I'll be seeing you, *love*."

Fenna moved to the tiny window at the rear of the cell. She stood on the edge of the bed and peered out, watching Burwardsley as he stomped past the children and pulled out his mobile. Fenna dropped down to the cell floor as Maratse unlocked the cell door.

"Time to go," he said and handed Fenna her

boots.

"Where?" Fenna sat on the bed and tied her laces. She reached up to take the leather belt from Maratse's hand. "Yours?"

"*Iiji*." Maratse waited. "I'll take you to Kula."

"Where is Kula?"

"Not *where*," he said and laughed. "*Who*. Kula is a hunter."

"Wait just a minute, Maratse," Vestergaard said and pushed his way past the policeman and into the cell. "She's staying here."

Maratse placed his right hand on the grip of his service pistol and pulled his smartphone from his pocket. "Nikolaj Petersen," he said and pointed the screen towards Vestergaard. He thumbed forward to the next picture. "Klaus Vestergaard. Dead in Kulusuk." Maratse popped the quick release snap open with his middle finger and gripped his pistol. "She comes with me. You stay here." He nodded to Fenna. "Get out of the cell."

"Big mistake, Maratse," Vestergaard said and pointed at Fenna. "You side with her and I won't be able to help you."

"Like you helped Fenna?" Maratse said and pointed at Vestergaard's feet. "Shoes. Belt."

"You're kidding?"

"Shoes." Maratse tugged the pistol a few centimetres out of the holster. "Belt."

"It's no real wonder Greenland will never be independent," Vestergaard said and tugged his belt through the loops of his trousers. "Such a backward people. You're just not smart enough to make the right friends. Friends who can help you get out of this frozen shithole." Vestergaard pressed the toe of his shoe against the heel of the opposite foot, slipped his ankles out of his street shoes. "I could be a good friend to you, Maratse. Get you anything you want. Help you out of this mess and get you set up for life. Money. Flat screen television. Anything you want."

"I have a flat screen television. Fifty inch," Maratse said and took Vestergaard's belt. He stepped back to close the door.

"Wait," Fenna said and pushed past the policeman. "Who do you work for, Vestergaard?"

"You'll see," Vestergaard said and lay down on the bed. He crossed his arms behind his head and rested one foot over the other. "If you live that long." Vestergaard closed his eyes and smiled.

Maratse slammed the cell door and turned the key in the lock. "Open the gun safe," he said and pointed to his office. Fenna crossed the room, reached around the desk and grabbed the handle.

"Combination?"

"It's open," Maratse said and grabbed his jacket from the hook by the front door.

Fenna pulled open the door and found an M1 Carbine leaning against the back of the safe. She swept her hand around the dusty shelves and found an empty magazine and a small box of .30 calibre ammunition. She pocketed the smaller items, pulled the semi-automatic carbine out of the safe and joined Maratse at the door.

"Where did you get this? It's ancient."

"Standard issue," Maratse said and pushed half a cigarette into the gap between his teeth. "Kula is waiting." He held out his jacket and nodded for Fenna to put it on.

"Where?" Fenna switched the carbine from one

hand to the other as she put on the policeman's jacket.

"On the ice."

"And where are we going?"

"To get Dina."

"They said she was dead?"

"Dina is not dead. You came by helicopter. Dina is north of here. She is coming by sledge."

"How do you know this?"

"Dina did not call Daneborg with your satellite phone. She called her grandfather."

"Kula?"

"Aap."

"How do we get to the ice?"

"We drive."

"Burwardsley is outside."

"We drive fast," Maratse said and shrugged. He reached beneath Fenna's arm and pulled a police issue wool hat from the pocket of the jacket. "Put this on. Hide your hair."

"It won't fool Burwardsley," Fenna said and pulled the hat over her hair, pushing the loose strands under the lip.

"Maybe not, but your hair won't get in the way when shooting." Maratse chuckled around the cigarette between his lips. "Ready?"

"You're enjoying this?"

"Better than picking up drunks on the weekend," he said and gripped the handle of the door. He pushed it open only to duck back inside the station as the first of Burwardsley's bullets thwacked into the door frame, the report of the *Browning Hi Power* ricocheting between the wooden buildings, echoing in the last clouds of fog. Maratse pulled his service pistol and loosed three rounds across the street at Burwardsley's position, the big lieutenant dropped to the ground and sought cover.

"Go." Maratse said and pushed Fenna toward the Toyota, the engine rumbling in the gravel.

Fenna pulled open the passenger door, hesitating at the sight of Petersen in the boot behind the rear passenger seat, his fingers curled around the square mesh of the dog guard.

"Don't worry about him," Maratse said as he jumped into the driver's seat.

"What's he doing there?"

Maratse threw the Toyota into reverse, gravel spewing from the front wheels, spattering the front of the station with stone shot. He reversed onto the street and shifted into first gear.

"He followed me," Maratse said as floored the accelerator. Fenna rocked into the policeman's shoulder. She gripped the carbine in her left hand, reached for the door and slammed it closed.

"You have to stop him, Fenna. He's breaking the law," Petersen said, his fingers gripping the dog guard.

"He's not the only one." Fenna shifted position to look out the rear window, flinching as the glass shattered and Petersen's head slammed into the guard, the crack of Burwardsley's Browning chasing the shot. She caught her breath at the sight of Petersen's blood, brain matter and bone fragments spattered across the plastic grille.

Maratse slewed the Toyota around the corner of the dirt street, sledge dog puppies and children scattering in front of the police car. He turned on the siren and the flashing blue light. A grin spread across the Greenlander's face. Fenna turned away from Petersen as the man's body slid into the rear and out of sight. She pulled on her seatbelt.

"Do we have a plan?" Fenna said and pushed her palm against the roof of the vehicle as Maratse bumped over an old sledge runner, shifted into fourth gear. "We're going to run out of road."

"No problem," Maratse said and pointed at the sea ice covering the fjord. "Lots of road there." He swung the Toyota into a right-hand turn, braked hard and wound down the window. Maratse pulled his service pistol and fired two rounds toward the red-striped yellow Hilux bearing down the dirt road. Fenna stared at the Nepali Sergeant behind the wheel.

"Where did they get a vehicle?"

"Stolen from the heliport," Maratse said and shifted gear. He stomped on the accelerator and slung the police car down the incline to the harbour. Fenna pushed one hand against the dashboard as Maratse bumped the Toyota up and over the ice foot. Once on the sea ice, Maratse shifted through the gears, surface melt-water spraying from the wheels, funnelling to each side of the car as he wound up the window. He turned to Fenna. "It's good? No?"

Fenna leaned into Maratse, tilting her head for a better view of the wing mirror. The yellow and red Hilux bumped over the ice foot, the rear end swerving left and right as Bahadur settled into pursuit. Burwardsley stood in the bed of the pickup, gripping the roll bar behind the cabin as he jostled the Nepali's SA80 onto the cab roof. Fenna watched as he leaned into the weapon and took aim.

The first burst from Burwardsley's SA80 raked the passenger side of the police Toyota. Maratse bounced up and down behind the steering wheel, cursing the ruts of the wheel tracks locking them in a straight line across the ice. He pushed the accelerator pedal flat to the floor, glancing at Fenna as the Toyota's engine growled - a mere thirty centimetres of ice between them and the Greenland Sea.

"We have to get out of this rut," Fenna said and banged her head on the window. She flinched at a second burst of lead to her right.

"Shoot back," Maratse shouted. "Crawl into the back seat."

Fenna threw the M1 Carbine onto the back seat, unclipped her seatbelt and squirmed between the seats into the back. She ducked behind the seat back and loaded the carbine, leaning her back against the passenger seat. Fenna poked the barrel of the carbine through the dog guard, resting the stock on top of the seat. She took aim.

Fenna's first bullet splintered the windshield, startling Bahadur into the same tracks they were caught in. With her target trapped in a static line of pursuit, Fenna took her time with each shot, anticipating the bumps and jolts in the ice road with well-placed rounds and the occasional near-miss. The Nepali slowed, the Hilux bumping further and further behind them.

"I made them cautious," Fenna called out as she peered along the sight.

"Maybe," Maratse said and adjusted the rear-view mirror. "Maybe not."

Fenna watched as Bahadur rolled the Hilux back and forth until the front wheel on the passenger side crept over the lip of the tyre tracks. The Hilux inched forward, bumped onto the surface of the ice and accelerated.

"They're coming back," Fenna said and pulled the M1 out of the grill. She slid over to the other side of the seat and took aim.

"Not long," Maratse called out.

"Until what?"

"Thin ice," he said and grinned at her in the rear view mirror.

Maratse shifted down through the gears and slowed the Toyota, rolling backwards and forwards until the police car bumped out of the tracks. With a volley of shots, Fenna pushed the Hilux to her left, further out to sea and wide of the Toyota. Burwardsley walked a long burst of 5.56mm into the ice and rear passenger window showering Fenna in a storm of glass.

"Maratse," Fenna yelled as she ducked.

"All okay," he said and accelerated, aquaplaning through a large puddle of surface meltwater. Maratse gripped the steering wheel as the Toyota spun one hundred and eighty degrees. When the Toyota stopped spinning the engine stalled.

The Ship

EAST GREENLAND

Chapter 17

"I'm getting out," Fenna said and slid across the seat. She opened the passenger door on the driver's side and dropped onto the ice. Fenna crouched by the rear wheel and took aim, firing single shots at the rapidly approaching Hilux.

The Toyota engine coughed and shuddered as Fenna ran back to the passenger door. The engine caught on Maratse's third attempt, exhaust fumes spattered the ice. Fenna climbed in behind Maratse as he shifted into first and spun the Toyota out of the puddle and in front of the Hilux just as Bahadur rammed the passenger side, crumpling the bonnet. Fenna fired blindly, emptying the carbine's magazine into the rear of the Hilux.

"Take this," Maratse ripped his pistol out of the holster and flung it onto the back seat. Fenna grabbed the Heckler and Koch 9mm USP Compact pistol, leaned into the back of the passenger seat and fired. Maratse flicked the finger at the Nepali as the police car and the Hilux roared alongside one another, alternating between jarring bumps and the *crack* and *thump* of incoming rounds.

"Shit," Maratse said and slammed on the brakes, spinning out to the left and away from the Hilux. He turned the Toyota toward the brown rocky coastline and accelerated away from a wide lead of black water splitting the ice in a long line before them. Fenna held her breath as Bahadur accelerated, throwing the Hilux over the lead and crashing into the sea ice on the other side, the rear wheels spinning, half on, and half off the ice. Burwardsley threw himself over the cab, sliding down the bonnet, spreading his weight over the front end of the vehicle. The Nepali turned the steering wheel back toward the ice, swerving toward the open water and back again, slinging the Hilux onto the safety of thicker ice. He accelerated in a course parallel to the police car. Burwardsley clambered back into the bed of the pick-up.

"We're going to run out of ice," Fenna said and crawled into the passenger seat beside Maratse. "It will be even thinner near the shore. The current around that point," she said and jabbed her fingers toward the granite coastline, where black lichen and bare rock peppered the snow above the ice foot. "It's bad there, isn't it?"

"*Iiji*," Maratse said and shifted to a higher gear.

"Then what?"

"Wait," he said. He jerked the Toyota into fifth and fished a crumpled packet of *Prince* cigarettes from his pocket. He tossed the packet into Fenna's lap.

"I don't smoke."

"I do," he said and pointed at his mouth.

Fenna pulled a cigarette from the packet and poked it between Maratse's lips. He rolled it into the gap between his teeth with his tongue and leaned forwards as Fenna lit the cigarette with the lighter tucked inside the packet.

"*Qujanaq*," he said. Maratse gripped the wheel with both hands and puffed at the cigarette.

Fenna turned to stare at the Hilux churning along the ice on the other side of the lead. Bahadur gripped the wheel. Burwardsley leaned against the roll bar, the stock of the bullpup rifle resting on his hip.

"What do we do about them?"

"Wait," Maratse said and swerved around a patch of thin ice. The Toyota buoyed as the pack ice bowed under the vibration of the wave building beneath the surface. Maratse slowed, driving in ever-widening curves around patches of ice too weak to hold the weight of the vehicle. "There," he said and pointed towards the shore.

"Where?" Fenna said and placed her hands on the dashboard. She leaned forward and scanned the coastline.

"Left of the point."

"A sledge," Fenna said and pointed. "I see it."

"Kula," Maratse said and grinned, smoke billowing out of the corners of his mouth.

"That's a big team." Fenna squinted, shading her eyes as the sun cut through the fog. A team of dogs running in fan formation pulled a long, broad sledge smartly across the ice. With an extra two metres of line, a small bitch led the team.

"Seventeen dogs," Maratse said and stabbed his chest with his thumb. "Seven of mine." He leaned over the wheel, staring at the ice as he accelerated.

Fenna twisted in her seat and looked across the lead of open water at the yellow and red-striped Hilux. She watched as Burwardsley banged his fist on the cab roof as he bent down to shout through the driver's window. The lieutenant pointed at the approaching sledge.

"Bad ice," Maratse said and pointed to the right as the Hilux slowed. "They won't make it."

"What's the plan?" Fenna said and rested the 9mm pistol on her thigh.

"You get on the sledge and go find Dina."

"With Kula?"

"*Iiji.*"

"What will you do?"

"Stop them," Maratse said and pointed at the Hilux crawling along the ice behind them. Fenna watched as Burwardsley jumped down from the vehicle and then walked ahead of it, directing Bahadur around the thin ice.

"You'll need this," Fenna said and slipped Maratse's pistol back into the policeman's holster.

Kula slowed his dog team to a stop. He leaped lightly from the sledge, curling the sealskin whip back and forth along the surface of the ice until the team dropped to their bellies. Maratse lifted his foot from the accelerator pedal, down-shifting and drifting to a stop by the side of the team.

"Out," Maratse said and nodded towards the sledge.

"Thank you," Fenna said and gripped the policeman's hand.

"Find Dina," he said and gave Fenna's hand a final squeeze.

"Be careful, Maratse."

"*Iiji.*"

Fenna stepped out of the Toyota as the policeman waved at Kula. Maratse stuck a new cigarette between his lips, lit it and crunched the Toyota into gear. He turned the vehicle through a slow circle on the ice as Fenna watched him leave.

"Fenna?" Kula said and pressed a firm hand upon her shoulder.

"Yes," she said and turned. The hunter cracked a smile in his weather-beaten almond-skinned face. His cheeks creased beneath bushy, black eyebrows.

"We must go," he said and hurried Fenna to the sledge and dogs.

The dogs stirred as she sat sideways towards the

front of the sledge. Fenna zipped Maratse's jacket and pulled up the collar as Kula pressed the patrol's satellite telephone into Fenna's hand.

"The battery is dead," he said.

"Where did you get it?"

"From your sledge." Kula pointed to the mouth of the fjord to the east. "Around the point."

"Dina sledged all that way?"

"Maybe," he said. "I haven't found Dina, only your sledge and team. I'll take you to them." He glanced over his shoulder at the Toyota, cracked the whip on the ice and leaped onto the sledge, his thin legs hidden within the thick fur of polar bear skin trousers. Kula curled the whip along the ice, distracting the dogs from the alternating crack of 9mm and 5.56mm rounds as Maratse harassed Burwardsley and his Nepalese Sergeant. Fenna started at the noise of another round close by. Kula grinned, and snapped the whip a second time. The team tugged at the traces, blurring into a mass of fur and bushy tails pulling the sledge across the ice towards the open lead of black water.

"That's a big lead," Fenna said and clenched her fists.

"*Iiji*," Kula said and shrugged. "They're good dogs." He reached into a sledge bag hanging between the uprights and handed Fenna a pair of sealskin mittens. He nodded for her to put them on. The sealskin blocked the wind and Fenna's fingers prickled as they warmed.

She looked up as a long, low blast of a car horn cut across the ice. Maratse waved from beside the Toyota. The Hilux crawled along the ice towards them, Burwardsley leading on foot from the front.

Kula leaped from the sledge as the team slowed in front of the lead. Larger floes of ice bobbed in the water, and it dawned on Fenna that the hunter intended to use them. She waited for instruction as he encouraged the dogs with whip curls on the ice and soft words. Kula guided the lead dog over a smaller crack in the ice and towards the edge where a large floe bobbed two metres away in the dark seawater. The hunter ran to the sledge and picked up a length of rope.

"Hold this," he said and threw one end to Fenna. "Stand here." Kula pointed at the edge of the ice before the floe, in front of the dogs. He walked the length of the team to the rear of the sledge.

Fenna stuffed the mittens in her jacket pockets, gripped the rope and planted her feet squarely on the ice. She took a moment to study the hunter, the sealskin kamiks on his feet, the polar bear-skin trousers and the blue fishing smock pulled snugly over a thick wool sweater. *He is shorter than me*, she realised, *and three times my age. At least.* She held her breath as Kula, the whip in one hand and the end of the rope in the other, ran to the edge of the ice and leaped onto the floe.

Fenna gripped the rope as Kula scrabbled to his feet, the floe seesawing as the skin soles of his kamiks gripped the surface. He dropped the whip onto the ice and pulled the rope, hand over hand, tugging the floe to the ice. Fenna held on and laughed as the hunter grinned at her. He had fewer teeth than Maratse.

At Kula's command, the dogs pulled the sledge onto the floe. He picked up his whip and gestured for Fenna to get on the sledge. The next floe was smaller, but wedged against the opposite side of the lead. There was a metre of black water between the floes, and Kula tossed his lead dog by the harness over the water and onto the floe. The bitch skittered for balance, claws rasping on the ice. Kula leaped onto the floe and slipped. Fenna gasped as he gripped his lead dog by the leg and pulled himself into the centre of the floe. Kula kneeled on the ice, and, with a firm grip of the gangline, he pulled the floes together. The dogs shuffled on the ice, their paws spread and claws splayed for purchase on the slippery surface.

"I'm impressed," Fenna said and walked to the rear of the sledge. She gripped the uprights and prepared to push the sledge as Kula directed. As the floes crunched together in the water, he turned to leap onto the ice on the other side of the lead. His lead dog followed and the fan-shape of the team narrowed into a cornet as the dogs scrambled from one floe to the other and then onto the ice. Kula curled the whip behind them and nodded for Fenna to get back on the sledge. He ran for a few metres more before leaping on to the sledge and settling on the reindeer skins beside Fenna. Kula tucked the whip beneath the cord criss-crossed over the sledge, and let the end of the whip trail along the ice. He clasped his bare, nut-brown hands in his lap and watched as Fenna coiled the rope. The ice thickened and the runners shushed across the surface layer of snow and Fenna relaxed to the familiar sounds and rhythm of the sledge. She placed the rope on the thwarts beside her and slipped her hands inside the mittens.

"We made it," she said and smiled at the hunter. Kula nodded and turned to look over the rear of the sledge.

"They didn't," Kula said and laughed. He pointed at the Hilux sinking through the ice on the other side of the lead. The two British soldiers scrabbled to get clear. Fenna looked beyond the sinking vehicle and saw the familiar shape of the police Toyota as Maratse drove back towards the settlement. Kula nodded at the sky. "The fog is clearing. It will be a good day."

"Yes," Fenna said and looked up. "Good flying weather."

The dogs leaned into their traces, the lines taut, pulling the sledge across the sea ice to follow the coastline east toward the mouth of the fjord.

Chapter 18

The snow reflected the late morning sun and forced Fenna's eyes closed. She felt the warmth on her eyelids, lulling her into a sense of security at once familiar and dangerous. She blinked in the sunlight, the weight of her eyelids feeling heavy after the previous day's interrogation and escape. She slipped into the rhythm of the sledge, her chin tucked inside the collar of Maratse's jacket and her mittened hands clasped between her thighs. Fenna dozed as the dogs *shushed* the sledge along the ice, encouraged with a soft double clap of Kula's gnarled hands and an accompanying whistle.

They rounded the corner of the fjord in this way, Fenna's nose resting against the rim of the stiff collar, her breath freezing in tiny pearls upon her cheeks and bleaching the ends of her hair with a rime of frost, stiff and white. If she dreamed it was the soundless dream of fatigue, her body too tired to seek a more comfortable position, her mind too exhausted.

She woke at the jerk of the sledge as the dogs laboured up and over the ice foot that marked the boundary between the sea ice and the land. Diamond hard it was a minefield of sharp edges, crazy paving flipped vertical. The ice foot rose and fell with the tide. The tide was out and the dogs had to work to reach the safety of the hunter's winter camp. They whined as the sledge runners caught, and the lines tangled around the mini bergs barring their way. Kula worked the dogs back and forth, lifting the lines and lifting the dogs when they stumbled, confused within the labyrinth of ice, as if the sea was reluctant for them to leave and the land was too stubborn to receive them.

Fenna opened her eyes and stepped off the sledge, stamping her numb toes to life and clapping her hands, urging the blood into her fingers. Her cheeks, the prominent parts just below her eyes, were thick like putty. She removed a mitten and pressed her fingertip against each cheek, cursing at the stubby resistance – the early stages of frostbite, her penance for fifty minutes of rest. She walked to the rear of the sledge and helped guide it up and over the ice foot as Kula untangled the dogs and led them into camp.

They were met with a chorus of whines and the familiar half-bark of Greenlandic sledge dogs, tethered with short lengths of chain to bolts hammered into cracks in the rock. Fenna recognised their voices and felt a tear begin to freeze beneath her left eye as she recognised one canine voice in particular.

"Lucifer," she whispered and choked back another tear. The remaining dogs from call-sign *Fever Dog*, tugged at the chains and lifted their paws in the air, snapping at the new arrivals and howling at the sight of Fenna. She let go of the sledge and let Kula lead his team up to the dirty canvas tent another twenty metres from where her team was anchored. Fenna dropped to her knees in front of Lucifer and buried her nose in the fur around his neck as he wriggled within her grip and strained to bump noses.

"I've missed you," she said, her words lost in the lead dog's fur. Lucifer leaned against her side and Fenna felt the reassuring weight of his body and the tickle of sharp claws pressing through her trouser leg.

"Fenna," Kula called and she pulled away from the dog and looked up. The hunter beckoned for her to come and help secure his team. He tugged the bight of rope leading to all seventeen dogs and freed it from the line attaching it to the centre thwart between the sledge runners.

"You don't want to tie them individually?" Fenna said as she helped him haul the dogs to a large iron ring sealed in a crack of exposed rock with cement.

"*Eeqqi*," he said and flicked his eyes towards the blue sky. "Good flying weather. We might want to leave in a hurry."

Fenna nodded and helped Kula secure the dogs in the fan formation. She knew they would twist the lines, as they roamed, but was surprised when they flopped to the ground as one and lay quietly, gnawing at the ice and wind-packed snow.

"We'll feed them later," Kula said and gestured for Fenna to follow him.

Inside the tent, Kula pulled Fenna's sledge bag out from behind a packing crate. He let her rummage through it while he lit the wood-burning stove, peeling off his smock as the temperature inside the tent rose. He picked at the holes in his thermal top while Fenna arranged the items from the sledge bag on the flimsy cot beside the stove. She placed the spare battery for the satphone beside the antenna, spare ammunition for the Glock and a handful of bullets for the Webley. She pulled the pistol out and handed it to Kula. He turned it one way and then the next.

"Good for bears," he said, admiring it in the yellow light of the tent.

Fenna nodded and pulled spare clothes out of the bag, together with the component she had unscrewed from the satellite. She tossed it onto the cot and unzipped her jacket. Fenna turned her back to Kula as she peeled off Maratse's spare clothes and replaced them with her own thermal layers, olive drab windpants, thick socks and a Norwegian wool sweater. She paused before pulling the sweater over her head and turned to look at the hunter.

"Dina wore this," she said. Kula raised his eyebrows in silent affirmation. "Where is she?"

"I don't know."

"But the sledge? The gear?"

"I found the sledge and your dogs on the ice. Alone. They were tired," he said. "I brought them here and fed them. Then I went to look for Dina."

"You found nothing?"

Kula pointed at the satellite phone Fenna removed from Maratse's jacket. "I found that," he said. "On the ice."

"But no trace of Dina?" Fenna sat down on the cot as Kula set a black kettle on the rusty stove. "Kula," she said. "Do you think Dina is still alive?"

Kula fiddled with two enamel mugs, preparing a mug of strong tea with lots of sugar for both of them before he answered. "*Iiji*," he said. And then, "Maybe."

Fenna thought about the distance the dogs had travelled. Even with a light sledge, it was a long way. A few hundred kilometres. When the going was good, a Sirius patrol with a fully-loaded sledge averaged fifty kilometres a day. Dina had travelled four times that distance, perhaps stopping to feed the dogs, and to dump the satellite. *That's what I would have done. It's just dead weight.*

Kula handed Fenna a mug of sweet tea and fished inside a cardboard box for a packet of ship's biscuits

– hard crackers full of fat. Fenna nibbled at one as she replaced the battery in the satphone. The cold had sapped it of energy, but there was just enough power to check the call history. She turned the display towards Kula and pointed at the last three numbers dialled.

"That's Daneborg," Fenna said and pointed at the last of the three numbers. "I made that call when we found the satellite." Kula nodded and pointed at the second number.

"Me," he said and took a sip of tea.

The last number was a long one that Fenna didn't recognise. "And this one?" she said.

Kula shook his head and brushed biscuit crumbs from between the hairs of his trousers.

Do I call it? Fenna wondered and rested the satphone in her lap. She powered off the phone and placed it on the cot. Kula handed her the Webley and she added it to her gear.

"What did Dina do for work?" she asked.

"She worked on a ship, as a guide."

"A guide," Fenna said and glanced at the satphone. *Then she would be familiar with satellite phones.* "Who did she work for?"

Kula shrugged and sipped his tea.

"She spoke Danish and English?"

"*Iiji*," he said. "and East Greenlandic."

"How long had she been a guide?"

"Three years," Kula said. He put down his empty mug and stood up. He reached behind the stove and plucked a faded photograph from its place on a wooden shelf tacked between two crates. He handed it to Fenna. "When she graduated school," he said. Fenna smiled at the glow of pride that flushed the hunter's wrinkled cheeks.

"She looks so young," Fenna said.

"1991."

"The year she graduated?" Fenna said and frowned.

"The year she was born."

"Okay," she said and handed the photograph to Kula. He smoothed a wrinkled corner with his thumb and returned it to the shelf.

"Dina," he whispered and sat down. On the cot opposite Fenna. She waited for him to speak, but Kula closed his eyes and took several breaths before he said another word. Fenna emptied the sledge bag while she waited. Other than the spare clothes and the Webley, the spare battery was the only other useful item. She slipped the pistol and phone into the bag and rolled it at her feet.

"Sorry," Fenna said as Kula opened his eyes. "I didn't mean to disturb you," she said and nodded at the bag.

"You didn't," he said and cocked his head to one side. "Listen."

Fenna listened as a breath of chill wind flapped at the tent door. She shook her head and opened her mouth to speak, stopping as Kula raised his hand.

"Helicopter," he said. "From the south."

Fenna heard it then and picked up the sledge bag. She glanced at Kula and he nodded, pulling the smock over his head as he stood up. As an afterthought, Fenna picked up the satellite component and thrust it into the sledge bag, pausing briefly to scan the tent for useful items before following Kula outside.

The dogs pricked their ears at the sudden activity

as Kula pulled Fenna behind the tent to where he had hidden the Sirius sledge. Kula ripped off the plastic tarpaulin and shoved the sledge past the tent, stopping for a moment as Fenna looped the sledge bag over the uprights and helped him slide it down to her team. They wrangled Fenna's dogs into harness and clipped them into the ganglines.

"There's nowhere to hide," Kula said and nodded towards the ice. "Best to keep moving."

"Where to?"

"Out there," he said and gestured into the distance. Fenna peered in the direction he pointed and squinted at the grey fog lapping at the ice to the east. "We can lose them in the fog."

"Okay," Fenna said and tugged Lucifer to the front of the team. Kula had arranged the lines in fan formation. *Or was it Dina?* Fenna wondered. Once they were through the ice foot maze, running in fan formation would be faster. *And speed*, Fenna realised, *was everything.* She turned at the click of a rifle bolt and watched as Kula slung it around his chest. It was a small calibre with a rusty barrel and a sling made of bailing twine, but Fenna didn't doubt the old man knew how to use it. Kula grinned and pointed two fingers at the sky, shaking his hands and spluttering like a machine gun.

"Yes," she said. "If only we had one of those." Fenna stopped as her stomach turned a somersault. She steadied herself with a hand on the uprights, before checking the sledge and walking the gangline to fuss the dogs.

"Fenna," Kula said as he joined her at the head of the team.

"Yes?"

"Go east, into the fog, all the way to the open sea."

"And then?"

"North, to Daneborg."

"Yes," Fenna nodded. It made sense to try to get to the Sirius base. "It's a long way."

"*Iiji*," Kula said. "And dangerous."

"Because of them?"

"*Eeqqi*," he said and wrinkled his brow. "Because of bears." He pointed at the sledge bag. "Keep the pistol close."

"I will."

"Good," he said and paused at a new sound whining beneath the *whop whop* of the helicopter. "Snowmobiles."

Fenna brushed her hair behind her ear and listened. "Two of them," she said.

"Go," Kula said and waved Fenna towards the ice. "I'll follow you."

Fenna watched as Kula jogged back to his own team. He slid the rifle from his shoulder and secured it between the cords criss-crossing the thwarts on his sledge. Kula pushed a plastic fish crate onto the sledge, fastened it and then heaved a clear plastic sack of dried fish into the crate.

He thinks of everything, Fenna mused before the whine of the snowmobiles forced her into action and she ran to the rear of the sledge.

"Come on boys," she yelled and pushed at the sledge uprights. Lucifer tugged at the harness and picked a route through the jagged barrier of the ice foot and down onto the sea ice. Fenna found her skis tucked beneath a cord on the sledge and clipped them into her boots as the dogs paused for direction. She turned to see Kula move his team through the ice to join her, and flicked her head to the south and west for sign of the snowmobiles. Fenna saw the helicopter first, the same one that had landed at the cabin. "Burwardsley," she said and suppressed a tremble through her body. She reached into the sledge bag and tucked the pistol into the waistband of her windpants. "This time, you British bastard," she said. "We'll see who owns the ice."

Kula whistled that he was ready and his sledge shushed past her. He tossed Fenna the sealskin mittens and clapped his hands for his team to pick up speed. Lucifer jerked Fenna's team into motion and she slipped behind the uprights as the helicopter worked its way overland towards Kula's camp. Fenna glanced over her shoulder as the snowmobiles whined around the point.

"Come on, boys," she yelled. "Let's go."

Chapter 19

The remnants of call-sign *Fever Dog* clawed at the ice. Nine dogs and one bitch raced after the hunter's team of ten lean dogs and Maratse's additional seven. The ice was smooth, with only the occasional ridge or bump to jar their progress. Fenna alternated from the left to the right-hand side of the sledge, correcting the team depending upon Kula's course towards the open sea.

The petrel grey fog licked at the ice in the distance and Fenna blinked at a cream blur ahead of the team. *Polar bear*, she wondered only to have Lucifer confirm it as the lead dog slowed to sniff the air, much like when the team had encountered the wolf. Kula's dogs had spotted it also, and the distance between the two sledges increased. The whine of the snowmobiles behind Fenna turned her head. The drivers hunkered behind the low plexiglas windshields and increased the throttle, leaping ahead and splitting up to flank the sledges, one on either side. Fenna reached for the pistol in her waistband, reassured by the weight. She tapped the butt and returned her hand to the upright as the snowmobiles closed the distance.

"Come on, boys," she shouted, her breath misting and freezing in front of her face, it pearled upon her sweater and froze on the fleece around her neck. She licked at the ice beading above her lip and cast another quick glance at the snowmobiles. Burwardsley, she observed, was on the one to her right, his large awkward frame instantly recognisable. She shuddered at the thought of what he would do when he caught up with her. But the fog, Fenna noticed, was thickening.

She scanned the horizon, twisting her neck to stare at the sky behind her, where the camp should be on the coastline. There was no sign of the helicopter and she couldn't hear the beat of its rotorblades above the grating of the runners on the ice and the incessant buzz of the snowmobiles. *And the bear,* she remembered and flicked her eyes to the horizon. *Where is it?*

Burwardsley was the first to draw his weapon, the snap of the bullet from his Browning caused Fenna to duck and ski to the other side of the sledge. She watched as Kula tugged his rifle free of the cords criss-crossing the thwarts. He dropped to one knee and leaned against the uprights, tracking the approach of the Gurkha on his snowmobile. Kula fired, chambered another round and fired again, forcing the Nepali to swerve out of range. Fenna reached for the Webley only to duck again as Burwardsley fired two shots in quick succession. The second splintered the right runner as it clipped the sledge and skittered across the ice.

"Fuck it," Fenna yelled and drew the Webley from her windpants. The handgun was heavy in her hand. She leaned into the left hand upright, curled her left arm around it, and straightened her right arm, pointing the Webley in the general direction of Burwardsley's snowmobile. She pulled the trigger and almost smiled at the reassuring boom, only to feel the shot go wild as her arm flicked with the recoil from the unsupported firing position. Lucifer skittered at the head of the team, but Fenna made her point and Burwardsley throttled down and swung further to the right. She thrust the pistol back into her waistband and swung to the right of the sledge, holding on to the uprights and yelling encouragement to the dogs.

"Come on, boys. Let's go."

In the confusion of the snowmobile chase and the exchange of bullets, the dogs had all but lost the scent of the polar bear. It came back with a vengeance as Lucifer changed direction, veering to the northeast, and the sledge surged ahead with renewed vigour. Fenna caught sight of the bear as she passed behind Kula's team. The hunter waved his arms into a cross above his head.

"I know," she shouted. "I can't slow them." She braked her skis into a vee only to feel the vibration rumble through the bindings and threaten to tear the skis from her boots. Fenna straightened them, placed them flat on the ice and held on.

Bahadur, she realised, had also seen the bear. He slowed his snowmobile to a stop and pulled the SA80 from the holster he had jury-rigged to the passenger seat. Fenna watched as he slipped off the snowmobile and stepped behind it, resting the assault rifle on the seat, tracking the bear as it loped across the ice. The Gurkha's first shot, however, lifted Fenna's wheel dog off the ice. It tumbled in its traces and slid across the surface as the team continued to chase the bear.

"Fuck," she said and drew the Webley. *He's going to take out my team.*

Bahadur's second shot clipped the end of the sledge, and Nansen, the second of the two wheel dogs, lost its footing, skidding to its knees and yelping as the rounded tip of the right sledge runner pressed into its back. The dog clawed at the ice and staggered into a running position as its running mate was dragged lifeless alongside it.

Fenna fired a random shot in Bahadur's direction.

As the Nepali ducked she gritted her teeth, rested the pistol on the crossbar between the two uprights, and fired again. The satisfying crack of the bullet piercing the engine casing of the snowmobile brought a smile to her face. She turned away from Bahadur to scan the ice for Burwardsley. She found him, in front of her and to her right. He was trying to cut her off. Fenna looked for the bear and realised that Lucifer had pulled the team to within a few hundred metres.

If I can get in front of it, I can use it. Fenna let Lucifer lead the team as she worked her way along the sledge towards the sledge knife the hunter had secured just behind the runners. "Thank you, Kula," she whispered as she pressed her bottom onto the sledge thwarts and let the ice bump her skis. Fenna inched forwards until she could draw the knife and cut the dead wheel dog from its traces. The sledge rode up and over the dog's body with barely a missed beat. Fenna slid the knife back into its scabbard and searched the ice for Burwardsley.

The Royal Marine was behind her, easing down on the throttle and signalling to Bahadur to run to him. Fenna watched as Bahadur jogged across the ice to Burwardsley. Behind them, the helicopter blurred into view as it thundered towards them, just twenty metres above the ice.

Kula, Fenna realised, was gone, enveloped by the fog and the snow clouds that had rolled in behind it from the sea. Fenna's world turned grey and thunderous, as the visibility decreased only to be replaced by machine noise and the excited clamour of sledge dogs. She caught a whiff of something feral and watched the bear's flight turn into fight as it slid to a stop and turned to face Fenna and her team.

"Fuck," she said and drew the knife again. Fenna sawed through the gangline and released the dogs. Once free of the sledge, the team leaped towards the bear as the sledge ground to a stop. Fenna kicked off her skis and ran to the rear of the sledge. She tugged the sledge bag free of the uprights and thrust her arms through the loops. She ignored the dogs as they baited the bear with half-barks, bared teeth and feints. Fenna caught a last glimpse of Lucifer as the bear batted a giant paw at the lead dog, only to be attacked from behind by Betty and Ninja. Fenna ran across the ice in the direction she imagined Kula had driven his dogs, towards the open sea.

The whine of Burwardsley's snowmobile increased in pitch, louder than the helicopter as it escaped the thunderous chop of the aircraft and followed Fenna into the fog and snow. As the air thickened, Fenna caught the static crackle of radio chatter between Burwardsley and the pilot as the Lieutenant ordered the helicopter to stay close. Fenna smiled at Burwardsley's frustration as the rotor noise diminished and the helicopter retreated from the fog. The dogs, she realised, had also disappeared. Fenna slowed as the fog enveloped her and her visibility decreased to a mere handful of metres. She stopped and turned a slow circle as she listened for the sound of the snowmobile, the dogs, anything.

"Not good," she whispered and raised the pistol in her right hand. She clutched the knife in her left.

Fenna heard the distant whine of the snowmobile to her left. It increased in pitch but diminished as if Burwardsley was accelerating in the wrong direction. She held her breath and cocked her head towards the other sound, the soughing breath and the huff of something large padding across the ice towards her.

Snow tickled Fenna's cheeks as the flakes thickened and swirled around her body. She imagined the bear to be to her right, and caught a whiff of wet fur, not dissimilar to that of the dogs. The scent was stronger and suggested something bigger, more powerful, faster. Fenna whirled at the first sight of the bear, its black snout pointed down toward the ice, its tiny ears alert and those great paws – Fenna could see the claws, black, thick as two fingers, sharp as pitons.

"Go away," she shouted and levelled the pistol at the bear. At one hundred metres Fenna had thought the bear to be huge, at ten it was mountainous. Fenna pointed the Webley at the ice, a metre in front of the bear and pulled the trigger. The bear reeled at the explosion, amplified as it was by the fog. The 11.6mm bullet punctured the ice in front of the bear, and it faltered. Fenna fired again, half a metre closer and the bear staggered back as a small crater cracked just a paw's length in front of its snout. The empty Webley wobbled in Fenna's grasp as the bear twitched in front of her, turned and loped back in the direction it had come.

Fenna slumped onto the ice and let the Webley rest in her lap. The knife slipped out of her grip and Fenna tucked her hand beneath her armpit to stop it shaking.

She sat there until the cold penetrated the seat of her windpants and forced her to stand up. She bent down to pick up the knife and slipped the Webley back into her waistband. Fenna turned to sniff the air and felt a fresh breeze with a subtle tang blow in from her right. She turned to face it and hoped she was walking east, towards the sea, to Kula.

She stopped after five minutes to slip the Webley into the sledge bag. She looked at the knife and placed that inside the bag too. She remembered the satphone and pulled it out. The phone flickered into life with a power warning. Fenna dialled Daneborg and waited. The phone burred through the number; the dial tone sounded to Fenna like it was being bounced around the world.

"Noa?" she said when a familiar voice answered her call.

"No, this is Kommandør Kjersing. Who am I speaking to?"

"This is…" Fenna started. She paused as a beam of light captured the fog in a brilliant white triangle and staggered in increments toward her. "This is..." Fenna tried again, but then the light caught her and she was at once blind and dumb as the familiar sound of metal biting into ice was magnified, far more than the metal edge of her skis when she braked, greater than the sound of runners on black ice. This was bigger than that; the noise was monstrous. A behemoth of marine industry. As the ice protested, the smell of diesel engulfed Fenna, reeking of industry, power, and man.

"Fenna? Is that you?" Kjersing said but Fenna was silent. She stared up at the massive bright red bow of a ship as it pressed down on the edge of the sea ice. Fenna was pinned to the spot with a searchlight from the deck of *The Ice Star*.

Chapter 20

The power warning on the satellite phone beeped and ended the call. Fenna lowered her hand and held the phone by her side as two men in full Arctic gear clumped down the accommodation ladder, zigzagging down the hull of the ship and stepped onto the ice. She watched as they walked towards her. The second the men stepped inside the cone of light from the deck, their shadows flanked Fenna on either side. Compared to the men, Fenna was underdressed. In the time it took them to unzip their fur-lined parka hoods, lift their goggles and tug their fleece balaclavas below their chin to speak, Fenna had made her decision – she would ask them to take her onboard the ship. Kula was gone, Burwardsley would realise his error and change course – *he might have done so already*, she realised – and the polar bear could return at any moment. With her survival instincts adapting and reacting to every new scenario, Fenna spent less and less time reviewing each new development since her escape onto the ice in the police Toyota. *One step at a time*, she reminded herself. *Just stay ahead – always at least one step ahead, and adapt. And*, she thought as she recognised the name of the ship, *find Dina.*

"My name is Bose," said the shorter of the two men in Indian-style English. "I am the ship's purser, and this is our head of security, Charlie Watts."

"We received a distress call for two hunters in trouble on the ice," Watts said. "Are you in need of assistance?"

"Yes," Fenna said and nodded. "I need assistance."

"Where is your sledge?" Watts said.

"Back there." Fenna pointed over her shoulder. "But there's a bear," she said and added, "A big one. I frightened it off, but I think it will be back." Watts reached behind his back and drew a large Magnum pistol.

"Mr Bose," Watts said. "Time to get back on the ship."

"Yes," Bose gestured for Fenna to follow him. "Do you have any belongings?"

"No," she said and fell into step beside the purser. He twisted at the waist to look at her, tugging at his hood with thick-gloved fingers.

"It's a little odd to meet a woman, alone on the ice. We were told to expect two hunters."

"Life is full of surprises," Fenna said and winced at her own cynicism. "I was with my grandfather," she said.

"You are Danish?"

"Yes, but my grandfather is Greenlandic." Fenna smiled at the thought of Kula and enjoyed the little white lie.

"I see," Bose said and stopped at the first step on the accommodation ladder. Watts joined them and nodded for Bose to go first. He lifted his foot onto the first step and stopped. "This is a private vessel. We will need to process you through security before you are allowed to venture further inside the ship."

"All right," Fenna said. "But I don't have any form of identification on me."

"We'll figure something out," said Watts. "Let's just get onboard before the bear comes back, shall we?"

Fenna followed Bose up the ladder, to the right, left and right again as they worked their way to the lower deck on the port side of the ship. She turned as the searchlight flicked in sharp increments across the ice before being extinguished with a soft thump.

"Where is your grandfather?" Bose asked as he guided Fenna to the security desk and a custom-sized baggage x-ray machine. Fenna paused to look at the security officer with a metal detector wand in his hand and a pistol holstered at his hip.

Fenna hesitated for a moment. "He is on his way back to camp. I called him on the satphone," she said and held up the phone in her hand.

"He doesn't require assistance?"

"No."

"But he didn't come back to get you?"

"We were separated in the storm. I called him as soon as I saw your ship. I told him I was okay." Fenna took a breath and continued, "The storm looked like it was going to get worse. I wanted him to get home."

Watts stepped inside the door and instructed the crew to raise the accommodation ladder. He holstered the magnum, pulled down his hood and removed his gloves. Fenna's pulse increased as Watts studied her. As head of security, she knew she was ultimately his responsibility, but his predator eyes were unsettling nonetheless. She slipped the sledge bag off her shoulders and handed it to the security officer standing beside the x-ray machine.

"I have a gun and a knife," she said. Watts stirred but Fenna tried a smile. "For protection. From bears."

"That's not a gun," the x-ray officer said as he pulled the pistol out of Fenna's bag. "It's a relic."

"Oh, I know someone who would like that,"

Bose said as he leaned around Fenna's shoulder for a closer look at the Webley.

"Is it loaded?" Watts said.

"With empty shells," Fenna said. "I used them all on the bear."

"Fair enough," Watts said and nodded at the crewmen to close and lock the door. He stepped around Bose and lifted a handset from the wall. "Captain, this is Watts. We're good to go." He replaced the telephone and returned to his position against the wall as his men ran Fenna's bag through the x-ray machine and checked her body with the wand.

"What's this?" the baggage security officer asked as he turned the satellite component in his hands.

"A bit of old radio," Fenna said and shrugged. "It was in my grandfather's bag. He is always collecting junk from old machines. It's difficult to get parts in the Arctic," she added. The officer slipped it back inside the bag along with the satphone.

"We'll have to keep your weapons," he said. "There is a safe in the hold the next deck down. We'll keep them there and you can have them again when you leave the ship." He reached for a clipboard and pushed it across the desk to Fenna. "Sign here." Fenna signed her name, conscious of Watt's scrutiny. "That should do it," the officer said and returned the clipboard to a hook on the bulkhead behind him.

"And this is your ID card," Bose said and showed Fenna a plastic card with a V for visitor stencilled onto the front. He clipped it onto her sweater. "Keep it on you at all times."

"Okay."

"Now, before we go any further, there are rules,"

he said. Bose paused as a forty-something woman wearing a stone-coloured alpaca dress and brown Bedford coat stepped into the security lounge. She paused to look at Fenna before addressing Bose.

"Who is our new guest, Kabir?" she said.

"Mrs Marquez," Bose said with a discreet dip of his head. "This is..."

"Fenna Brongaard," Fenna said and held out her hand.

"Vienna," said the woman. She held Fenna's hand and studied her fingers. "My dear," she said. "Have you been in battle?"

"Something like that," Fenna said and smiled. The woman's touch was feather-light and yet firmer than Fenna had imagined. She reached for Fenna's left hand and held them both under the light. "Your skin deserves more, Fenna," she said and looked up. "Did I pronounce your name correctly, dear?"

"Yes," Fenna said and caught her breath. The woman's eyes glittered like ice, as the corners twitched in a smile. Fenna restrained the impulse to flinch as Vienna let go of her hands, reached out and teased her hair into single strands.

"Just what *have* you been doing?"

"We found her on the ice, Ma'am," said Watts.

"Charlie," Vienna said as she studied Fenna's face. "You know how I detest that title."

"Yes, Mrs Marquez."

"And that one is hardly any better," she said and flicked her eyes at the head of security. "Mr Bose?" she said and turned away from Watts.

"Yes?"

"How long will Fenna be staying?"

"Ah, that is as yet..."

"Undecided? Good." Vienna took a step back and nodded at Fenna. "My husband is away, and you shall be my guest."

"Your guest?"

"Of course," Vienna said and plucked the visitor card from Fenna's sweater. "G for guest," she said and took Fenna by the arm. "Do you have any luggage?"

"Just my sledge bag," Fenna said.

"Bose will bring it to my apartment, while I show you around."

"Mrs Marquez," Watts said and took a step forwards. "With respect, this woman has not been vetted. Neither has she been briefed on ship protocol, or even dress code. I really don't think..."

"And I don't care, Mr Watts. You know what my husband does for a living."

"Yes," he said.

"Then you should know the types of *guest* I am familiar with. I think we can both agree that my current guest, despite her cosmetic needs, fits a rather different category than those I am accustomed to receiving in my home."

"I was just doing my job," Watts said and sighed.

"And you do it admirably," Vienna said. "And I trust you will continue to do so. If I require more assistance, and if my guest," she said and paused to squeeze Fenna's arm, "should prove to be troublesome, I trust you to do your job, Charlie, as per your contract."

"To the very letter, Mrs Marquez," Watts said and pressed his hands inside his belt. Fenna caught the look he shot at Bose as she was whisked out of security and into the reception lounge.

"Such bores," Vienna said as she pointed out the grand piano, waving to the pianist as he experimented with *Rachmaninoff Concerto No. 2*. "The pianist, however," Vienna said and pulled Fenna close, "is far more interesting. He only plays Rachmaninoff for me – it's my signature tune."

Vienna guided Fenna through the lobby and into a corridor lined with a few select shops. They paused in front of a window and Fenna marvelled at the jewellery on display.

"There's no price tag," she said.

"If you have to ask the price, my dear, then you simply can't afford it," Vienna said and gently pulled Fenna along the corridor past the delicatessen and the ship's general store. It reminded Fenna of *Meyer's Deli* in Copenhagen. "People are starting to stare," Vienna whispered as they passed two couples coming out of the store. "It must be your authentic rustic look," she said and giggled. "I couldn't care less, but chins will wag if we don't do something about it. We'll take the lift to my deck and you can relax while I find you something to wear."

"I don't want to trouble you," Fenna said as she tried to gently prise her arm free of Vienna's.

"Nonsense," Vienna said. "It's my pleasure. Besides, as long as you join me for dinner, then you will have repaid me a thousand times more than I can expect."

"Dinner?" said Fenna.

"Yes," Vienna said and sighed. "I have been summoned to dine with the ultimate of bores, his partner and their wives." Vienna stopped at the lift to press the button set in an elegant brass panel. "It seems that Richard thinks a woman is incapable of eating alone. It's the same thing every time Alejandro is away on business, I am summoned."

"By who exactly?" Fenna said as the door to the elevator slid open.

"By that bastard, Humble," Vienna said and stepped inside the elevator. Fenna's boots stuck to the floor, like sledge runners caught in a patch of meltwater freezing on the ice. "Well, come on, my dear. We can't keep the bastard waiting. And," she added, "I fear it will take more than a quick shower to rinse away the grime of battle." Vienna laughed and held out her hand. "Don't worry," she said as Fenna took her hand and let herself be pulled inside the elevator. "I won't let the bastard bite."

Fenna watched as the door closed and her reflection slid into view. She studied her face beside Vienna's and willed her cheek muscles into a smile. *Humble is here.* The thought crowded her mind as the elevator purred upwards through the decks.

Chapter 21

The elevator whispered open and Fenna paused before stepping out of the mirrored interior and into the plush-carpeted passageway. Everything about *The Ice Star* was plush, she realised. Plush and functional. It was also over-designed, sailing in a class of its own, the brainchild of a group of rich Norwegians looking to combine five star comfort with an insatiable lust for adventure. Few ships of its size could cope with the ice, fewer still could afford to. *Don't let yourself get sucked in*, thought Fenna as she followed Vienna to her cabin door. *Stay sharp*.

"Did you hear me, dear?" Vienna said as she slipped her keycard from her jacket pocket.

"No," Fenna said and shook her head. "I'm sorry. I was just trying to take it all in."

"All what? Oh," Vienna said with a nod to the passageway. She smiled. "My dear, you really have been in the wilds far too long if a bit of brass, a couple of oil paintings, and a thick carpet throws you for six." The door unlocked with a beep and Vienna closed her fingers around the handle. "Do you have a problem with dogs?" she said and waited for Fenna to answer.

"Dogs?" she said and peered through the gap in the door as Vienna opened it. "I'm fine with dogs," Fenna said and suppressed a laugh.

"Good for you," Vienna said and opened the door. The shrill bark of a small dog cut through the hum of the warm air conditioning as they stepped inside the cabin. "Personally," she said as she closed the door, "I can't stand them. The dulcet tones you can hear are from Alejandro's beast. I keep the little mongrel in the bathroom. Over there," she said and shut the cabin door. Fenna glanced behind her as the door locked with a beep.

Vienna took off her jacket and hung it on a wire-frame mannequin by the door. She ushered Fenna beyond the pine finish of the hallway and into the cabin proper. Fenna caught a gasp in her throat as she followed Vienna inside, her eyes flitting from the leather sofa to the mirrored wall, beyond the spacious kitchen and back to the black hardwood table facing the balcony. The cabin was twice the size of Fenna's family flat in Esbjerg. She took a few steps towards the sofa as Vienna walked into the kitchen and prepared two mugs of coffee. The polar bear rug beneath the glass and birch coffee table was the only item in the flat Fenna could identify with, that and the view of the thick fog pressing against the cabin window.

"The crew call us guests," Vienna said as she waited for the coffee machine to finish preparing the first mug.

"Guests?"

"Yes. Instead of passengers. Although, I rather like to think of myself as a resident," Vienna said as she placed Fenna's coffee on the kitchen counter. "I spend all my time here. It keeps me away from Alejandro and his dreadful business." She turned back to the machine.

"What business is that?" Fenna asked as she curled her fingers around the mug.

"Cocaine," Vienna said as she sipped at her coffee. She raised her eyebrows, and Fenna caught the twitch of a smile in the corners of her eyes.

"Seriously?"

"Fenna, my dear," Vienna said as she guided her into the lounge. "How else do you think I can afford to live here?" Fenna sat down in the corner of the sofa as Vienna shushed at the dog whining from the bathroom and then sat down opposite her. "I speak for myself, of course," she said. "Most of the residents aboard *The Ice Star* are thoroughly reputable. Incorrigible and ruthless, but reputable all the same. You seem surprised?"

"Yes, perhaps," Fenna said and put her mug down on the coffee table.

"Take off your boots, dear. You are stiffer than one of Alejandro's dead rivals."

Fenna paused as she reached down to untie her laces. Vienna wore that smile again, the one that threw a coal of warmth upon her ice-bright eyes. She undid her laces and hesitated before removing her boots.

"I'm not quite dressed for your apartment," she said.

"Nonsense. Take off your boots, my dear. Relax. I have too few guests to complain. You are my first since October. Alejandro comes once a month or so, just for a few days," she said as Fenna placed her boots behind the sofa and, at Vienna's urging, curled her feet beneath her legs and settled onto the cushions. "He never stays long. Always on the move. Of course, I make sure to feed up the dog before he comes."

Fenna lifted the mug of coffee to her lips and looked around the cabin as Vienna talked. She lingered over a painting hanging on the bulkhead to the right of the balcony.

"Monet?" she asked and pointed at the painting

with her finger.

"Yes," said Vienna and kicked off her own boots. "Do you like it?"

"I recognise it," Fenna said. "I'm not sure what to make of art."

"It's a fake. Alejandro has the original at home, but wouldn't settle for a print, so he had a local artist make a copy." Vienna sighed. "It's all about the *look*, the *feel* of money and what it can buy. These clothes, for example," she said and tugged at the hem of her dress. "I am from Switzerland, but I dress like Katherine Ross."

"Who?"

"From *Butch Cassidy and the Sundance Kid*," Vienna said and smiled. "Before your time, I'm sure."

"Yes," Fenna said. She uncurled her legs and stood up. Vienna followed her to the balcony. The ship's engines thrummed through the floor, tingling Fenna's toes as she studied the fake oil painting.

"I even married a bandit," Vienna said as she stood beside Fenna. "Only he's from Colombia, not Bolivia." She waved her hand as Fenna frowned. "Don't mind me," she said. "More film references. I see far too much television. That and books are all that keeps me sane on this damned boat."

"Why do you stay?"

"Why? Ha," Vienna said. She walked around Fenna and placed her mug on the dining room table. "I don't stay, my dear, I am kept. I am an amusement," she said and glanced at the bathroom door. "Like the fucking dog."

"I'm sorry," Fenna said and raised her hands. "It's not my place."

"No, perhaps not, but..." Vienna paused as if to

erase a shadow from her mind. Fenna watched as her host made a decision. "Yes," she said. "It was rash of me to invite you into Alejandro's den, but I'm so very lonely, Fenna. I don't know how long you will be aboard – as short a time as possible if it's up to Charlie – but let us relax this evening at least. Within these walls, we can tell each other secrets, and pretend that no-one is listening."

"Pretend?" Fenna said and looked around the cabin.

"Oh, no, silly me," Vienna said and placed her hand on Fenna's arm. "It's not bugged. There are no cameras. Believe me," she said and let go of Fenna's arm. "I've had plenty of time to look. No, there are others onboard that like to film things." She shuddered for a moment and then continued, "But Alejandro can't risk having anything on file. For obvious reasons."

"I can imagine," Fenna said and smiled.

"What the other guests do with their cameras, well, that's up to them. I'm sure that one day," she said with a sneer that Fenna could feel as easily as she could see it, "those bastards will realise they made one film too many."

"Is there anyone onboard that you like or is likeable?" Fenna asked.

"Oh, yes, I'm sure there is. I just don't mix with them, my dear. No, Alejandro has vetted my circle and that's why we must suffer the likes of Richard Humble tonight."

"Who is he?" Fenna forced herself to ask.

"Humble?" Vienna said and paused to tap her fingers on the table. "Richard is as Canadian as Alejandro is Columbian. Impeccable manners, polite and generous. He is a charmer. His only public flaw, the only chink in his armour, is his partner, Mark Lunk." Vienna curled her fingers into a brief fist before smoothing her palms over her dress. "I don't know what it is that binds the one to the other. But Lunk is a pig with..." She stopped at the curl of her lips. "Excuse me," she said. "That's enough for now. No matter the company, it does not do to speak ill of dinner guests before the meal. Let's find something for you to wear, then I'll let the dog out of the bathroom and you can relax and freshen up. You'll have the cabin to yourself," Vienna said as she led Fenna to the bedroom. "I'll take the mongrel upstairs."

"Upstairs?"

"Yes," Vienna said and nodded. "Alejandro has bought the cabin above. He's hired a marine architect to draw up plans to put in a staircase, over there," she pointed, "right where the coffee table is."

Fenna pushed the image of a two-storied cabin out of her mind and waited as Vienna let the dog out of the bathroom. She caught a smile at the sight of the Pekingese as it yapped at her feet. The thought of a Colombian drug baron tickling the dog behind the ears made her laugh out loud, causing the dog to yap even louder.

"It is laughable, isn't it," Vienna said and tried to call the dog to her. She gave up and fetched a treat for the dog from a ceramic pot on the kitchen counter. "Like its master it has a high opinion of itself," she said as she held out the treat and clipped a leash from her pocket into the dog's collar.

"When you breed the wolf into a dog that size," Fenna said, "You're asking for trouble."

"A wolf?" Vienna said as she stood up, tugging at the leash every time the dog barked.

"All dogs come from the wolf," Fenna said with a shrug. The thought of Betty and the wolf flashed through her mind, as did the image of her team as they raced towards the polar bear. *If they are smart*, she thought, *then they will follow the scent back to Kula's camp.*

"You look distracted, dear. Let me get rid of the dog, then you can clean up. We're about the same height," Vienna said as she glanced at Fenna. "And you are a size A?"

"As flat as they come, yes," Fenna said and glanced down at her chest.

Vienna laughed and tugged at the leash. "We're going to get along well, Fenna, my dear. I might just have to encourage the Captain take the long way back to the mainland." She pointed at the bathroom. "Fresh towels are on the rack. The maid was in earlier, but who knows what the dog has done since then. Watch your step."

"I will."

"I'll be down later to find something for you to wear." Vienna looked at her one last time and nodded as if she had already decided on Fenna's evening attire.

The dog erupted into a new round of shrill barks as a porter knocked at the door. Vienna fumbled with the leash as she opened the door and received Fenna's sledge bag. The porter nodded and retreated down the passageway towards the elevator as the dog nipped once at his heels.

"Damn this animal," Vienna said. She gripped the sledge bag as Fenna took the leash from her hand, reached down and flipped the dog onto its side.

Fenna slipped her right hand over the dog's muzzle and held it firmly as the dog settled beneath her grip.

"I know dogs," she said and smiled up at Vienna. "I think that's mine." Fenna gestured towards the sledge bag.

"Yes," Vienna said and closed the door. "May I look inside?"

"Sure, go ahead," Fenna said. "There's not much."

"There's nothing at all," Vienna said as she reached inside the bag. "Oh, wait. There's a phone. That's all."

"That's all?" Fenna relaxed her grip on the dog as she did a quick mental inventory. The Webley and the knife were locked in the safe. Vienna had the phone. The muscles of Fenna's stomach tightened as she realised the satellite component was missing. She let go of the dog and checked the sledge bag, sweeping her fingers around the inside, and fighting another round of muscle cramps as she confirmed that it was gone.

"You look pale, dear. Is something missing?"

"Yes," Fenna said and took a step back. She held out her hand as Vienna gave her the satellite phone. She looked at it, bit her lip and nodded. *Next step*, she thought to herself. "Do you have a USB charger?"

"Now that," Vienna said, "is something I do have."

Fenna nodded as she glanced at the satphone. "Time to call for backup," she whispered as Vienna led the dog across the cabin floor in search of a charger. "But who do I call first?"

Chapter 22

Fenna's mind raced with questions. She showered, dressed in a robe and towelled her hair, then she walked into the lounge area of the apartment – she couldn't call it a cabin – and checked the battery level of the satellite phone. She frowned at the single solid black bar, one of five. *Not even enough to turn it on.* Fenna put the phone down, sat on the sofa and hugged her knees to her chest.

"*Think*," she said to herself, the single word lost in the upholstered interior. Fenna leaned back on the cushions and closed her eyes. She imagined Kula on the ice, running his dogs on the thinnest layer where the sea bit at the edge, where snowmobiles could not follow. She saw Burwardsley then, his face a mask of professional hatred, eyes piercing the fog, searching for Kula, for Fenna, for Dina. "Dina," Fenna said and opened her eyes. The room drifted into focus and she gripped the hem of her bath robe. She slipped her legs over the side of the sofa and checked the phone battery once more, shaking her head as she pushed it back onto the surface of the small table next to the power outlet. *Who did you call, Dina?* she wondered. *Who would you call after your grandfather?*

Fenna chewed on the thought and returned to the sofa. She closed her eyes again, thinking through what she knew, rejecting her best guesses. Her thoughts returned to the ship, and how it came to be there, at the edge of the ice, at the right moment. A blurred image of Burwardsley's handwritten note pressed its way into the fore of Fenna's mind. The logo, a ship. A ship with a name. *The Ice Star.* A ship for the rich and the infamous. A home from home at sea, beyond borders, beyond the law. *A haven*, she realised as her mind wandered and her thoughts drifted, merging with the incessant fog pressing at the windows.

Fenna woke at the sound of the lock beeping. She sat up as Vienna let herself in, the keycard in her right hand, a dress draped over her arm, and a pair of high heeled shoes in the other.

"Did I wake you, dear?" she said as she bumped the door closed with her hip. "You must be exhausted."

"No. I'm fine. Really."

"You sure you're up for dinner?"

"Yes," Fenna nodded. *I need to meet him.*

"Good," Vienna said. She hung the dress by its hanger from a shelf and held out the heels. "I hope we have the same size."

Fenna slid along the sofa and took the heels, slipping the left one onto her foot. "They fit," she said. "But I've no idea how I'll walk in them."

"I am sure your boots will be more comfortable, but there is a dress code, and you simply won't be allowed into the restaurant unless you are dressed for it."

Fenna put on the right heel and stood up. She took a breath and walked around the sofa. "I haven't worn heels since gymnasium," she said and laughed. It felt good to laugh, to be distracted.

"Try on the dress," Vienna said. "I'll fix us a drink."

The heels left deep impressions in the carpet as Fenna willed her way across the floor of the cabin. She lifted the dress from the shelf and noticed the panties and bra folded over the inside of the hanger.

Black, like the dress. Fenna took it into the bathroom. She put on the panties and bra and then pulled on the dress. After almost a year of olive drab cotton windpants, wool sweaters that scratched at her skin until she learned to ignore the itch, and the cling of week-old thermal layers, the dress slipped across her skin like spindrift. Fenna caught herself smiling in the mirror. She teased out her hair, curling a handful into a loose ponytail and letting the sides hang in bangs to frame her face, and hide the bite of the Arctic wind and the slap of a Nepalese fist. She twisted to the left and the right, enjoying the swish of the side panels and the tickle of rayon on her legs. With a last look in the mirror she stepped out of the bathroom. Vienna sighed as she walked into the lounge.

"Stunning," she said and pressed a gin and tonic into Fenna's hand. "Truly, stunning. Do you like it?"

Fenna curled her fingers around the glass and nodded. "I do. Although the heels," she said with a guilty glance to where they lay on the bathroom floor.

"You can kick them off under the table."

"Yes."

Vienna walked over to the kitchen and placed her glass on the counter. She returned with a pair of black elbow-length lace gloves. "The final touch, before make-up," she said.

Fenna exchanged her glass for the gloves and slipped them over her frost-beaten fingers. She slid her thumb into the loop and tugged the gloves to her elbows. The thumb loop was at least familiar, but her mind raced with that which was not – the clothes, the apartment, the ship.

"Think of it as camouflage," Vienna said and took a sip from Fenna's glass. "You are simply getting ready for battle." She reached out and teased a few more strands of Fenna's hair, letting it fall across her cheeks. Fenna's stomach turned over as Vienna's fingers brushed her cheek. Vienna caught her eye and withdrew her hand. "Drink up," she said and gave Fenna her glass. "I'll change in my room and then we can go to dinner."

Fenna waited until Vienna had closed the bedroom door before putting down her drink and checking the battery level of the satellite phone. "Two bars," she whispered. She unplugged the charger and took the satellite phone to the window. The door was unlocked and Fenna stepped out onto the balcony. The chill wind tugged at the fine hairs on her skin as she powered up the phone and scrolled down to the second to last number, the one between her call to Daneborg and Dina's grandfather. She checked the signal, wrinkled her brow at the poor reception, and pressed the button to dial. Vienna's shadow flickered in the light from her bedroom window next to the balcony as the dial tone burred in Fenna's ear.

"Come on," she said, the fog beading her hair as the wind tugged at the strands. The dial tone ended and the sound of wind crashed through the earpiece.

"Dina?" said a man's voice. The single word clamped around Fenna's chest before the satellite phone beeped with the loss of signal.

"Fuck," Fenna said and lifted the phone from her ear. She held it above her head and looked up as if searching for the satellites through the fog, above the earth. The phone beeped as the call ended and the words NO SIGNAL flashed across the screen. A rumble that could have been rotor blades caught her attention before Fenna slipped back inside the cabin and pushed the charger into the micro USB port. She stepped away from the phone as Vienna walked out of her bedroom.

"Were you just outside?" she said. "I was sure I felt a draught."

"Yes, I needed some air." Fenna felt the blood rush to her cheeks. Her mind wandered back to the call. *Dina, whose voice was it?*

"What do you think, my dear? Will I do?" Vienna turned on the spot, the graphite ribs of her dress hugged her body above the waist, flaring above her knees.

"Stunning," Fenna said.

"That's my word, dear. You shall have to think of another over dinner, or there will be a forfeit. Now," she said as she joined Fenna in the lounge. "Make-up." She gave Fenna a tube of lipstick and a powder blush for her cheeks. Fenna stared at them. "May I?" Vienna asked and took a soft brush from the purse hanging from her arm.

"Yes," Fenna said and nodded. She held her breath as Vienna applied powder to her cheeks.

"You seem distracted, dear," Vienna said as she finished with Fenna's left cheek and dusted her right with the bristles of the brush.

"I'm fine, really," she said as Vienna stepped back to give Fenna a look.

"If you say so. Although, I must admit, you know rather more about me than I do about you."

"There's not much to tell," Fenna said. She stopped talking and closed her eyes as Vienna pressed the tip of the lipstick to her lips.

"No? The Captain came by while you were showering," Vienna said. Fenna flicked her eyes open.

"He said it was highly unusual for a woman to be sledging on the ice, even more so that she should be alone. In fact," Vienna paused to roll the lipstick along Fenna's bottom lip, teasing at the vermilion borders. "He said that the only white women to sledge on the East Coast of Greenland were tourists or," she smiled as she smoothed an errant smudge of lipstick from Fenna's skin, "soldiers."

Fenna could feel the weight of the lipstick tugging at her lips. She stood, lips parted, her face barely two hand lengths away from Vienna's, close enough to catch the diamond scrutiny of her eyes and the crow's feet concealed beneath a dusting of powder.

"Do you trust me, Fenna?"

"No," she breathed.

"Good," Vienna said with an enigmatic nod. "Then we will be the perfect partners this evening."

"Why?"

Vienna closed the blush with a snap and stepped back to perch on the arm of the sofa. She slipped the make-up into her purse and tossed it onto the cushions.

"If Alejandro has taught me anything," she said and plucked at the edge of one of the ribs of her dress, "it is that partners must never trust one another. That way neither partner can be disappointed or surprised."

"I am a soldier," Fenna said.

"I know."

"A sailor, actually, with the Danish Navy."

"With the sledge patrol?"

"Yes."

"The Captain said as much," Vienna said and

rested her hands in her lap. "Do you intend to steal from me?"

"No."

"Use me?"

Fenna paused for a beat. "If I can."

Vienna nodded. "An honest answer." She tugged at a hair tickling her eyebrow, pulled it from her head and twitched it out of her fingers onto the carpet. "Do you know Richard Humble?"

"I know of him, yes."

"And you've heard of *The Ice Star*?"

"Yes."

"But not of my husband?"

"I have no interest in your husband."

"That makes two of us," Vienna said. She chuckled as she stood up. She glanced at Fenna's hands. "I'm afraid no amount of cream or varnish will help those nails of yours. But then, in tonight's company, it might be appropriate to show a little of your wild side. Just to keep the bastards in check."

Fenna nodded towards the bathroom. "I'll get my shoes."

"Yes," Vienna said. She caught Fenna's wrist as she passed. "I won't pretend to know your plan, I'm not even sure you have one, but I will help you."

"Why?"

"Because if you came aboard this ship knowing the name Richard Humble, then you, my dear, are in a lot more trouble than I will ever be."

"Thank you," Fenna said, and nodded. She tugged her wrist free of Vienna's grip and pointed at the bathroom door. "My shoes."

"Of course," she said and let go.

When she walked out of the bathroom, Vienna

gave her a keycard and a raisin coloured shawl. Vienna, she noticed, had an identical one wrapped around her shoulders.

"I bought two by mistake," she said and shrugged.

Fenna let Vienna wrap the shawl around her. She ran her hands over her hips, biting her lip at the lack of a weapon. *I have never felt so naked*, she thought, *not even when Mikael pulled me out of the ice*. She shivered at the memory as Vienna opened the door.

"Ready?"

"Yes," Fenna said and tucked the keycard inside the glove on her left arm. She stepped into the passageway and ignored the scrape of shoes on her heels. Vienna held out her arm and they walked to the elevator. Fenna smiled at the ship's guests, singles and couples, as they passed them in the passageway and squeezed beside them in the elevator. Vienna chatted and exchanged pleasantries as Fenna studied the ship's schematic hanging at numerous positions on their route to the restaurant. She let Vienna guide her through the lobby, the notes of the piano altering key as they passed, and then they were past the jewellery boutique and delicatessen. The glass doors of the bar were open and the restaurant, one of two onboard, was only a few metres away when Vienna stopped.

"Fenna?"

"Yes?"

"Do you see them?"

Fenna looked beyond the entrance to the restaurant and searched the tables for anyone that might resemble Humble and his partner.

"No," she said.

"There are three men and two women at the table

furthest from the bar."

Fenna found the bar and looked to the right of it, towards the windows, and there, sitting beside two men and their wives, was Burwardsley. She faltered on her heels as he caught her eyes and glared at her.

"Bathroom," Fenna said and tugged at Vienna's arm.

"Here," she said and led Fenna out of the passageway and into the ladies' restroom. Fenna stumbled to the sink and retched.

Chapter 23

Fenna wiped her mouth with a cloth hand towel and checked her face in the mirror. To her amusement, her lipstick wasn't even smudged. Unlike my confidence, she mused. "Fuck," she said and stared at herself in the mirror. "He doesn't have the right to make me feel this way," she whispered. *But he does.*

"Do you want some water, dear?" Vienna said and filled a glass from the drinking fountain. She handed it to Fenna. "I thought you had never met Richard?"

"I haven't," Fenna said and sipped at the water. She set the glass by the sink and stood up straight. "I'm okay. Let's go," she said and nodded towards the door. She followed Vienna into the passageway and to the front desk of the restaurant. Fenna caught the name *Starlight* above the door and then her attention was consumed by the table the waiter led them to. He stopped as the men at the table stood as they approached. Vienna kissed each man on the cheek. She paused beside Burwardsley.

"Mike," she said. "I didn't know you would be joining us."

"Neither did I," he said and winked at Fenna.

"Mike just got in on the chopper," Humble said. Fenna studied him as he stepped around Vienna to pull Fenna's chair out from the table. The cut of his tailored suit matched his cologne, delicate but sharp. Fenna caught herself admiring his jawline and the way he wore his black hair, casual but neat. "I don't know any man that can slip into a tux faster than Mike Burwardsley," he said and gestured for Fenna to sit. "Richard Humble," he said and took her hand.

"Fenna," she said and caught the lump in her throat. She forced a smile upon her lips and made a point of looking at each of the guests seated at the table. Vienna waited for Humble to pull back her chair and Fenna realised he would be sitting next to her.

"So glad you could join us, Fenna," he said as he sat down. "When the ship stopped to pick you up we were intrigued, only to discover our luck that Vienna had taken you in." He glanced at Vienna as he poured Fenna a glass of wine. "How's that dog of yours?"

"You know perfectly well how he is," she said and held out her glass. Humble filled it, put down the bottle and picked up his own glass by the stem.

"To Vienna's dog," he said and raised his glass.

"Vienna's dog," the party chorused and then stilled as they drank. Fenna sipped at her wine and forced herself to look at Burwardsley. She tried to anticipate the rules of the game but was distracted as Humble interrupted her thoughts.

"Introductions," he said and placed his glass on the table. "To your left is my lovely wife, Stella." Humble waited for Stella to smile. "Mike has just been introduced," he said and gestured at Vienna sitting next to him. "Vienna you have met. And sitting beside her is Mark Lunk."

"Richard's partner," Lunk said and nodded at Fenna. She caught his gaze as it rested on her chest. The colour in his fat cheeks and his blatant stare suggested to Fenna that he was drunk, or doing his best to become so.

"Yes, for my sins," Humble said and flicked his hand to the woman sitting to Mark's right. "Madeleine, Mark's wife, completes the circle, and," he added, "no circle would be complete without her."

"Thank you, Richard," Madeleine said and blushed. Fenna imagined it was not the first time she had been the last to be introduced.

The waiter gave Fenna a moment to think as he returned to take their orders for starters. Humble ordered the same main dish for all of them, *something French*, she thought as she struggled with the unfamiliar words. Bread was served and Fenna forced herself to eat as the conversation returned to Vienna's dog and then to her guest.

"Of course," Stella said, "we're dying to know all about you."

"Me?" said Fenna and swallowed.

"Oh we know all about her already," Lunk said and reached for the bottle of wine. He frowned as Humble moved it away from him, emptying the last drops into his own glass. Fenna caught the look Humble shot at his partner as he set the bottle down on the table. Lunk's lips snarled as he turned to Fenna and said, "Jane fucking Bond herself."

"Mark," Humble said with a nod at Burwardsley.

"No, it's all right," Lunk said. "I'll explain." He lifted his palms and made a slowing sign towards Burwardsley. "I was just going to say that our guest is like a spy."

"A spy?" said Stella.

"That's right," he said. "I mean, who else turns up in the middle of fucking nowhere with a gun, a phone and a radio, eh?" He looked around the table. "Jane Bond," he said and thrust his arms across the table. Madeleine reached for her glass as he knocked it over, the wine stained the tablecloth. Lunk chuckled and took the napkin from his lap to dab at the wine.

"I'll do it," Madeleine said and brushed his hands away. Burwardsley suppressed a smile and took a long sip from his glass. He watched Fenna over the rim.

"Mark," said Humble.

"What?"

"Why don't you go and get a drink at the bar."

"You sending me away, partner?" Lunk said and lifted his finger to stab at the space between them. "You're starting to make a habit of that..."

"A habit I would dearly like to quit." Humble nodded at Burwardsley. "I think Mike might like a drink. It's thirsty work out on the ice." Burwardsley pushed back his chair, but Lunk lifted his hand.

"No," he said and wobbled to his feet. "I prefer to drink alone. Either that, or maybe I'll drink with that savage whore in the hold." He looked up and grinned. "Eh, Richard?"

Fenna held her breath as Humble smoothed his fingers on the tablecloth. Burwardsley stood and dropped his napkin onto his seat. He ignored Fenna and moved to stand right behind Lunk, his eyes focused on Humble, waiting for a nod.

"I really don't know why I put up with this," Humble said. Lunk stopped grinning, his face paled and he jerked his head around to look at Burwardsley.

"Hey, I'm sorry, Richard. Really," he said and pressed his knuckles on the tabletop. "I was out of line." He turned to his wife. "Out of line, *again*," he said. Madeleine turned away as Burwardsley placed his huge hands around Lunk's shoulders and guided him away from the table to the bar. Fenna turned in her chair to watch as Burwardsley found an empty stool for Lunk and slipped a tip to the waiter to keep an eye on him. He waited until Lunk ordered a coffee and then returned to the table.

"Madeleine," Humble said as Burwardsley picked up his napkin and sat down. "Would you like another glass of wine?" She nodded and Humble raised his hand to attract a waiter. He ordered two bottles of wine and more bread. Fenna looked at Burwardsley only to find his attention was fixed on Lunk as he sipped his coffee at the bar.

The savage whore in the hold? Dina? she wondered. Fenna turned to glance at Lunk and, forgetting for the moment the voice on the other end of the satphone, she made a decision. She looked up at a brush of toes on her legs. Vienna caught her eye and mouthed the word, *sorry*. Fenna shrugged and took a sip of wine as Stella made another attempt at conversation.

"I don't believe you are a spy," she said. "But do tell. Who are you and how did you come to be on the ice, so far from civilisation?"

"Civilisation?" Vienna said and laughed. "That is assuming that Greenland is civilised. Personally," she said and took a sip of wine. "I find that hard to believe."

"There is plenty of civilisation in Greenland," Burwardsley said without taking his eyes off Lunk. "The capital, Nuuk, has a concert hall, museums, cafés," he turned to look at Vienna. "They even have a court and a bank. Just how civilised do you want them to be? The population of Greenland is about the same size as Hereford, in England. But they are spread out over an island about nine times the size of Britain." Burwardsley turned to continue his observation of Humble's partner. He flicked his gaze towards Fenna for a moment and she thought she caught the briefest of smiles.

Conversation halted as the waiters brought the food to the table. Fenna studied Burwardsley as she turned his words over in her mind. She lifted her hands as the waiter placed a plate in front of her. As he arranged her cutlery, Burwardsley pushed back his chair to stand.

"Bugger," he said and moved around the waiter for a better view of the bar.

"Mike?" said Humble.

"He's gone. I can't see him."

"Really?" Humble said and twisted in his seat. "I shouldn't worry, Mike. He's probably gone to the restroom." Humble thanked the waiter as he turned back to the table. "He'll be back shortly. Sit down and enjoy your meal."

Fenna waited until Burwardsley sat down before excusing herself. She felt Burwardsley's eyes on her back as she walked to the restaurant entrance. She paused to wait for a group to walk through the door and then used them as cover to enter the men's restroom. She slipped around the door and let it close softly behind her. She found Lunk at the sink, washing his hands. He looked up and caught her eye in the mirror.

"Mrs Bond, I presume," he said and grinned. "What brings you in here?"

Fenna walked to the centre of the bathroom, glanced at the stalls to her left, the urinals to the right and then back to Lunk as he turned around and leaned against the counter. She could see the sweat plastering his black hair to his forehead, smell the alcohol on his breath. She blotted out the image of the man and focused on Dina. *Find Dina. Get off the ship. Clear my name.* Fenna recalled Mikael's surprise at finding Dina in the cabin, a cocktail dress tucked beneath their spare clothes. She glanced down at her own dress and looked up to find Lunk staring at her breasts, his mouth drooping into a sadistic leer.

"You said something at the table," she said. "I want to hear you say it again."

"Say *what* again?" Lunk pulled his eyes from Fenna's chest and wiped spittle from his chin. He leered at Fenna and shook his head. "I'm a little drunk. Although," he said and pushed himself off the counter and took a step towards her. "Not *that* drunk."

Fenna slipped the shawl from her shoulders and wrapped the ends around her fists, pulling the shawl tight like a rope.

"Ooh, little girl wants to fight," Lunk said and feinted with a lurch to Fenna's right. Fenna wobbled on her heels and moved to kick them off just as Lunk launched himself at her chest and slammed her to the tiles. The air *whumphed* out of Fenna's body as she scrabbled for breath beneath Lunk's massive frame. Where Burwardsley was all muscle, Lunk's advantage was in the pounds of fat rolled around his belly, jowls and arms. He crushed Fenna with his weight and fumbled his right hand around her throat.

"You want to know about the whore, eh? The little savage? Well," he said and grunted. "Why don't I just show you what I did to her." Lunk gripped Fenna's throat as he pressed one knee after the other onto her thighs. Fenna clawed at Lunk's fingers, but her broken and battered nails left only the slightest impression. Lunk laughed as he grasped a fistful of Fenna's dress in his left hand and tugged it upwards. "Just let it happen like a good little Bond Girl," he said and tugged again, higher this time.

Fenna let go of Lunk's hand at her throat and stretched her arms to reach for the door of the closest stall, or the wall between the door and the urinals. Anything. Her left hand swished across the tiles, empty, but her right caught hold of her shoe and she turned it within her hand and slammed the point of the heel into Lunk's head.

"Fucking bitch," he said as he reeled under the impact. The drool of spit dripped from his chin as he renewed his grip on Fenna's throat. With her last breath Fenna hit him again, this time the heel entered Lunk's ear and he screamed, rolled onto his side and pulled the shoe out of her grasp. Fenna squirmed to her knees and slammed her lower arm onto the shoe before Lunk could remove it. Blood fantailed out of his ear and she slipped on it as she straddled Lunk's body and gripped the shoe in her hand.

"Where is she?" Fenna shouted. "Where's Dina?"

"Fuck," Lunk said and screamed as she turned the heel in her hand. His hands spasmed around Fenna's as he tried to wrench her hands free of the heel, but the pain kept him pinned helpless to the tiles, now bloody.

"Where is she?" Fenna lifted the heel slightly and then pressed it home again, squinting through another shriek of pain and a skeletal geyser of blood. Lunk trembled beneath her and Fenna realised his was not the only body that was shaking. She pushed herself off Lunk and trembled to her feet. The blood on her legs clung to the gauze panels of her dress. She turned to the mirror and pressed the bloody fingers of her right hand to her throat, staring at the red shadow of Lunk's grip. The door opened and Fenna looked into the mirror. Burwardsley stared back at her.

Chapter 24

Fenna watched Burwardsley in the mirror as he stepped into the restroom and walked across the floor to check on Lunk. He prodded the lawyer with his foot and nodded as he moaned. Not once did he look away from Fenna. She noticed the bulge at his hip and wondered why she hadn't seen it earlier. Burwardsley followed her gaze and opened his jacket just a little, enough to reveal the Browning and to ratchet the tension to the next level. He let his jacket fall, straightened his back and smoothed his hands down the front of his jacket.

"You had every opportunity," he said, "more than once, to end this. And now," he gestured at Lunk lying in the foetal position on the floor, bloody hands clasped to his ear.

Fenna shuddered as she opened her mouth to speak. The rush of adrenalin peaked with each breath, her body ready to fight, as her eyes flickered in the mirror, looking for an alternative, a way out.

"There's nowhere to go, *love*," Burwardsley said. He lingered over the last word and scratched the side of his nose, casually brutal. *A monster.*

"He mentioned a girl," Fenna said as she gripped the edge of the counter. "You know who he means, don't you?"

Burwardsley clasped his hands in front of his stomach. Fenna studied him through the mirror, not daring to turn, as if her back was a shield, a line he would not cross. So long as she held that position...

"That was before," he said. "Not now. I don't know about now."

"He spoke in the present tense. My English is

pretty good, you know."

"He was drunk."

"Not that drunk," Fenna said and lifted her head to let the light shine on her neck. Burwardsley shrugged.

"He didn't know what he was saying."

"Humble didn't think so."

"Konstabel," Burwardsley said and sighed. "What do you think is going to happen here?"

"That depends on you."

Lunk moaned and mumbled something about help and a doctor. Burwardsley glanced down at him and took a step back as Lunk fumbled a bloody hand towards his shoes.

"How do you figure that?" he said. "You think I call the shots?"

"Maybe," Fenna said and hoped, just for a moment, to appeal to Burwardsley's human side – the one she glimpsed at the dinner table.

"Then you're just as stupid as this thick fuck," he said and pressed the sole of his shoe onto Lunk's outstretched hand. "Humble's the boss, love. I go where he points, do what he says."

"And you call me stupid?" Fenna said and gripped the counter again, harder now as the shivering rippled through her body.

Burwardsley turned at the sound of voices outside the door. He slid his hand to the Browning and slipped the holster further around his belt, almost behind his back. He let go of his jacket as Watts stalked into the restroom together with a man Fenna assumed to be the Captain, the chevrons on his shirt epaulettes suggested as much.

"You," the Captain said and stabbed his finger at

Burwardsley. "I told you to get off my ship. You and your Nepali friend."

"His name is Bad," Burwardsley said.

"I don't care what his name is. You have no authority on this ship. Mr Watts is in charge of security."

"Hey, Charlie," Burwardsley said, ignoring the Captain. "How's things?"

"Fuck off, Mike," Charlie said and walked around the Captain to kneel beside Lunk. He lifted Lunk's hand from his ear and was rewarded with a moan and a string of curses. "He'll live," he said to the Captain. But he'll be deaf in one ear."

Fenna caught the disappointed look in Burwardsley's eye and turned to face the Captain.

"You're the one we picked off the ice?"

"Yes," Fenna said.

"You followed this man into the restroom?"

"Yes."

The Captain paused to look at Fenna's bloody knees. She flinched as he reached forward to lift her hair from her neck. "He did this?" Fenna nodded. "And you defended yourself?"

"Yes."

"With a shoe?"

Fenna said nothing. Burwardsley smirked.

"Charlie, get this man out of my sight and confine him to his quarters."

"Be seeing you, *love*," Burwardsley said as Charlie took his arm and led him out of the restroom.

"I'll need your pistol, Mike," she heard him say.

"Fuck off, Charlie."

The door closed with a snick of the lock behind them, leaving the Captain alone with Fenna and Lunk.

The Captain walked to the door and locked it. He turned to face Fenna and gestured at Lunk as he moaned on the floor.

"I don't care for any of these men," he said. "They operate around my command, disobey my rules, and, together, they bring a bad name to a magnificent ship. If I had my way..." He stopped and took a breath. "I'll let the medics in, shortly. But before then," he said and glanced at Fenna, "before I have you locked in a cabin, I want you to do something for me."

"What can I possibly do for you?" Fenna said and frowned.

"One of the guests said he heard a woman shouting. It was you, wasn't it?" he said. Fenna nodded. "He said you were asking about a woman, wanting to know where she is. Is that right?"

"Yes," Fenna said and held her breath.

"Then before I lock you up, I want you to push past me and get down to the lower deck. Below that, the orlop deck, there is a compartment, a hold, towards the bow. It's on the port side. That's the..."

"The left," said Fenna. "I know."

The Captain sighed. "This voyage will be my last. Humble intends to kill my career. Dares to call me insubordinate..." Fenna watched as a tick worried at the Captain's left cheek, just below his eye. "I won't be able to help you very much. I can do little more than bark a few orders, but maybe you will find something down there. Or someone."

"Thank you," Fenna said and stepped around the Captain.

He shook his head and said just one word, "Go."

Fenna grasped the handle, unlocked and opened

the door. She saw a gap in the crowd gathered in the passageway that ran from one side of the ship to the other. Fenna stepped over the lip of the doorway and shoved her way through the guests.

"Fenna," said a man. She recognised the voice as Humble's and kept going. The carpet was smooth beneath her feet and she ran to the nearest elevator and launched herself at the stairs going down to the lower decks. The rustle of jackets whispering down the passageway behind her warned Fenna of the security officers giving chase. Fenna saw a crewman coming up the stairs. She gripped the handrail and swung herself around the corner, kicking the man off balance as her feet crashed into his chest. She landed on the landing between the stairs and continued down to the next deck.

Beyond the carpeted stairs, the lower deck favoured form and function over comfort and style. Fenna raced down the wide passageway, weaving between bedding hampers and catering trolleys pushed by Filipino crew members. She ran past the crew canteen and ducked into the passageway leading to the bow of the ship. A metal ladder on the port side of the passageway led down to the orlop deck and Fenna ran towards it.

She paused at the sound of her name, turned and gripped the handrail for support as she recognised Burwardsley's Nepalese thug as he raced towards her, his kukri glinting in the overhead lights.

"Fuck," she said and stomped down the ladder, gritting her teeth as she pounded her soles on the metal. The orlop deck was darker, lined with lengths of spare cable, wires bunched and secured with plastic ties. Fenna ran forwards, past the dark workspaces of tool-pushers and modern day grease monkeys. The Gurkha's boots clattered down the ladder and Fenna ducked through a passageway. She crossed the ship to the starboard side, clambered over a coil of cables and squeezed into a body-sized crevice that even the Filipinos would struggle to fit inside. It wasn't a question of fitting, but surviving. Fenna waited until the ring of Bahadur's boots along the metal passageway had disappeared. She pressed her nose into a gap between the coils and turned her cheek to scan the passageway with her right eye. Bahadur came back, paused at the cable and ran to the ladder on the starboard side, the opposite of the one Fenna had used. Fenna waited until the ring of his boots had cleared the ladder and squirmed out of her hiding space.

She wiped a smear of blood from her cheek, a cut from a stray twist of cable, and padded along the passageway to the bow. She crossed to the port side of the ship and stopped at a door, closed and secured. The light flickered above the door – a loose connection or a failing bulb. Fenna grasped the wheel in the centre of the door and turned it, the dogs in each corner slid open and the door creaked as she opened it.

Fenna cupped her nose and mouth in her hand and hesitated before stepping over the lip of the door. She waited for the light to filter through from the faulty bulb, and for her eyes to adjust to the darkness. A shudder of movement made her jump and Fenna took a breath of foetid air and fought to steady her pulse.

Her mind raced with warnings, as if her very nerves extended from her body, wrapped around the handrail by the door like a lifeline, ready to pull her back from the brink and into safety. Fenna took another step. She saw a flicker of movement to her left and pushed her bare feet ahead of her, testing the floor. She slid on a puddle of liquid and fell onto her knees by the side of a crate, and a body, the naked form of a woman with long hair glued to her skin in matted twists and knots.

"Dina?" Fenna whispered and held out her hand. "Dina, is that you?"

Fenna paused at the thought of how many kilometres she had sledged, how far she had run, fought and bled to get to this point, in a dank, black hole of the richest ship afloat, the hold where even the brightest star would never shine. She let her fingers brush against the woman's shoulder, smoothed her hand into a firm grip and crawled forwards to pull the woman into her arms.

"Dina," she said. "I found you."

Dina choked a response and flung her arms around Fenna, clucking and clicking the stub of her tongue at the back of her mouth as she squeezed with what little strength she had left.

"I won't let you go," Fenna said and smoothed her hands through Dina's hair to free her face. "I've got you," she said and kissed Dina's forehead. "Bloody hell, I've got you." The echo of Mikael's words jerked tears onto her cheeks and she pulled Dina closer still as the door to the hold squealed shut and the last of the light was extinguished. Fenna closed her eyes and let her tears mix with the Greenlander's. *They can do what they want with me now. I have found Dina.*

The deck vibrated as the Captain ordered more

thrust from the *The Ice Star*'s engines as he turned the ship in a lazy curve away from Ittoqqortoormiit and set a course for the southernmost point of Greenland, Cape Farewell.

Chapter 25

The cold from the metal deck seeped into Fenna's body, pressing raised diamond shapes into her skin. She opened her eyes and moved her arm, only to have Dina clutch it once more. The Greenlander curled her naked and bruised body into Fenna's, her long black hair flowed in knotted strands and greasy twists across her back and was lost in the black fabric of Fenna's dress. The dogs on the door squealed as someone unlocked them and Dina shivered. Fenna closed her eyes, squinting through her lashes as Humble, Burwardsley and the vicious Nepali were framed briefly in the lowlight from the passageway before they stepped into the hold. Bahadur carried a chair for Humble. He moved around the two men and placed it just a few metres from where Fenna and Dina lay curled on the floor. Fenna closed her eyes and listened to Humble's voice as it drifted through the dark hold.

"The Captain played his part well," he said. "I'll give him that, although it will count very little towards his career." Fenna heard Burwardsley grunt a reply as Humble scraped the chair along the deck, and moved it closer to her. He sat down and she opened her eyes. "Konstabel," Humble said as Fenna blinked to focus. She kept her head low, behind Dina, until a pang of guilt reminded her that the Greenlander had been used enough. She prised her arm free of Dina's grip and sat up.

"I see you're just like him," Fenna said and nodded at Burwardsley.

"What? Oh," Humble said and made a show of looking around the hold. "You don't like your accommodation?"

Fenna said nothing. She flicked her eyes from Humble to the two men he used for muscle, and back again.

"What do you think, Mike?" he said. "She seems pretty quiet."

"She's learned when to keep her mouth shut."

"And yet, that's not enough, is it?"

"No, Mr Humble. Not nearly enough."

Humble clicked his fingers and Bahadur handed him an object. Fenna recognised it as he held it up and twisted it in the light. Humble tossed it onto the floor in front of her.

"Do you know what that is, Konstabel?"

"Part of a satellite, made by Humble Industries," she said. "Your company."

"You're right, in part," he said and gestured at the component. "My father's company did make it, but it's not from a satellite," he said, smirking. Humble turned to look at Burwardsley. "I've been looking forward to this."

"It should never have gotten this far," Burwardsley said.

"Oh, Mike, stop beating yourself up. A loose end is a loose end. Besides, she's here. They both are. All tied up, figuratively and," he laughed, "literally, in a little while anyway."

"Still," Burwardsley said and shuffled his feet. "It should have gone smoother."

"No matter," Humble said and turned back to Fenna. "In fact, I like it this way because I get to gloat."

Burwardsley bristled as Fenna shuffled forwards and picked up the piece of metal. She moved back to sit beside Dina and studied the component in the gloom. Dina kept her eyes shut, her knees tucked into her chest, and her elbows jammed into her thighs. Her skin goosebumped as Humble talked. He ignored her, but for a casual glance at her body. Fenna threw the component at Humble's feet.

"I don't understand," she said and waited for him to respond.

"What was your mission, Konstabel?"

"To retrieve that," she said and pointed at the component.

"What would you say if I told you it was a fake, that, in fact, the entire satellite was a fake, dropped out of a plane, a matter of hours before you were tasked to pick it up?"

Fenna felt a surge of adrenalin prickle through her body. It raised her pulse, pressed her heart against her chest, confused her lungs into thinking she needed more oxygen. "What plane?" she said, but she already knew. "The Chinese..."

"No," Humble said and laughed. "A stolen transponder on a charter plane, made to look like it was from China. You see," he said and rested his elbows on his knees. "The Danes aren't the only ones who can play games in the Arctic."

"I don't understand."

"Hans Island," he said. "In 2005 we sent our Minister of Defence, Bill Graham, with a bottle of whisky and a flag to that pathetic rock in the Nares Strait. The Danes responded with a delegation of their own, putting a battleship in the strait, and a bottle of booze beneath *their* flag."

"It's an island," Fenna said and shook her head. "I don't understand what it has to do with a fake satellite."

"Of course you don't." Humble paused to flex his fingers. "But it didn't stop with the island. Did it? It's not enough to mock the Canadian presence in the Arctic, now you want the fucking Pole."

"This is about the North Pole?" Fenna shook her head. "You're insane."

"No," Humble said and leaned back in his chair. "Not insane. Not even close to being slightly mad. You see, while you and your teammates are laughing it up over failed manoeuvres in the Canadian north – mocking our so-called Rangers – you are missing the bigger picture. The future economy. Hell, Konstabel, the Northeast and Northwest Passages are open, it's only a matter of years before the Pole itself is ice-free. And if you think for a minute that we're just going to sit back and let you take it..." Humble took a breath. "No," he said. "It's not going to happen. You've had your fun in the Arctic, Konstabel, you and your Sirius boys. Welcome to the real world of geopolitics. It's time to get serious, and for Denmark to realise it is seriously out of its depth."

Fenna snorted, "You *are* mad. Canada is our ally. We're not at war..."

"No? Like we're not at war with Russia? Or China?" Humble leaned forwards. "Understand this, if an independent group of patriots can drop a piece of junk from an aircraft and have your navy task a mission to pick it up, just imagine what we could do if we decided to bring some real resources into play. It's only a matter of time, Konstabel. Greenland is begging to be independent, free of its Imperial masters. What if Canada were to step in and offer it a way out? What if we were to create such a scandal that the whole world was forced to question Danish sovereignty and their competence as a ruling power in the Arctic? How long do you think it would take, how many years, before you were out and we were in? Denmark would be a very small country all of a sudden, wouldn't it?"

Fenna swallowed a rebuke, and focused on her breathing. Her head was beginning to spin and she felt small, as small as Denmark, just a pawn in a political game. "But Mikael…" she said.

"A piece of the puzzle," Humble said and turned to look at Burwardsley. "A counter to be moved around the board. A loose end."

"Like me," she said.

"Exactly like you, and the girl," said Burwardsley and nodded at Dina. "You were just unlucky – you were chosen to be in the right place, at the right time."

"And Kjersing?"

"Ah," Humble said and smiled. "Commander Kjersing. Our man in the Arctic."

"Your man?"

"Ours, yes. He was proving to be troublesome. I needed to test him, and this was the perfect test. If he could sweep this little incident under the rug then he would indeed prove his worth." Humble paused. "He failed, of course."

"You set him up," Fenna said and resisted the urge to shout. "You concocted all this as a test? For one man?"

"With the added benefit of creating a scandal if he couldn't resolve it. Yes, that's exactly what we did." Humble pushed back his chair and stood up. "I need Kjersing driving a desk at Arctic Command in Nuuk, not driving dogs in some East Greenland armpit. He's no good to me there."

Fenna looked up at Humble. She felt the energy and adrenalin drain from her body. "Who *are* you?"

"A good question," he said. "You can take it to the grave, Konstabel."

Fenna blocked Humble's words from her mind. *Not yet*, she said to herself. *I need to know.* "Vestergaard," she said. "What about him? He works for you?"

"Vestergaard?" Humble said and turned to Burwardsley.

"You know him as *The Magician*," Burwardsley said. Fenna recognised the look on his face, as if it was more information than he wanted her to know.

"Yes, yes. Now *he* proved his worth."

"But he's Danish?" said Fenna.

"Yes. So was Kjersing."

"Was?"

"Mike?" Humble said and looked at Burwardsley.

"Not yet," he said.

"Oh, come on, Mike."

"Mr Humble, sir," Burwardsley said and sighed. "What with her and the Greenlander..."

"Fine," said Humble. "I'm sure you'll get around to it."

Burwardsley nodded as if it was one more task on a very long list. Fenna watched him and then turned her attention to Bahadur as he shuffled closer, his hand grasped around something. Fenna squinted to see what it was but failed. She glanced at Dina. The Greenlander had not moved. She was completely locked down, as if Humble's presence had tripped a switch and short-circuited her body. Humble took a step to one side and cocked his head. Fenna looked up as she became aware of him staring at her. She met his gaze and placed her hand on Dina's leg.

"And her?" she said. "What about Dina?"

"What about her?" Humble said and shrugged. "She heard too much."

"So you cut out her tongue?"

"Christ no," he said. "She bit it off herself. Some foolish attempt at suicide."

"Why would she do that?"

"It's in the Greenland psyche…"

"You're a bastard. An evil piece of work," Fenna said and spat.

"All the same, Konstabel, Dina heard far more than was good for her, or you," Humble said as his lips curled into a smile Fenna wished she could erase from her memory. He leered at her, looked at Dina and then licked his top lip. "There are some rewards in this line of work, and I have certain needs, things I desire that I would not wish on my wife. Dina satisfied those needs," he said and Fenna shuddered at the matter-of-fact manner in which he said it.

"You're an animal."

"And she is a savage," he said and shrugged. "Your country treated them as savages for years, why shouldn't I?"

"She's a human being."

Humble shook his head and turned his back on Fenna. He walked across the deck to Burwardsley and nodded. "Drug her," he said. "The guests have forced a vote. Apparently they're tired of the east coast and want to go to the west. That suits me fine. I'll get a plane to pick me up once we get there. They can fly me over to Canada. You can reach me at the Toronto office if you need me."

Burwardsley nodded and clicked his fingers at Bahadur. Fenna watched as the Nepali opened his hand to reveal two syringes. She shuddered as he held them up to the light.

"Just the Dane, Bahadur," said Humble. "I have to talk to the Captain, but when I'm done," he said and nodded towards Dina. "I might have some appetite left." He turned towards Fenna and said, "They're no good if they're drugged. It's like having a limp fish on your cock." Humble slapped Burwardsley on the back and laughed as he walked towards the door of the hold.

"You bastard," Fenna shouted at his back. She scrambled to her feet as Burwardsley pulled a Taser gun from behind his back and fired. Two probes punctured Fenna's dress and knocked her to the floor as the electroshock incapacitated her. Burwardsley tossed the Taser onto the deck and kneeled down beside her.

"You haven't got much time left, Konstabel," he said. "There's been a bit too much drama these past few hours. The guests are all on edge and dumping two young women over the side will only make them nervous. They might be rich, but not all of them are stupid." He waited as Bahadur pressed the needle into Fenna's neck and depressed the plunger to pump the sedative into her body. Fenna's teeth chattered as she tried to focus her eyes on Burwardsley, Dina, anywhere.

"Done, *Saheb*," said Bahadur.

The Nepali moved to stand up but Burwardsley caught his arm. Fenna fought to focus on his words as he nodded in Dina's direction.

"Do me a favour, Bad," he said.

"*Saheb?*"

"Shoot her up too."

"But Mr Humble..."

"Fuck Humble," Burwardsley said and waved his finger in front of Fenna's eyes. She followed it as best she could. "You think I'm a monster, Konstabel," he said. "But even monsters have days off." Burwardsley stood up and shrank out of view, and the thrum of the ship's engines seeped into Fenna's mind as her body let go.

The Schoolhouse

WEST GREENLAND

Chapter 26

UUMMANNAQ, WEST GREENLAND

The light from the passageway tugged at Fenna's eyelids, pressing, insistent, painful. She rolled her tongue within her mouth, it flopped to one side and lay heavy in her cheek. She tried to open her eyes and caught a glimpse of a man with the head of an elephant, huge ears, before her lids failed and her eyes shut. Something kicked at her feet and she felt the deck beneath her legs as they were spread apart.

I must wake, the thought tumbled within her head. *Wake up, Fenna. Wake up.*

"Wake up," a voice said. "Open your eyes, bitch."

Fenna opened her eyes as the shadow of Lunk towered above her, extinguishing the light from the passageway, extinguishing hope.

"No," she said, the word mumbled from her lips.

"Oh, but I say yes," Lunk said and laughed. He moved his head and the light caught the elephantine bandage covering his left ear. Lunk unbuckled his belt and slipped it out of the loops of his trousers. He huffed for breath as he kneeled beside Fenna and bound her hands in front of her stomach. "Payback's a bitch, *bitch*," he said, his breath ragged with excitement.

Lunk gripped Fenna's jaw within his meaty hand and squeezed her mouth open. He spat in her face and lumbered into a standing position. The muscles in Fenna's face trembled into a limp grimace as her body fought the drugs.

Wake up, Fenna.

Lunk unzipped his trousers and reached inside the fly, pleasuring himself with one hand as he wiped a swathe of sweaty hair from his forehead. He leered at Fenna, the smile on his face dimpling his fat cheeks. He hawked and spat again, the spittle and phlegm landing squarely on Fenna's breast. Lunk twisted to free his penis from his trousers, sneering as the tip caught on the teeth of the zipper. He sighed as he stroked himself above Fenna, pleasure flooding his body, dulling all other senses, blinding him to the chair that crashed into the back of his head.

Fenna blinked as Dina raised the chair a second time, gutter noises clucking from her mouth as she hit Lunk again, and again. She turned as he lifted his right arm in defence. Dina slammed the chair into his bandage. Lunk screamed and collapsed to the deck. She hit him again and the chair bounced out of her grasp, it skittered across the deck as she leaped upon Lunk, curling the fingers of her right hand into a fist full of greasy hair as she punched his left ear. Fenna blinked at the vision of Dina, cat-like, her hair streaming like a banshee's, rising and falling as she lifted Lunk's head and hit him again and again.

"Dina," a man's voice shouted from the passageway. Dina hit Lunk again as the man leaped over the lip of the door and ran across the deck, the stomp of his boots echoing around the hold, drumming into Fenna's body. She lifted her head as the man turned and the dim light flickered across the face of *The Ice Star*'s head of security.

"Dina, stop," Watts said. He dropped the bundle of clothes and boots in his hands and wrestled Dina off Lunk's back. She screamed a gargle of abuse and fought back, pushing Watts to the floor. He tried to stand but Dina pressed her knee into his chest, fumbled for the pistol at his waist, ripped it from the holster and pointed it at Lunk's head. Fenna squirmed to one side, out of the line of fire.

"No, Dina," Watts said.

Dina flicked Watts a look through slitted eyes, turned to face Lunk and pulled the trigger. The report of the 9mm boomed through the hold as the bullet punctured the back of Lunk's head and pulped the left side of his face. Dina lowered the pistol, slipped off Watts' chest and kneeled on the floor.

"Fuck," Watts whispered as he pushed himself to his feet. He reached down and pulled the pistol from Dina's hands and holstered it. The echo of the shot lost momentum and faded into the depths of the hold as Watts ran a hand across his chin. He took a breath, nodded and crouched by the side of Dina.

The Greenlander's body trembled as Watts wiped the hair from her eyes and slipped a t-shirt over her head. He lifted Dina's limp arms and guided them through the holes. He did the same with a sweater then walked around her, slipped his arms beneath hers and lifted her to her feet.

"How are you doing, Konstabel?" he said as he helped Dina step into a pair of military trousers.

Fenna licked her lips and coughed a reply, "I am okay."

"Can you stand?"

"My hands," she said and lifted her wrists, Lunk's belt pinched the skin, the buckle digging into the back of her hand.

"Give me a minute," Watts said. He glanced towards the passageway as he lowered Dina to the deck, tugged socks over her toes and shoved boots onto her feet.

Fenna wriggled into a sitting position, wobbled

onto her knees and stood up.

"All right, Dina. I am going to help the Konstabel now," Watts said as he tied the laces of Dina's boots. "Do you hear me?" Dina stared at the deck. Watts tied the last bow, cupped Dina's face in his hands and kissed her brow. He reached for the second set of clothes and boots, stepped over Lunk's body and nodded at Fenna. "Let's get that belt off," he said and dropped the clothes and boots onto the deck. He glanced for a second time at the doorway and then unbuckled the belt around Fenna's wrists.

"It was your voice on the satphone," she said as Watts freed her hands. "It was you Dina called, wasn't it?"

"Yes," Watts said and tossed the belt onto the deck. The dim light reflected the tears welling in his eyes as he tried to smile. "She is *my* ice star. Not this fucking ship. Not these people. I can't live without her. I won't live without her..." he wiped away a tear with his finger, then palmed it away with his hand. Fenna dressed as Watts recovered. "We met only a few months ago, when she first came onboard. I got to know her as she guided the guests. Then she got sucked in by Humble's charm, and the next thing I know, she is gone for days. I overheard one of the Filipinos say they saw Burwardsley dragging her into the chopper. I guess he was tying up a loose end. He was off the ship when she called me. I found her on the ice with a dog team," he said as Fenna fastened the buttons of her windpants. "They found her, of course, in my cabin." Watts clenched his fists. He looked away as she pulled the dress over her head and slipped her arms into the sleeves of her thermal top. She sighed as the sleeve caught on Vienna's gloves.

Watts looked up and tugged the gloves free. He slipped the fold of the top over her breasts and pulled it down to her waist.

"Thanks," she said and took the sweater from his hands.

"We don't have much time," he said and glanced for a third time at the doorway. Fenna tugged her boots over her bare feet. "No socks," Watts said. "I couldn't find them. Sorry."

"It's fine," Fenna said. "You got all this from Vienna's cabin?"

"She gave me the key," he said and nodded. "I also have this." Watts tugged the Webley from the waistband at the back of his trousers. "I even found a single bullet in the bottom of your sledge bag." Fenna fumbled the pistol as Watts handed it to her. "You sure you're okay?"

"I'll be fine," she said and pressed the pistol into her windpants. "Just a little groggy."

"Okay," he said and nodded towards the door. "We have to be going." Watts walked around Lunk's body and pulled Dina to her feet. "You've been out for four days. They gave you at least one more shot that I know about. Maybe two. You don't remember them feeding you?"

"No."

"Food and water. They even forced you to pee."

"Thorough," Fenna said as she blocked the image from her mind. "Where are we?" she asked as she followed Watts and Dina to the door.

"Uummannaq fjord. We're anchored just outside the harbour. It's a popular stop for tourists and the guests got tired of Humble planning their itinerary. He's rich, but not *that* rich," Watts said and smirked, but Fenna could see no amusement in his expression.

"So what happens now?"

Watts paused at the lip of the door. Her curled his arm around Dina and kissed her gently on the side of her head. "I have a Zodiac waiting to take you into town. You can trust the driver," he said as Fenna frowned. "He owes me a favour."

"And then what?"

"I called ahead to the hospital. It's the yellow building right on the water's edge. They are expecting you. I told them you were both in need of medical attention, and that they might want to inform the police."

"Okay," Fenna said as she processed the information. "Okay, let's get to the boat."

"You'll have to do that," Watts said and pressed Dina into Fenna's arms.

"You're not coming with us?"

Watts shook his head and tugged the pistol from its holster.

"He'll kill you." Fenna caught the edge of fear in her voice.

"Burwardsley? Maybe," he said and smoothed his hand through Dina's hair. "But I can't live with the knowledge of what they did to her," he paused to swallow, "on my watch."

"You're not responsible."

"Yes, Konstabel, I am," Watts said. "I practically delivered her to them." He let go of Dina and pressed his fingers into his shirt pocket. He pulled out a micro SD card in a tiny plastic case.

"What's this?" Fenna said as Watts placed the card in her palm.

"Humble likes to watch," he said and gave Fenna

a grim smile. He closed her fingers over the card and nodded. "I'll get you off the ship. Just promise me you'll get the bastard. For Dina," he said and let go of her hand.

"I promise," Fenna said and zipped the card inside the chest pocket of her thermal top.

Watts stepped over the lip of the door and pointed to the ladder halfway down the length of the passageway. "Take the ladder to the next deck. The door is open and there is a ladder down to the Zodiacs. There will be a crowd," he said. "Guests going into town. Go past them and get on the last boat."

"Got it," said Fenna as she guided Dina through the door. She flexed her fingers and smiled as the feeling returned to the tips beneath her scratched and broken nails. She caught Watts' arm as he took a step down the passageway. "Vienna?" she said, "Is she with Humble?"

"I don't think so. She let me in to her cabin and helped me find your clothes," he said and shrugged. "She is also a prisoner aboard the ship. Just not Humble's."

Fenna took a breath and nodded. With one hand curled around Dina's back, her fingers gripping the waistband of the Greenlander's trousers, Fenna walked down the passageway behind Watts. He held his pistol low but ready, his index finger tapping the trigger guard.

Dina stumbled along beside Fenna, all the way to the ladder. Fenna took a step and tugged at Dina's trousers. Dina shook her head and looked at Watts.

"It's okay," he said. "Go with her. I'll find you later."

Dina stamped a foot on the deck.

"Dina," Watts said. "Go."

She stamped again and Fenna winced at the ring of her boots echoing down the passageway. Watts pressed his hand against Dina's cheek. He smoothed a strand of hair from her eye with his thumb. Dina's eyes glistened and a tear rolled onto Watts' thumb, seeping into the pores of his skin.

"Go," he said.

"Come on, Dina," Fenna said and took a step up the ladder. She pulled at the waistband of Dina's trousers, yanking the Greenlander up and onto the first step as Dina clawed at Watts' jacket. Dina choked and the guttural sounds of her cries were painful for Watts to hear. He took a step back, out of reach. Fenna yanked Dina onto the next step as the sound of someone jogging along the passageway from the stern of the ship forced Watts into a defensive stance. He held the pistol in a two-handed grip as Bahadur slowed to a walk and lowered the British SA80 rifle to a casual position.

"Charlie, Charlie, Charlie," said Burwardsley as he stepped out of a workspace between the hold and the ladder.

"Mike," said Watts as he glanced over his shoulder. Bahadur slipped behind a fire hose mounted on the bulkhead, his rifle raised as Watts flicked his attention away from Burwardsley, searching for the Gurkha. Fenna tugged Dina onto the next step.

"The Captain chose the right side," Burwardsley said. "Why couldn't you?"

"Oh, I don't know," Watts said as he stepped backwards around the base of the ladder and pressed his back against the side of the ship. "I guess I have principles."

"Principles?" Burwardsley said and laughed. "That's rich." He nodded at Bahadur and took a step towards Watts. "You sold out, just like the rest of us."

"Maybe I did, but..." Watts flicked his eyes from Burwardsley to Bahadur as the Gurkha inched forwards. Fenna pulled Dina up the ladder, just three steps from the deck above. She looked over Dina's shoulder just as Burwardsley drew the Browning, straightened his arm and fired.

The crack of the shot thundered along the passageway, drowning Dina's scream as Fenna dragged her up the last steps and onto the deck. Watts tumbled to the floor, raised his pistol and fired two shots in quick succession only to be silenced by a three-round burst of 5.56mm from the Gurkha's rifle. The impact flipped the security officer against the bulkhead. He slid onto the deck as Burwardsley leaped over him and ran up the ladder. Fenna shifted her grip to the front of Dina's waistband and dragged her into a stream of crewmen as they bustled about the passageway, heads bobbing around one another for a better view. Fenna crashed through the crowd, located the open door and pushed Dina out of the ship and down the ladder to the Zodiacs, squinting in the brilliant light, and stumbling past the guests and into the Zodiac at the end of the pontoon dock.

The Filipino driver clicked the Zodiac into gear and pressed the throttle lever as Fenna tumbled Dina over the rubber sides of the boat and grabbed the safety line. The wind flicked at her hair as she turned to see Burwardsley charging down the ladder only to be stopped by the throng of excited guests filling the pontoon. Fenna turned her head as she heard the *thunk thunk* of small chunks of ice hitting the rigid hull of the Zodiac, and she let the wind blow her hair free of her eyes. The heart-shaped mountain that gave Uummannaq its name towered above the yellow hospital. Fenna plucked a strand of hair from her mouth and dared to breathe.

Chapter 27

The driver of the Zodiac powered the inflatable craft in a wide arc around an ice floe, a sheet of ice that defied the warm sea temperatures. The bow waves of the small blue fishing trawlers chopped the water as they motored past. Fenna noticed the patches of blood on the floe, the remains of a hunt when the fjord was frozen. The island of Uummannaq, 650 kilometres above the Arctic Circle, had been locked in for the brief, unseasonable but increasingly common, winter. Fenna scanned the road and shivered in the cool breeze. She didn't have enough layers for sailing despite the warmer weather. The ice may have melted but it was still sub-zero.

She spotted a familiar blue police Toyota parked outside the hospital, a Rav4 minus the bullet holes. A policeman was leaning against the door, smoking and watching the Zodiac slip between the hunters' dinghies. Fenna held his gaze as the man finished his cigarette and walked down the road to the concrete slipway. The hull of the Zodiac crunched over a layer of ice as the Filipino driver cut the power and raised the outboard motor. Fenna waited for the boat to bump to a halt, then stood up and helped Dina to her feet. She nodded at the driver and stepped over the side of the boat, tugging Dina's sweater and encouraging her to follow. The policeman stopped at the top of the slipway and waited.

Fenna realised that Dina was walking with the weight of the dead, as each step took her further and further from Watts. She barely lifted her toes from the ground, sliding her feet forward, up the slipway, away from *The Ice Star*, away from the scene of so much horror. *And love*, Fenna thought as she remembered the security officer's tenderness, the light kisses he placed on Dina's forehead, the wet sheen to his eyes as he looked at her.

"It's going to be okay, Dina," she said and pulled her another few steps.

"Konstabel Brongaard?" the policeman said and pulled his hands out of his pockets.

"Yes," Fenna said and studied the man. She thought of Maratse and realised she would have preferred a Greenlander, but also that it was quite normal for the more senior ranks to be Danish. She stopped a half metre in front of him and circled her arm around Dina's waist.

"My name is Simonsen. I'll take you to the hospital."

"Okay," she said and glanced over her shoulder as the Filipino slipped over the bow of the Zodiac and pushed it back into the water. She waited for him to wave, but the man dipped his head low inside the high collar of his jacket, his breath misting over the lip as he lowered the outboard, started the motor and weaved between the dinghies on his return to *The Ice Star.*

We're on our own again, Fenna thought as she guided Dina along the road behind the policeman. Simonsen waited for them beside the Toyota, pausing as a second policeman, a Greenlander, walked out of the side door of the hospital and held it open.

"We'll go in the back way," Simonsen said and nodded towards the policeman. Fenna took a last look at the ship and the two Zodiacs heading towards the harbour. She relaxed when she couldn't see Burwardsley's massive frame; the Zodiacs were full of guests, six to each boat.

The policemen kicked the snow off their boots before entering the hospital. Fenna did the same, but Dina dragged each toe as if it was frozen to the floor, as if she had to break every step free before she could move on. The dim light of the corridor cast a yellow light on the white walls as they passed the tiny morgue and skirted around a gurney. Simonsen stopped as the mobile in his pocket rang. Fenna smiled as Europe's *The Final Countdown* rang louder and louder before he swiped the screen and nodded for his assistant to take them into the room off to the left.

"In here," the policeman said and opened the door to a small storage room with a chair in one corner. Fenna guided Dina between the packing cases and plastic storage boxes and helped her sit down. She turned to the policeman as he stepped out of the room and gripped the handle of the door.

"What are we doing in here?" she said. "I thought we were going to be seen by a doctor?"

"Maybe," he said and shrugged. He nodded towards Simonsen, out of sight but within earshot. Fenna strained to hear his voice as he continued to speak on the phone.

"Yes," he said. "I understand." Simonsen's mobile beeped as he ended the call. Fenna listened as his boots clumped along the corridor. The policeman let go of the door and took a step back, making way for his boss. Simonsen stepped inside the storage room, glanced at Dina and then fixed Fenna with a steel gaze.

"You're not going to help, are you?" she said.

Simonsen unzipped his jacket and wiped his

sleeve across his brow, strands of thin grey hair caught in the Velcro at the wrist. He cocked his head to one side and called the policeman over.

"Danielsen," he said.

"Yes?"

"Stay here while I go back to the office. No-one comes in. Not even a nurse."

"Not even a nurse?" Fenna said and took a step forwards. Her elbow nudged a cardboard box and it crashed to the floor, spilling its contents of vacuum-packed needles capped in plastic.

"Settle down, Konstabel," Simonsen said. Fenna watched as the man's hands moved to the ready position. "I'll be back very soon, and we can sort all this out."

Fenna caught his arm as he turned. "Who was that on the mobile?" she said as he brushed her hand from his sleeve. "Who was it?"

Simonsen held up his palm and waited for Fenna to take a step backwards. She glanced at Dina and then back at Simonsen's hand. *I could snap his wrist*, she thought as she played out the move in her mind. *Snap it and pull the Webley, force him to give me his pistol. And then what?* She took another look at Dina and then a slow step backwards.

"That was your commanding officer," Simonsen said. "Kommandør..."

"Kjersing?" Fenna said and resisted the urge to spit. "He's crooked. Working for Canadian Intelligence," she said.

"Really?" Simonsen said as his mouth creased into a grin. Fenna saw the flecks of tobacco between his teeth as he laughed. "He said you might say something like that."

"It's true," Fenna said and glanced at Dina. She wished she would at least lift her head so that she could see her eyes, but Dina kept her face covered. Fenna flexed her fingers as Simonsen laughed. *As soon as I see my chance – we have to go*, she thought.

"I find it difficult to imagine that the leader of Sirius is a secret agent, Konstabel." Simonsen's last word cackled out of his mouth, his cough rasping and his chest rattling. Danielsen grinned behind Simonsen's back.

Fenna slipped her left hand behind her back and closed her fingers around the handle of the Webley. *A metre and a half*, she calculated, *from me to Danielsen, through the laughing policeman. Down the corridor and... where?* She paused for a moment as Simonsen doubled over in a second bout of coughing. *The boats, and into the fjord.* She smiled as Simonsen caught her eye. Then she drew the Webley, changed her grip and pistol-whipped Uummannaq's Chief of Police on the side of his head. Fenna leaped over Simonsen as he crashed to the ground and threw herself into Danielsen's chest. She dropped the Webley and gripped the policeman around the throat with her right hand, slapping his hand away from his pistol with her left. Fenna changed her grip again, grabbing the policeman by the ears with both hands and slamming his head on the corridor floor as she wormed her knees onto his arms. Danielsen moaned until Fenna smacked his head for the fourth time. She felt his body go limp beneath her knees. Fenna let go and tugged the USP Compact, the same model as Maratse's pistol, from his holster, cursing at the spiral of plastic securing the pistol to his belt. She searched Danielsen's utility pockets and found a folding knife. Fenna flicked it open with her thumb and sawed through the plastic. She slipped the pistol into the side pocket of her windpants, stepped over Danielsen's body and picked up the Webley. Fenna whipped the butt of the handle into the side of the policeman's head and pushed the Webley into the waistband of her trousers. She found two spare magazines and shoved them into her pockets. Simonsen's pistol had no security loop so Fenna could pull it free of the holster and shove it into the front of her windpants, leaving the handle poking out of the waistband. She searched his belt and removed another spare magazine and fished his lighter out of his pocket. Fenna remembered how cold it had been on the water and unzipped Simonsen's jacket. She rolled his body from one side to the other and pulled the jacket free. She did the same with Danielsen as Dina lifted her head and stared at the two policemen.

"Put this on," Fenna said and gave her Danielsen's jacket. She slipped her arms into Simonsen's jacket, folded the knife and stuffed it into the pocket with the lighter. Fenna flicked her eyes upwards and mouthed a quick *thank you* as Dina zipped her jacket and tucked her hair inside the collar. Dina stamped her foot and pointed at Simonsen.

"I had to," Fenna said. "He got a call from Kjersing," she said and held up her hands. They trembled and she clenched her fists to suppress the adrenalin pumping through her system. *Not for the first time*, she realised. *And probably not the last. Not before this is over.*

Dina nodded and walked towards the door. She skirted around Fenna, stepped over the policeman and turned towards the door at the end of the corridor. Fenna followed her and pulled the pistol from her waistband. The grip was familiar in her hand and she slipped her finger alongside the trigger guard.

"Dina," she said. Fenna waited until Dina turned to look at her. "We have to finish this."

Fenna's chest ached as Dina took a step towards her, reached out and cupped her hands either side of Fenna's cheeks. She raised her eyebrows, *yes*.

"We can't keep running. You understand?"

Dina raised her eyebrows again. *Yes*.

"I don't know how it will end."

Dina shrugged and smoothed her thumbs on Fenna's cheeks. She nodded, let her hands slide down Fenna's face, onto her shoulders, along her arms and to her hands. Dina slipped the fingers of her right hand into Fenna's left and lifted her chin towards the door. She tugged Fenna along the corridor and Fenna let herself be guided to the end, realising as they walked towards the light filtering through the salt-stained window, that an end was all Dina wanted.

They stopped at the door and Dina moved to give Fenna space to look through the window. She lifted her hand but Dina did not let go. Beyond the Toyota the road wove to the right along the harbour towards the stone church and *Pilersuisoq*, the supermarket. To the left, Fenna remembered, was the slipway and a fleet of dinghies. She bit her lip and scanned the road once more. Fenna could see the bright red jackets and the slim lifejackets worn by the guests from *The Ice Star*. The tourists clumped in small groups along the road, and Fenna held her breath in anticipation of seeing Burwardsley or Bahadur among them. Dina stamped her foot and Fenna turned as a nurse entered the corridor at the opposite end of the hospital. The nurse cried out at the sight of the two policeman as Dina increased her grip on Fenna's hand, pushed the door open and pulled her outside.

The cold air caught Fenna's breath for a moment and then they were running and sliding, slipping the soles of their boots along the slick snow, which was compacted and ground into the road, all the way to the slipway. Fenna paused at a single shout. She turned towards the hospital and saw Burwardsley running towards them, one hand tucked beneath the parka he wore over his Arctic camouflage pants, the other waving at the Nepali in the Zodiac powering through the water towards the slipway. Fenna tugged her hand free of Dina's. She gave the Greenlander a short shove down the slipway and pointed at the dinghies. As Dina picked her way across the ice to the boats, Fenna gripped the pistol in two hands, fired two shots in Burwardsley's direction and then turned to empty the magazine into the pontoon of the Zodiac as Bahadur increased speed. The pontoon deflated with a violent gasp as Greenlanders nearby and the guests on the road began to scream and shout. Fenna changed the magazine and fired two more shots at Burwardsley as Dina tugged at the start cord on an outboard. The motor coughed to life and Fenna fired once more as Dina untied the dinghy and waved for Fenna to come quickly.

The *boom boom boom* of Burwardsley's Browning barrelled along the road as he walked the rounds across the ice-coated rocks, puncturing the dinghies between him and Fenna. Plastic jerrycans of fuel in adjacent dinghies popped and burst just a metre from Dina's back as she twisted the throttle arm and turned the bow of the greasy and blood-stained hunter's vessel into the fjord. Burwardsley cursed as he changed magazines and yelled for Bahadur to come and pick him up.

"Go, Dina," Fenna said and pointed towards the tip of an island in the middle of the fjord. Dina planed the dinghy to the left and right of the larger floes and growlers at the entrance to the harbour, lifting the bow of the dinghy as she increased speed and steered a course away from the island, away from *The Ice Star*, towards the end.

Chapter 28

UUMMANNATSIAQ, WEST GREENLAND

The outboard motor failed ten metres from the curved point of Ikerasak island. Dina gripped the throttle arm of the motor and used the remaining forward motion to steer the dinghy closer to the ice lining the shore. Fenna twisted in the seat at the bow, the pistol pointing at the deck in a loose grip. She looked over Dina's shoulder and scanned the fjord, searching for the black hulls of *The Ice Star*'s Zodiacs. She knew Burwardsley would follow just as soon as he got a replacement for the one she hoped she was lying on the sea floor in Uummannaq harbour, preferably with the bloody Gurkha inside it. She turned and faced forward as Dina bumped the dinghy into a flat growler grounded on the rocks just a few metres from the shore. Beyond the ice and rock of the coastline, Fenna could see wooden buildings, painted red and blue, sitting on granite foundations. She focused on a red building, the largest and furthest from the shore, across a wide open field of snow with little to obstruct a bullet, a killing ground should anyone wander into it. She nodded at Dina, tucked the pistol into her windpants and scrambled over the side of the dinghy, her feet sliding for purchase on the ice as she held the boat steady for Dina to climb out of it. As Dina clambered around her and onto the island, she kicked the boat free. *One way or another, we won't need it*, she reasoned. Fenna watched as the boat drifted out between the growlers of ice and into the fjord. The tide might take it deeper into the fjord, *if we're lucky*, she thought. She turned and followed Dina towards the red building.

It was a schoolhouse, with thick square rafters of dark hardwood in the roof space, long benches around broad tables, and bunks at the rear. Dina walked from the door into the kitchen and searched the cupboards, pulling tins and dried goods onto the counter. She found a tin of peaches and pulled open a drawer, rattling through the cutlery until she found a tin opener. She beamed at Fenna as they sat down opposite each other at the table closest to the kitchen. It was the first time she had seen Dina smile, Fenna realised. She watched as Dina chiselled her way into the lid of the tin and twisted it open, turning the tin with one hand at the base and cutting the lid with the blade and quick flicks of the tin opener. The syrup spilled onto Dina's hand and she smiled as she licked it from her fingers.

"Dina," Fenna said as the Greenlander prised back the lid and fished a peach slice out of the tin. "You're going to need this," she said and slid Simonsen's pistol across the table. Dina flicked her eyes at the pistol and shook her head. "Yes," Fenna said and placed one of the two extra magazines next to the pistol. Dina ignored Fenna and ate two more slices of peach. Syrup dribbled down her chin and dripped onto the tabletop.

Fenna sighed and made a play of wrestling the tin from Dina's grasp. She tried to smile, then slipped a slice of the preserved fruit into her mouth. Dina nodded and then grabbed the tin. They shared the last of the slices until there was only syrup remaining. Dina drank half of it and pushed the tin to Fenna.

"No," she said. "You finish it." Fenna waited until Dina had wiped the last drop of juice from her chin. The twenty-five year old woman grinned like a cheeky toddler and Fenna smiled at her. Then she placed her hand on the pistol and pushed it all the way to Dina's chest. "I can't do this alone," she said.

Dina's hair shook as she frowned and looked away from the pistol as Fenna wrestled with the image of Dina shooting Lunk in the head, only hours earlier.

"They are coming," she said. "You understand, don't you?" Fenna reached across the table and tugged at Dina's arm. "Don't you?" she said as Dina turned to face her.

Yes, Dina raised her eyebrows. She scowled and took the pistol and the extra magazine, pushed them into the voluminous pockets of her jacket. Dina lifted her right leg over the bench, stood and walked to the window. She picked at the sealskin cord of a dog whip hanging on the wall – there was another on the wall opposite – and stared out across the snow towards the fjord. Fenna joined her and realised she could just see the dinghy before it floated out of sight behind a large berg. The tide had cleared this area of the fjord, carrying the larger floes deeper into the black waters, around the peninsula and out to sea. Apart from the numerous bergs, the sea was clear and free for sailing. The sun was low in the blue sky, and the glaciers on the mountains were tinged with pink. If it wasn't for the drone of the outboard motor that drifted towards the schoolhouse on the wind, Fenna thought she might have enjoyed the view.

"I have no plan," she said to Dina as the Greenlander cupped her mouth and nose in her hands, staring through the window at the sea. "But I will finish this," she said. "For Mikael, for you..." Fenna stepped behind Dina, wrapped her arms around her and smoothed her hands through her long, black hair, tugging it free of the jacket collar and letting it flow down her back. "I will finish it for you, Dina," she said. "And Charlie," she whispered.

Dina trembled as Fenna stroked her hair. The pink glow of the late Arctic afternoon spread down the mountain and disappeared into a cold shadow, black like the water, black like the hull of the Zodiac that drifted around the corner, black like death. Dina turned away from the window and buried her head against Fenna's chest as the driver of the Zodiac cut the power and the hull bumped against the ice. Fenna recognised the four men who clambered out of the inflatable. She watched as Bahadur secured the Zodiac to the rocks with a length of rope. She recognised the two policemen. They wore non-regulation jackets and carried the same model of antiquated rifle that Fenna had fired from the back of Maratse's police car. The scowls on their faces and the bandages around their heads were new. Burwardsley, she noted, stood apart from the rest as he removed the magazine from the SA80 rifle he carried, checked it and slapped it home. Fenna shuddered as she heard the click, as if all her senses were wired to that one man. A second click caught her attention and she flicked her eyes from Burwardsley, scanning for his Sergeant, the merciless Nepali with the curved blade.

"These men," she whispered, "are the single most important men in my life." She watched as Bahadur nodded at Burwardsley and stalked towards a lip of rock, an elevated position above the schoolhouse to Fenna's left. "But it is *my* life," she said and sank below the window. She eased Dina to the floor to the right of the window, and took the pistol and magazine from Dina's pockets as she leaned her back against the wall. Fenna crouched. She moved to the door, keeping low, and opened it. She peered around the frame as the policemen stopped in the snow, five metres from the boat and just thirty to the schoolhouse. Burwardsley didn't move.

"Konstabel," said Simonsen. He coughed and spoke again in English for Burwardsley's benefit, raising his voice. "Fenna," he said. "Throw out your weapons and come out. There's nowhere to go," he added and gestured at the fjord with his left arm.

Fenna stood and pressed her body to the wall. She shouted through the open door, "Get rid of your friends and I might consider it." She glanced at Dina while she waited. The Greenlander looked at Fenna through the strands of her hair, as if she was peering through a blind in the jungle, shallow breathing, hoping the tigers would go away.

"I'm not going anywhere, Konstabel," Burwardsley said. "You know that."

Fenna took a breath and a firm grip of the pistol in her left hand. *I knew that*, she said to herself. With a quick glance at Bahadur's position, she snapped off a single shot at the Gurkha and ducked back inside the schoolhouse.

Dina clucked the remains of her tongue and pressed her hands to her ears. She looked at Fenna and then crawled the length of the table and hid at the end furthest from the door. Fenna leaned against the wall and listened as the policemen swore in Danish, thumping the snow from their trousers and jackets as they picked themselves up and moved into cover. Fenna smiled until she heard Burwardsley's laugh, deep and indulgent, as it broke against the schoolhouse wall, slamming into Fenna's gut like a boulder.

"We've been here before, *love*," he said. Fenna heard the snow crunch beneath his boots as he walked forwards.

"Get down, you fool," Simonsen shouted. Burwardsley ignored him and Fenna counted his strides. "She has two pistols."

"Yes," Burwardsley said. "Both of them yours."

Fenna imagined Bahadur settling into the stock of his gun and lining his sights on the door. *I'll give him ten strides.* "And then I will kill him," she said and shifted her position to the second of two windows, furthest from the door and closest to the kitchen. She counted five more strides, scooted a metre from the window, popped up and fired twice. The window shattered and she fired twice more at the British Lieutenant as he crashed to the ground and rolled to Fenna's right. She tracked him with the pistol, stepping to the left and firing again. Fenna felt the impact of her fifth round as if she controlled its flight with a wire, slamming into Burwardsley's right shoulder and spraying blood across the snow like a reckless painter.

"Bad," Burwardsley yelled as he switched his grip on his rifle. "Take her."

Fenna dropped to the floor and rolled into the kitchen unit as the Nepali shredded the exterior of the schoolhouse and the windows disintegrated under his sustained burst of fire. *This isn't for me*, Fenna realised and forced herself to move. She cut her hands and knees on the glass as she crawled to the door. "It's covering fire," she breathed and thrust the pistol around the door frame, firing blind and emptying the magazine as she sprayed the approach with lead.

"Fuck," Burwardsley shouted.

"You like that, eh?" Fenna shouted as she switched pistols, stuffing Simonsen's into her pocket.

"Laugh it up, *love*," Burwardsley shouted and opened up with three-round bursts that splintered the door frame and tore the door from its hinges. Fenna rolled onto her side as the door crashed onto the stone floor and fell against the remains of the frame. Another burst from Burwardsley's rifle splintered the door in the middle and it collapsed into two pieces, flat on the floor.

Fenna ignored the glass splinters in her hands and popped up behind the first window, firing two shots blind and sighting the third as she found Burwardsley, as close to the schoolhouse as he dared, too close for Fenna's liking. She aimed. Squeezed the trigger and then paused at a *whush* of air behind her and the sound of wood creaking and leather snapping like a whip on the ice. She turned as Dina's feet brushed the surface of the table, her neck noosed within a dog whip lashed by her own hands around the beam above her.

"No," Fenna screamed and clambered onto the table top. She gripped Dina's feet and pushed them upwards, trying to lift her body as the British rifles pulped the side of the schoolhouse. Fenna screamed again as a tornado of splinters cycloned around the room, piercing her cheeks, stabbing at her body, pricking Dina with jagged chips as her almond face paled into blue and she swung beneath the beam until a burst of bullets severed the sealskin cord and she fell onto the table and rolled onto the floor. Fenna dropped the pistol and scrambled after her, lifting her head and tearing at the cord around Dina's neck with bloody fingers. It was tight, cinched, she pinched Dina's skin as she tried to pull it free.

The whip was no ornament. Cut from the skin of a ring seal, it was cured, greased in blubber, finger-wide at the base, it fluted to the diameter of a square pencil at the end where it was bound tight around the Greenlander's neck. Fenna held Dina's head in her arms and then, as the splinters withered to the floor, she pulled Simonsen's pistol from her pocket and slipped the last magazine inside the grip. She let go of Dina and reached for the other pistol beneath the table. She tapped the barrel into the floor to remove any stray splinters. With a pistol in each hand, Fenna stood up and walked to the door. The glass crunched beneath her feet, blood trickled from the cuts in her hands, from the ends of the splinters embedded in her cheeks, but her focus was elsewhere. Fenna raised the pistols and stepped over the remains of the door, pulling the trigger of each weapon alternately, first left, then right, searching for targets with a haphazard sense of apathetic justice, letting the bullets fall where they may. She was done. There was no more, and this was the end.

“Sergeant,” Burwardsley shouted as Fenna cleared the schoolhouse.

“Yes, Saheb,” Bahadur said and pulled the trigger.

Chapter 29

Fenna lay in the snow as the blood pulsed out of her left arm. The beat was stronger than the pain. The flesh of her right leg was clipped below her knee and a third shot from the Gurkha's rifle had broken at least three of her ribs. Glancing blows, all of them. Crippling but not mortal. She would recover, she realised, and that was the last thing she wanted. Fenna stared at the fading light above her as the sky turned from pale blue to bruised purple, fading to black, unlike her memory. In her mind's eye, Dina swung from the beam still as Burwardsley pressed his boot on Fenna's wrist, plucking the pistol from her right hand. He repeated the action for the one in her left. Fenna ignored him, staring past his face, and the blood staining the shoulder of his parka. She heard the policemen as they entered the schoolhouse and called out Dina's status.

"She's dead," Fenna said, speaking the words at the same time as Simonsen, as if they had rehearsed. But they hadn't. *It wasn't meant to be like this*, Fenna told herself, admonishing herself with another image of Dina swinging from the cord whipped around her neck. Dina swung back and forth, even as the snow crunched beneath the policemen's feet as they carried the Greenlander's body past Fenna to the Zodiac. As the sound of their boots and Simonsen's huffing and grunting receded, Fenna heard the Gurkha arrive, his light step revealed only by the slap of the rifle against his back as he slung the SA80 and stopped at her feet.

"Saheb?" he said and nodded at Fenna. "What we gonna do?"

Burwardsley stepped over Fenna and crouched

beside her. He prodded her ribs with two stiff fingers, smirking as she winced, ignoring the pain in his own shoulder. He lifted his hand. Fenna watched as Bahadur pressed a field bandage into it. Burwardsley lifted Fenna's arm and, with Bahadur's help, he bound the wound, pressing the bloody sleeve of the jacket beneath the bandage. He bound her leg with a second bandage from Bahadur, flicking the Gurkha's hand away as he tried to plug the wound in Burwardsley's shoulder.

"It can wait," he said. "Like her ribs."

"Policemen coming back, Saheb," Bahadur said.

"Stall them. I need a minute with the Konstabel." Burwardsley reached down and turned Fenna's face towards him as Bahadur met the policemen and discussed when they would leave. Fenna stared past Burwardsley until he pressed her cheeks together, his finger and thumb squeezing between her teeth and forcing her lips to part. "Look at me, Konstabel," he said. Fenna flicked her eyes past the swinging shadow of Dina's corpse and stared at Burwardsley. "That's better," he said and relaxed his grip.

Burwardsley pulled the glove off his left hand and searched Fenna's body. She waited for him to violate her, to cup his hand around her breast, to grope between her legs, but Burwardsley was professional, thorough but fast. He dug the Webley out from beneath Fenna's back and tossed it towards the policemen. His fingers lingered over the square of plastic tucked inside her thermal top. He unzipped the pocket and pulled out the SD card.

"Interesting," he said and held it up in the last of the evening light. "Charlie give you this?"

"Yes," Fenna breathed. Her eyes flickered from

the card to Burwardsley's face, and then back to the image of Dina in her mind.

"Do you know what's on it?" he said. "Hey, Konstabel." Burwardsley slapped her face with the back of his hand. "I said do you know what's on the card?"

Fenna flicked her eyes towards his. "I have an idea," she said.

"Will you use it?"

"I don't understand..."

"Yes you do," he said. "Will you use it?"

Fenna listened to the throb of her blood, pulsing past her temples and pressing at her wounds. She ignored Burwardsley until, a second slap later, and he had her attention.

"Yes or no, Konstabel."

"Yes," she said.

"Good."

"Why?" Fenna said.

"Because I'm done," he said and flicked the lapels of her jacket to the side. Burwardsley reached beneath her sweater and slid the card inside her pocket. He zipped the pocket halfway as Simonsen crunched through the snow. He removed his hand and stood up.

"Is she hurt?" Simonsen said and stared around Burwardsley at Fenna.

"She'll live," Burwardsley said. "What about the Greenlander?" he said and nodded towards the Zodiac. Bahadur helped Danielsen shove the boat off the ice and into the water. The policeman held the rope as Bahadur crawled over the side and started the motor.

"Hmm," Simonsen said and cast a glance at

Fenna. "I'd love to pin it on her, but honestly don't know how she could have done it." He shook his head. "She was pretty intent on killing you."

"I have that effect on women," Burwardsley said. Fenna waited for him to laugh, and couldn't decide if she was surprised when he didn't.

"Lieutenant," Simonsen said and lowered his voice. He gestured for Burwardsley to step away from Fenna. "What happened here today, I need to write it up. If it hadn't been for the call from Premierløjtnant..."

Fenna stiffened, the throb of blood forgotten as she strained to hear what Simonsen was saying. Burwardsley turned his back to her and leaned in close to the policeman. He towered above the Dane and Fenna gave up on trying to hear what was said, the look on his face confirmed it. It was a done deal, she realised. Bulletproof. Fenna let her head flop back onto the snow. The back of her neck cooled and she looked up at the first stars, closed her eyes, and imagined Dina's face. The image of the Greenlander stayed with her as the policemen lifted her up, cuffed her, and marched her to the Zodiac.

Dina was her focus as Bahadur sailed across the fjord, weaving slowly around the ice, and steering past the bergs as they threatened, in all serenity, to crumble at a glance. Fenna crumbled each time the image of Dina in her mind was replaced with the sight of her slumped in the bow of the boat, a red welt around her throat, the sealskin whip hanging loose around her neck. The lights of the town flickered into her vision as the Zodiac idled at the slipway, long enough for the policemen to drag Dina's body out of the boat and into the back of the ambulance, long enough for them to return and march her into the Toyota waiting at the top of the slipway.

Burwardsley walked alongside the policemen, leaning on the door as they shoved her into the passenger seat. He waved Danielsen away as the policeman tried to shut the door.

"Give us a minute," he said and the policeman walked away to smoke quietly next to Simonsen. Burwardsley took a breath and Fenna watched as he favoured his left arm. She hoped the right hurt like a motherfucker. He followed her gaze and laughed. "Yes, love, you finally got me."

"I'm not your *love*," she said. "I never was."

"No," he said and glanced over the roof of the car at the mountain, its features snow-cut and stark in the distance. "It's a pretty country. Brutal and unforgiving but pretty. Don't you think so, Konstabel?" Burwardsley said and looked down at Fenna.

"I used to," she said as the bump of sledge runners in her mind forced her to think of Mikael, Dina...

"Listen, Konstabel, shit happens and jobs have to be done." Burwardsley shrugged. "Bahadur and I, we're just good at what we do. More or less. We were meant to gather all the loose ends at the cabin. Kjersing arranged for you to bring the satellite to us. We brought Dina. Only," he paused and winced at the wound in his shoulder, "things didn't go quite to plan."

The twinge of satisfaction Fenna felt at the obstacles she had overcome, how she had evaded the British Lieutenant, again and again, was banished by the guilt of Dina's death and Mikael's murder. "What did you mean when you asked me if I would use the card?"

Burwardsley glanced at the policemen as they finished their cigarettes and took a step towards the Toyota. He leaned inside the car and said, "Humble pays for everything, but the things he takes for free still have a price. The girl should never have been involved," he said and glanced at Fenna. "I'm not a complete monster. Use the card, Konstabel. Make the bastard pay." Burwardsley nodded once, turned and walked down the slipway to the Zodiac. Fenna watched as he slipped his long legs over the side of the boat and waved for Bahadur to take them back to the ship. Danielsen closed the door and Fenna pressed her face to the window, watching as Bahadur ploughed a course through a patch of brush ice towards *The Ice Star.* The ship stirred in the fjord, the navigation lights sparkling as the propellers maintained its position in the face of the tide. Fenna lost sight of the Zodiac as it disappeared in the black water and Simonsen backed the Toyota onto the road and drove the short distance to the hospital.

She let them drag her from the back of the car. She let them stand in the room as the nurse undid her bandages and stripped Fenna to her underwear, tossing her dirty, blood-stained clothes onto a chair in the corner of the room. Fenna sat on the bed at the nurse's instruction and lifted her arms for her to clean and bind the superficial wound in her chest where Bahadur's bullet had glanced her ribs. *He was surgical*, she realised. *And I got off lightly.* Unlike Dina down in the morgue. Danielsen and Simonsen stepped out of the room as the nurse undid Fenna's bra. She cleaned her skin and bound a fresh bandage over her arm before slipping a gown over her head. Fenna noticed that Simonsen had found a seat in the nurse's office in the adjacent room. He stared at her through the observation window, and Fenna realised she was in the island equivalent of Intensive Care, a pane of glass and a spit wad from the medical staff.

The nurse dumped Fenna's bloody bandages and her own surgical gloves into a yellow medical waste bag and helped Fenna onto the bed and beneath the sheets. Fenna lowered her head onto the pillow and stared up at the ceiling as Danielsen entered the room, closed his fingers around her left wrist and cuffed her to the rail of the bed. He tugged at the chain once and then walked out of the room without a word. The nurse followed him and turned out the light. Darkness, Fenna realised, was not the friend she'd hoped for.

She tried to sleep, tried to force the image of Dina from her head, but she was trapped in the room with the ghost of the Greenlander. And when the image of Dina did fade, Mikael sledged into her mind, his red beard dark with blood, and the back of his scalp flapping as they crested the top of a gulley, or pushed the sledge over the ice foot and onto the frozen sea. The howl of the dogs kept her awake, as did the *crack crack* of 9mm rounds and the maniacal grin of the elephant man as he bled from his ears and pleasured himself, one stroke after another until Dina returned, swinging in front of Fenna through the long, dark polar night and into the morning. It was only the bustle of the nurses and breakfast that forced her to accept that sleep was gone and the nightmares were not confined to the night.

The lights came on and Fenna turned her head

towards the nurse. The woman paused at the door, her short body half inside the room as she turned her head to talk to a policeman in the corridor. Fenna heard the nurse switch from Greenlandic to Danish and then tut to allow the policeman to enter the room. The tears that Fenna's nightmares had held at bay, welled in her eyes at the sight of Maratse. He grinned as the nurse scolded the unlit cigarette from between his lips and into his jacket pocket. Maratse stepped aside and let her pass, closing the door behind her with his foot.

"Konstabel," he said as he fished the cigarette from his pocket and pushed it into the space between his teeth. "I've come to take you home."

Fenna nodded and sniffed once before lifting her wrist and rattling the cuffs chaining her to the bed. Maratse grinned and fished a key from the pocket on his belt. He tossed it to Fenna and nodded at the clothes in the bag on the chair.

"Get dressed," he said. "We have to take Dina to the heliport."

And there she was, Dina, again, but this time Fenna wasn't alone.

Chapter 30

There was a crowd outside the hospital when Fenna walked out of the front door. She tugged the collar of Simonsen's jacket high around her neck and dipped her head, covering her face with her hair. Her leg was stiff but she was determined not to limp. Maratse opened the taxi door as Fenna slid her feet along the smooth surface of the snow. She noticed that Simonsen was sitting in the driver's seat of the police Toyota, watching her from where he was parked on the road, outside the light blue offices of Nukissiorfiit, Greenland's energy utility company. Maratse waited for Fenna to get inside the car and closed the rear passenger door. He sat down next to the driver and told him to wait on the road. Dina's body, Fenna had heard the nurse say, was sealed inside a zinc casket and loaded onto the back of a pickup. She saw the vehicle outside the side entrance to the hospital, the early morning sun reflecting on the shiny surface as the driver secured it with straps to the pickup's bed. Maratse nodded for the taxi driver to follow the pickup as it pulled out of the hospital parking area and onto the road. Simonsen followed in the Toyota.

The road to the heliport wound around the mountainside, cut into the rock. Wooden houses painted blue, red, green and yellow, leaned over the edges. They drove past the town scrap yard and an assortment of sledge dog houses, drying racks, snowmobile carcasses stripped for parts, and the ubiquitous plastic fish crates borrowed indefinitely from the Royal Greenland fish factory. Fenna took it all in, her face pressed to the passenger window as she avoided looking through the windscreen, avoided the thought of Dina, and tried to block out the shoot-out at the schoolhouse.

The taxi slowed as the pickup drove up the slight rise beside the heliport and through the gates onto the landing pad. The ground crew helped the driver unload the casket and secured it inside a net to be slung beneath the red Air Greenland Bell 212 helicopter. Maratse paid the driver and got out of the taxi. Fenna waited for him to open the door. He pressed a small backpack into Fenna's hands and waited for her to look inside.

"I can't take that on the plane," she said and opened the pack to show Maratse the Webley. He shrugged and fished a cigarette from the packet in his pocket.

"It's all you have," he said.

Fenna closed the backpack and slung it over her shoulder as Simonsen parked the Toyota beside the heliport building, stepped out of the car and bummed a cigarette from Maratse. He stared at Fenna's jacket as he lit the cigarette.

"Konstabel," he said and paused to blow out a lungful of smoke. "I don't pretend to understand what happened before you arrived in Uummannaq. All I know is I want you off this island. You are now in his custody," Simonsen said and nodded at Maratse. "He'll see you all the way to Kangerlussuaq. You'll fly to Denmark later today."

"That's it?" she said. "What about Kommandør Kjersing?"

"Dead," said Maratse.

"What?"

"Shot himself yesterday," he said and shrugged.

Fenna's shoulders sagged as she processed the information. The distant beat of rotors *whopped* through the air and she thought about Humble's *man in the Arctic* and the cost of the Canadian's test, the number of dead, and the potential implications for the Sirius Patrol should the story ever find its way into the papers.

"You are advised to keep your mouth shut, Konstabel," Simonsen said, raising his voice as the helicopter settled into a hover over the helipad, buffeting them with the wash of the rotors as it landed. "There are no journalists on the island," he said. "And, fortunately for you, no-one thought to film your gunfight outside the hospital. If someone had posted this on YouTube..." Simonsen shrugged and took a last drag on his cigarette. He flicked the butt into a snowdrift.

Maratse tugged at Fenna's elbow and nodded towards the helicopter. The ground crew had finished attaching the net to the bottom of the aircraft and the pilots were signalling that they were ready.

"You can keep the jacket," Simonsen said as he walked beside Fenna to the gate. "Consider it a souvenir, a reminder. I have mine," he said and smoothed his hand over the purple welt on the side of his head. Fenna nodded and followed Maratse through the gate and across the helipad. They ducked instinctively as they walked beneath the rotors and climbed into the helicopter. Fenna slid along the bench beside Maratse, dumped the backpack on the floor and buckled her seatbelt. Maratse handed her a pair of ear defenders and she tugged them over her ears. Simonsen waited by the gate until they were in the air before returning to the Toyota. Fenna watched him drive along the road as the helicopter lifted off the helipad and into a hover, settling the weight of the casket before gaining altitude and dipping the nose of the aircraft. The island was busy as people walked along the roads to the supermarket, glancing up at the helicopter as it chopped through the air above them.

The flight to the mainland took less than twenty minutes. Maratse was silent and Fenna closed her eyes. She immersed herself in the high pitch and tremor of the rotors, blocking out images of the schoolhouse, and focusing on Kjersing's abrupt death. She thought about Humble and pressed her hand against the pocket in her thermal top. She felt the card at the bottom of the pocket and pulled the zip closed. Maratse tapped her shoulder and pointed out of the window at a whale breaching the surface between the icebergs in the dark waters of the fjord below the helicopter. Fenna noticed the pilots exchanging gestures and felt the aircraft dip to the left as they angled for a better look. The pilots levelled the helicopter and raised the nose of the aircraft, losing speed and altitude as they settled above the gravel landing strip at Qaarsut airport. More ground crew guided Dina's casket to the ground before stepping back as the helicopter shifted position and landed. The rotors whined as the pilot powered down, reaching up to apply the rotor brake as the helicopter shuddered and the motor ticked cool. Fenna grabbed her backpack and followed Maratse out of the helicopter as the ground crew jarred the door open, sliding it alongside the fuselage. Dina waited to one side.

"I told Kula I would bring his granddaughter home," Maratse said. Fenna stood by his side as the ground crew removed the net and straps. They paused at the roar of the four-engined Dash-7 aircraft as it touched down on the gravel strip, air-braking all the way to the airport building. Maratse turned away from Dina's casket and stuck a cigarette in his mouth. He walked towards the building and Fenna fell in step beside him. The aircraft turned at the end of the strip and taxied to the terminal, a small wooden building with a tiny tower.

Fenna's bag was shoved in the hold with the other passengers' luggage. Maratse sorted her boarding pass and they waited in the small lounge as the crew removed several rows of seats inside the aircraft to make space for Dina. When they climbed onboard, Fenna was relieved to sit in the seats directly in front of the casket. While the first sight of the casket had troubled her, she now realised that Dina was finally at peace, and that no man could ever hurt her again. She smoothed her hand over her breast pocket, not for the last time, and imagined how she could use the card inside it.

What was it Burwardsley had said? She tried to remember as the aircraft taxied to the end of the strip, powered up and lifted into the air. The short take-off thrust Fenna back into her seat. *Toronto*, she recalled. *That's where Humble will be.* Fenna closed her eyes as Maratse fidgeted beside her. When the stewardess brought coffee, Fenna shifted her position and winced at the pain in her ribs. Maratse stared out of the window as they flew over Disco Island. Fenna tapped him on the arm and beckoned for him to lean in close.

"Vestergaard?" she said. "What happened to him?"

"Gone when I got back to the station," Maratse said.

"Where to?"

He shrugged and took a sip of coffee.

"And the dead Danes in Kulusuk?"

"Navy," he said and reached inside his jacket for a newspaper clipping. He unfolded it and presented it to Fenna. She read the headline and shook her head at the caption citing *an unfortunate boating accident* – the two men supposedly drowned when sailing in a hunter's dinghy from Kulusuk to Tasiilaq on the mainland. Fenna furrowed her brow and returned the clipping.

"Cover up," she said.

"*Iiji*," he said and stuffed the clipping inside his jacket. He sipped his coffee and then grinned.

"What?"

"Us," he said and finished his coffee. "They said it was an exercise."

"The gunfight on the ice?" Fenna said and laughed.

"*Iiji*," Maratse said and smiled. "The Chief of Police flew in from Nuuk. He said we had to be prepared to fight terrorists, even in Greenland."

"Terrorists? Really?" Fenna laughed again and felt her cheeks begin to ache.

"*The world is changing*," Maratse said. "*And Greenland with it*."

"He said that?"

"*Iiji*."

Fenna leaned back in her seat. She warmed her hands on the paper cup and sipped at the coffee. The world was indeed changing. The Arctic, and Greenland, she realised, was, now more than ever, firmly in the spotlight. It had started with global warming, when hundreds of politicians and journalists had been encouraged to visit the glaciers calving in Ilulissat, to see climate change in progress. *And then came oil*, she mused, or the promise of it. And minerals. Tourism alone will never support an independent Greenland. *And everyone wants a slice of the pie. Before it's too late.*

The plane landed to pick up more passengers in Ilulissat, before touching down at Greenland's main hub: Kangerlussuaq. Maratse escorted Fenna out of the aircraft once all the passengers were gone. She lingered by the side of Dina's casket and turned to look at Maratse. He nodded.

"I will tell Kula what you did for Dina," he said.

"It wasn't enough."

Maratse shrugged and gestured towards the exit. Fenna smoothed her hand on the casket and then turned her back on Dina, nodding at the stewardess as they climbed down the steps and onto the layer of firm snow that covered the tarmac. The dense, inland cold bit at her lungs and she thrust her hands inside the pockets of her jacket, the tips of her ears prickling as she followed Maratse to the terminal. He waited by her side as airport security processed her, presented her with a boarding pass and queried her backpack.

"Evidence," Maratse said and waited as the officer inspected the Webley.

"It will have to go in a strong box," he said. "And then someone will have to sign for it in Copenhagen."

Fenna watched the man place the Webley inside an aluminium box, a strip of yellow warning signs blazed on the lid, and a combination padlock that secured it. *What was it Bose had said? 'I know someone who would be interested in that.'Humble*, she realised and then smiled at Mikael's words, mumbled in disgust inside the tent. *'Fuck eBay.'*

"I have to go," Maratse said as Fenna was shown to a secure waiting room. He shuffled his feet and Fenna saw the awkward flicker of his eyes.

"Thank you," she said and held out her hand. Maratse ignored it and pulled Fenna into a brief hug. She caught her breath as he managed to trap her arm and squeeze her ribs in his embrace, but the tears rolling down her cheeks were not from pain. She smiled as he let her go.

"I won't forget," she said.

Maratse nodded once, turned and walked away. Fenna watched as he walked through the security door and was lost in a sea of passengers. The sense of being alone clamped her stomach and she stumbled towards the nearest seat. The dead had departed, and now the living had abandoned her. She sucked at the air through her teeth and tapped her hands on her knees. It was going to be a long flight to Denmark.

The Office

TORONTO, CANADA

Chapter 31

KASTRUP AIRPORT - COPENHAGEN, DENMARK

Fenna woke at the light touch of the flight attendant on her shoulder. The woman left her hand there as Fenna blinked and fidgeted beneath the blanket. She nodded at the attendant that she was awake and squinted out of the window at the baggage handlers moving into position alongside *Norsaq*, Air Greenland's Airbus 330. The passengers bustled out of their seats as Fenna retrieved her temporary passport – a hastily printed official document – from the sleeve of the chair in front of her. She waited until the aircraft was all but empty, unfastened her seatbelt, slid out of the seat and into the aisle. Fenna smoothed her hand around the outline of the SD card in her shirt pocket, grabbed Simonsen's police jacket from the overhead locker and made her way out of the aircraft. The cleaners had already entered the aircraft to prepare it for the following day's flight to Kangerlussuaq.

Fenna winced at the bullet wound in her leg as she worked the pins and needles out of her system, picking up the pace along the jet bridge to the terminal. She ignored the passengers waiting at the gate, barely noticing the airport luggage trolleys as she weaved her way between them. Fenna blinked at the image in her mind of Dina swinging from the rafters of the schoolhouse, and every black-haired woman in the terminal thereafter wore the Greenlander's almond death mask. Fenna stopped and pressed her hand to her forehead, her temporary passport clutched between her fingers. She looked up and searched for a toilet. Fenna pushed through a group of aircrew and burst into the ladies' restroom. The cubicles were occupied. Fenna threw up in the hand basin.

"You all right, love?" Fenna whirled around at the word, fists clenched, only to glare at the face of a middle-aged British woman. Fenna unravelled her fists and did her best to ignore her. She wiped her mouth with a paper towel and waved her hand beneath the tap to rinse the sink. Fenna scrunched the towel into the wastepaper bin and walked out of the restroom.

"Feeling better, Konstabel?" said a man standing by a vending machine.

"Who are you?" Fenna said and wiped her cheek with her hand as she studied the man in the jeans and suit jacket. He wore a graphite wool sweater beneath the jacket and, Fenna noticed, a 9mm pistol in a shoulder holster rig on the left side of his body. *Old school*, she thought and almost laughed at the observation.

"My name is Per Jarnvig," he said and waved a hand towards the nearest café. "Can I buy you a coffee? You look like you need it."

"Sure," Fenna said as she scanned the crowd of passengers. "Let's go." She folded the passport and slipped it into the inside pocket of her jacket. Jarnvig nodded at the jacket and smiled.

"Souvenir?" he said as he led Fenna to an empty table near the huge windows overlooking the runway.

"Something like that." Fenna waited for Jarnvig to order two coffees. She decided to let him talk, and waited for him to flash his badge tucked inside a leather wallet. She recognised the logo of *Politiets*

Efterretningstjeneste, the Danish Intelligence Service of the Police. "PET?" she said and sighed as the waitress returned with two black coffees.

"Yes," said Jarnvig and slipped his badge inside his jacket.

"Then you knew I was coming." Jarnvig nodded, and took a sip of coffee. "And you know everything that happened?"

"Most of it, although I am sure you can elaborate," he said and held up his hand as Fenna started to speak. "But that's not why I'm here."

"No?"

"No," he said and shook his head. "There's a lot about this case that needs investigating, and just as much that will be swept under the carpet. No," Jarnvig said and leaned back in his chair. "I'm much more interested in you."

Fenna warmed her hands around the coffee cup, turning it slowly within her fingers. She blinked an image of another coffee and another interrogation out of her mind and focused instead on Jarnvig and the man's forty-something stubble of white hair on his chin and the groomed cut of grey on his head. The butt of the 9mm peaked out of his jacket and Jarnvig adjusted his position to conceal it.

"What do you want?" she said.

"I'm just curious as to what you plan to do next," Jarnvig said and waited as Fenna turned the coffee one more revolution.

"What I really want," she said, "is a flight to Toronto."

"Canada? Are you sure that's a good idea?"

"You asked me what I want," Fenna said and looked up. "Can you get me what I want?"

"Well," Jarnvig said and leaned forwards. "That all depends on you." Fenna lifted the paper coffee cup to her lips and waited for Jarnvig to explain. The hot coffee stung her broken lips. "I need a young woman with your expertise..."

"Expertise?" Fenna said and spluttered the coffee onto the table. "You think I am an expert?"

"I could have said *experience*," Jarnvig said and wiped the coffee from the table with a napkin.

"You know what happened?"

"Like I said, I know enough," he said and dropped the wet napkin onto the floor. "Konstabel," Jarnvig continued, "you're going to have a tough time adapting to life after Greenland." He held up his hand as Fenna opened her mouth. "Hear me out," he said. "You'll need a place to stay, money, a job – I can set you up with all these things."

"And a diplomatic pouch?"

"What?"

"One of those bags they won't open at the airport."

"I know what a diplomatic pouch is."

"I'll also need a ticket to Toronto, and one more thing."

"Fenna," he said and leaned over the table. "Forget Humble. He's untouchable."

"I think he'll listen to me," she said and pressed her hand against her shirt pocket.

Jarnvig rubbed his hand across the stubble on his chin. Fenna heard the rasp of hair on his fingers as he stared at her.

"What do you want a diplomatic pouch for?"

"That's for the other thing," Fenna said and took another sip of coffee. She swallowed. "You're recruiting me, aren't you?" She smiled at Jarnvig's curt nod of the head. "Then this is the price. Plus, the other things you mentioned."

Jarnvig tapped his fingertips on the table. Clipped and filed, Fenna noticed and looked at her own broken nails and scarred fingertips. Greenland was still ingrained in the pores of her skin. *I'll carry it forever*, she realised.

"All right," he said.

Fenna almost spilled her coffee for the second time. "All right?"

"Yes," Jarnvig said and shrugged.

"You do know what I am going to do?"

"I have a pretty good idea."

"Fuck," she said as the realisation of what he wanted in return sank in.

"Fenna," he said. "There's no going back after this. I'm willing to turn a blind eye to your business in Toronto..."

"Because your *business* is much worse? Is that right, Jarnvig?"

"There's that possibility."

Fenna turned her fingers within the light from the window. Gone were the icebergs and the harsh polar light, the sting of ice splinters on the wind, and the howl of the sledge dog beneath the pitch black winter canopy of the Arctic. *But there are things to be done*, she reminded herself. *Debts to be paid*. She looked up and nodded.

"I am twenty-four," she said. "My father is dead, my mother is an alcoholic and may as well be dead, and my sister probably hates me for leaving her to cope with our mother by herself." She looked at Jarnvig and sighed. "Everyone else I ever cared for, I lost in Greenland."

"Greenland has its price," Jarnvig said and nodded. "I've heard that before."

"And so does the rest of my life," Fenna said and stood up. "I need to pee."

Jarnvig's chair squealed as he pushed back from the table and stood up. He pulled a card from his pocket and handed it to Fenna. "When you're done, go to customer service and ask them to show you to this room. I'll have the things you need, a change of clothes, luggage..."

"And the other thing," Fenna said. "The Webley. It was sent with my personal effects on the same flight – addressed *care of* Airport Authorities. I think that means you."

Jarnvig shook his head. "That's not going to be possible."

"And yet, that's the price," she said and turned to walk towards the nearest toilet. Fenna smiled as she savoured the last look on Jarnvig's face, and her own renewed sense of strength and purpose.

PEARSON INTERNATIONAL AIRPORT - TORONTO, CANADA

Fenna shrugged her backpack higher onto her shoulder and waited for the Canadian Border Services Agency officer to return with her documents. The officer's shoes whispered along the airport carpet as she approached Fenna, a clipboard and several documents in her hand.

"Miss Brongaard?"

"Yes," Fenna said, ignoring the mispronunciation of her name.

"If you'll come with me?"

"Sure." Fenna followed the woman into a tiny room. She noticed her diplomatic pouch and the new duffel bag Jarnvig had bought for her on a table in the corner. Fenna waited for the officer to close the door before sitting at the table.

Another table, another interrogation, she mused. *This seems to be my lot in life.*

"So," the officer said. "This is just a formality."

"Okay."

"All your papers are in order, and I must admit, my supervisor and I are impressed at the speed at which they were prepared."

"The Danes can be quite efficient when they want to be," Fenna said and tried a smile. She regretted it as a fresh scab on her lip began to split. She reached into her pocket and smoothed some salve from a tube onto her bottom lip.

"So we can see," the officer said. "Your first stop?"

"Is the Consulate General," said Fenna. "Here in Toronto."

"All right." The officer checked her notes and placed the clipboard onto the table. She pressed her fingers together and took a breath. "We only have one question."

"Go ahead."

"More of a concern, really."

"Yes?" Fenna said and nodded. She had a feeling she knew what was coming.

"Your appearance worries us a little," the officer said and smiled in such a way that Fenna could feel the sympathy pouring out of her. "We don't have a lot of information about you, Miss Brongaard, but, if you need any assistance," she said and gestured at

Fenna's face.

Fenna almost laughed. *My papers are in order, but they are worried if I am not?That's a first*, she mused and turned her head to look at her reflection in the glass. *Fair enough.*

"I can assure you I'm all right," she said. "It's not as bad as it looks."

"I don't know," the officer said and, testing, she added, "If my husband..."

"Husband," Fenna said and laughed. "If only." She took a breath, scratched a broken fingernail through her hair and looked at the officer. "I work for the Danish Navy. I have been on exercise and this," she said and nodded at the diplomatic pouch, "is a comfortable job they have given me while my body mends." *That sounded good – almost plausible.*

"I see," the officer said. Fenna could see that she didn't, but that her questions, for the moment at least, were satisfied. "How long are you planning to stay in Canada after you have visited the Consulate?"

"I'll be leaving tomorrow evening, on the first available flight," Fenna said. *All being well*, she thought.

"Then we're done. Thank you, Miss Brongaard." The officer stood and gestured at Fenna's luggage. "You'll find a taxi outside, unless the Consulate is sending a car?"

"A taxi will be fine," Fenna said. She walked around the desk to the table with her luggage, nodding at the weight of the diplomatic pouch as she picked it up. She slipped it inside her backpack and turned for the door.

"Your duffel bag, Miss Brongaard," the officer said. "Don't forget it."

"Right," said Fenna. She turned back for the duffel. "It's been a long flight." *Maybe I'll sleep on the return*, she wondered. *But then, that all depends on tomorrow*. Fenna thanked the woman and walked out of the room in search of a taxi.

Chapter 32

DOWNTOWN TORONTO, CANADA

The office building of Humble & Lunk was as space-age as the technology its parent company created. The huge glass plates reflected the summer sun, much like the icebergs off the coast of Greenland. Fenna pulled on her sunglasses and pressed the bridge against her nose. She shrugged the backpack onto her shoulder and climbed the marble steps in front of the building. She waited for two men and women in suits to walk out of the revolving doors before dipping her head to her chest and walking beneath the security camera and into the foyer of the lion's den. Like *The Ice Star*, the building reeked of money, all the way from the door to the mahogany reception desks and into the elevators. Fenna walked to the desk closest to her and gripped the strap of her backpack.

"I have an appointment," she said and fiddled with a lock of her hair as the receptionist checked the computer.

"Name?"

"Gregersen."

"And who are you here to see, Ms Gregersen?"

"Richard Humble," Fenna said and tapped her finger on the surface of the desk. "He is expecting me."

"Not according to his schedule," the woman said and looked up from the computer screen. "I suggest you wait while I contact his office." She pointed to the area of the foyer closest to the door, the sofas, Fenna realised, were longer than Sirius sledges.

"I'll wait," she said and turned towards the sofas. The receptionist picked up her phone and dialled through to Humble's office. Fenna heard the name *Gregersen* as she crossed the marble floor to the sofa. She sank onto the cushions and leaned back as the receptionist clicked her heels across the floor and looked down at Fenna.

"Rachael will be down to see you shortly," she said.

"Who's Rachael?"

"Mr Humble's secretary."

Fenna shifted position and pulled the backpack closer. "Is Mr Humble here today?"

"He is in the building, yes," the receptionist said and gestured at the coffee machine and water dispenser. "Please help yourself to coffee. Rachael will meet you here."

"Thank you," Fenna said and watched as the receptionist returned to her desk.

This will go one of two ways, she thought as her pulse quickened. Fenna looked around the foyer and flicked her eyes from the security man by the door to another by the elevator. *And then there's the Toronto Emergency Task Force. And everything that entails.*

But I got this far, she said to herself. *I just need to get a little further.*

The elevator door opened and Fenna turned her head to see a young woman, perhaps the same age as Fenna – chestnut hair and a flat chest. *My city double*, she laughed.

"Ms Gregersen?" the woman said as she approached. "I'm Rachael. Mr Humble's secretary."

"Mikaela," Fenna said as she stood. She shook Rachel's hand and pulled the backpack over her shoulder.

"Mr Humble was intrigued by your email,"

Rachael said as she led Fenna to the elevator. "It came quite out of the blue."

Because I wrote it last night at the hotel. Fenna pinched her thumbnails into her index fingers and nodded. "He is interested in the piece?"

"Oh, yes," Rachael said. "There are very few things that he would cancel a meeting for, but a handgun from The Great War is one of them. You're lucky he's in town. He has a flight scheduled for the afternoon. And then he will be flying on to meet his ship..."

"*The Ice Star*?"

"Yes," Rachael said and frowned as she stepped into the elevator. "You know of it?"

"In passing," Fenna said and felt the hairs on her neck rise as the elevator door whispered closed.

The security guard pressed the button for the twenty-eighth floor and clasped his hands in front of his waist. He stared at Fenna through floors two and ten until Rachael nodded that it was okay and he turned his attention to the control panel.

"You're from Europe?" she asked. "Your name, is it Norwegian?"

"Danish," said Fenna and smiled. She gestured at the control panel and said, "I thought Mr Humble would have an office on the top floor?"

"No," Rachael said and laughed. "He's always getting teased about that," she said and paused. "Mr Lunk used to say it was like going down to the basement, every time they held a meeting in Richard's office." The corners of Rachael's lips soured at the mention of Lunk's name. "Of course, after Mark's death..." At a look from the security guard, Rachael stopped talking and Fenna bit back a smile. The elevator slowed to a stop and the doors opened into a modest reception with two sofas identical to the ones in the foyer. Fenna followed Rachael through the doors and into the main office area of the twenty-eighth floor. She waited until the elevator doors had closed before opening her backpack.

"I'll just let Mr Humble know you're here," Rachael said as she walked to her desk.

"That won't be necessary," said Fenna as she pulled the Webley out of her backpack and pointed it at Rachael's head. Rachael's assistant screamed, but, to her credit, Fenna mused, Humble's receptionist stayed cool and nodded. "Which office?"

"That one," Rachael said and pointed at the double doors in the centre of the office space.

"Is he alone?"

"Yes."

"Okay," Fenna said and took a breath. "Let's do this." She nodded towards the doors and let Rachael lead the way. Fenna followed Rachael inside as she knocked and opened the door.

"Rachael," Humble said as he looked up from his desk. "And Konstabel Brongaard," he said. For a brief moment, Fenna enjoyed the lack of composure on the man's face, and then he was all business and she knew what she must do.

"Surprised?"

"Yes," he said. "I really thought you were dead." Humble leaned back in his chair. Fenna kicked the door closed. She waved the Webley at Rachael and nodded for her to stand beside Humble.

"Burwardsley finally choked on your money and had a change of heart," she said and pulled the SD card from her shirt pocket. She handed it to Rachael and nodded at the computer. "Put it in and let me show you who your boss really is."

"Fenna," Humble said as he removed his glasses and wiped them on his tie. "I see you brought the Webley."

"That's not all," she said as Rachael clicked on the folder icon on the computer to open the SD card.

"Really? You have something to show me?"

"Oh yes," Fenna said. "I remember how you like to watch." Humble paled and reached for the mouse. Rachael moved to one side only to pause at the click of the pistol's hammer as Fenna cocked it. "There's a movie file," she said. "Click on it."

"Burwardsley," Humble said and stammered. Sweat beaded on his brow and he pushed Rachael away from the computer.

"Yes," Fenna said. "Like I said, he finally got sick of your shit, just a few minutes after the woman you tortured hung herself from the rafters in the schoolhouse on that island."

"What is she talking about, Richard?" Rachael said and stepped away from the computer. Humble said nothing. He stared at Fenna as she centred the pistol on his face.

"Are you going to tell her?"

"Security has called the Emergency Task Force by now," Humble said and swallowed. "You know that?"

"I'm counting on it," Fenna said.

"In the time you've wasted on this," he said and gestured at the screen. "I could have bought the Webley and you could be safely on your way."

"This isn't about money."

"It's about the girl?"

"The girl, my partner, Oversergent..."

"Gregersen," Humble said and sighed. "I should have guessed at the name."

"You didn't know his name."

"No," Humble clicked his tongue. "You're right, I didn't."

"What about the girl? Do you remember *her* name?"

"Diana," Humble said and shrugged.

"Dina," Fenna shouted. "Her name was Dina, you fuck." Rachael backed away from the table and Fenna swung the Webley towards her. "Stay there. Open that movie file."

Rachael clicked the file and stared at the image on the screen. Her lips paled as the phone rang. Humble looked away from the screen and focused on Fenna.

"That's ETF," he said and reached for the phone.

"She answers it," Fenna said and walked to the side of the desk furthest from the window. Rachel picked up the phone. She held it to her ear, trembling as the grainy image of a woman chained to a pipe twisted on the screen, the only sound a whimper and the chatter of two men as they tore the clothes from her body with their hands. Humble flicked his eyes to the screen and back to Fenna.

"Keep watching," she said.

Stifled cries of pain wept out of the computer's speakers. The image on the screen blurred back and forth from the picture of a young woman, naked but for her own panties gagging and choking her. Tears streamed down her face, mixing with the saliva spooling out the corners of her mouth.

Rachael held out the phone and nodded at Fenna. "They want to speak to you, Richard."

Humble turned away from the screen.

"You will look, you bastard," Fenna slammed the Webley onto the table top, took two steps and gripped Humble's head between her hands, turning and pushing the lawyer until his head was a hand's width from the screen. "This is your boss, Rachael."

Rachael gasped as Dina screamed, the blurred motion of the camera focusing and refocusing on the face of the Greenlandic woman and the man penetrating her from behind, the sweating, heaving, grinning face of Richard Humble.

The metallic clack of weapons and the shuffle of feet on the other side of the door turned Fenna's head. She let go of Humble, paused the video and picked up the Webley. "Get back on the phone, Rachael." Fenna pointed the Webley at Humble's crotch. "It's time to negotiate."

"They really want to speak to Richard," Rachael said. The telephone trembled in her grasp.

"Tell them they can open the door," said Fenna.

"Wait," Humble said and looked up at Fenna. "Just wait a second."

"I'm waiting."

"Just wait. Rachael," Humble turned to his secretary. "Tell them we will be out in five minutes. She is here to negotiate," he said and turned to Fenna. "You want something in return for the video? Right?"

"Something like that," said Fenna.

"Then tell me what you want."

Fenna pointed at the image of Humble, mid-thrust, as he penetrated Dina's tied, torn and twisted body. "You can't bring her back. Can you, Richard?"

"No," Humble said and shook his head. "You know I can't."

"Oversergent Gregersen, then. Can you bring him back?"

"No."

"Then I don't know what you can give me," Fenna said and pressed the gun to Humble's head, the barrel depressing the skin beneath the lawyer's receding hairline.

"Ms Gregersen." Fenna turned at the shout from outside the office door. "We need to talk to Mr Humble."

"Your friends are impatient, that wasn't five minutes," Fenna said and lifted the Webley from Humble's forehead.

"Rachael," said Humble. "Set up a transfer of $1,000,000 to an account of the Konstabel's choice." Humble looked up at Fenna. "In return," he said, "I get all the copies of that video."

"That's what Dina's life is worth? And Mikael's? 1,000,000 Canadian dollars?"

"I can't give you their lives back, Fenna. I am buying my reputation. You know that."

"Yes, I do," Fenna said took a step back. "You pay and I walk?"

"Yes."

"Then make it $2,000,000 and you can have all the copies." Fenna turned to Rachael. "You'll find the account number in my original email with the title 'Webley'."

"There are two numbers here," she said.

"There are two families."

"And what about you, Konstabel?" said Humble. "What do you want?"

"Your assurance you won't press charges. That will be enough for me."

Humble nodded his head at the door. "You have my word," he said and reached for the mouse.

"Not for that," Fenna said as Humble closed the movie file. She took a step backwards, away from the desk. "For this," she said and pointed the Webley at Humble's crotch and fired.

Chapter 33

At the crash of the bullet and the combined scream from Humble and his secretary, Toronto's Emergency Task Force breached the door. Fenna closed her eyes and opened her mouth a second before the flash grenade rolled into the room, detonating in the centre of the office. Two ETF officers tackled Fenna to the ground, pulling the Webley from her grasp; they cuffed her and pressed her body to the floor with a knee in her spine. Two more officers assisted Rachael out of the office while a third attended to Humble's bleeding crotch. The tactical team leader stepped around Fenna. He pointed to the door with the gloved thumb of his right hand. The officers holding Fenna changed their grip and pulled her to her feet.

The team leader looked down at the medic cutting away Humble's trousers with medical shears. "How bad is he hurt?"

The medic looked up at Humble. He turned to the team leader. "The bullet has severed his penis and blown one of his testicles to mush, sir." Humble groaned.

"But he'll live?" said the team leader.

"Yes. I'll give him a shot of morphine," the medic said and looked up at Humble. "Are you allergic to morphine, sir?"

"No," Humble said and gritted his teeth. The medic pressed a needle into a phial from his pack and drew the clear liquid into the syringe. He jabbed the needle into Humble's thigh and depressed the plunger.

"Wait," said Humble. He gasped and pointed at Fenna. "Please, wait."

"What is it, sir?" the ETF team leader walked around Fenna and stood in front of Humble.

"She didn't do anything," said Humble, his chest rising and falling with rapid movements.

The team leader pointed at an ETF officer unloading and securing the Webley. "She shot you, sir. With that pistol."

"No," said Humble, his face contorted, his cheeks wet with sweat and tears. "It was an accident." He gritted his teeth and continued. "I wanted to see if it was in working order." Humble looked at Fenna. "It went off in her hands."

"You're saying she *accidentally* shot you with a loaded pistol?"

"Apparently," said Humble and took a ragged breath.

The team leader rubbed his face with his glove. "Okay, sir. Are you sure you want us to release this woman?" he said and pointed at Fenna.

"Yes," Humble said and twisted as the medic applied a large bandage over his crotch. Humble glanced at the medic's hands as he packed the wound and then averted his eyes. "I have already bought the pistol. It is mine. Ask my secretary."

"All right then, sir. We'll get you to a hospital and she..." the team leader said and shook his head. "She walks free." Fenna stared at Humble.

"Thank you, officer," said Humble.

"Ms Gregersen. If you'll come with us."

Fenna's body shook within the ETF officers' grasp as the rush of adrenalin in her body dispersed. She sagged within their grip and the men pulled her to her feet and marched her towards the door. She willed her legs to hold her as she stopped and turned to face Humble. He stared at her, biting back a spasm of pain as the medic bound his groin.

Fenna took a breath and let the men lead her from the room. The irony of being captive in the hands of men once again, was not lost on her. As they neared the door she heard Humble begin to choke. The ETF officers paused and Fenna turned as they did to see Humble start to convulse in his chair. The medic pressed his hands to Humble's shoulders and nodded for the team leader to help him.

"It must be an allergic reaction," he said.

The team leader shook his head. "But he said..."

"I know what he said." The medic's voice faltered. "Shit. We're going to lose him."

The team leader turned and waved at the men guarding Fenna. "Get her out of here," he said.

The officers pulled Fenna from the room as she twisted for one last look at Humble, his face turning a shade of blue, a stark contrast to the white froth bubbling at his mouth. The image of Humble's last minutes flickered across Fenna's mind as she was escorted into the elevator. Fenna suppressed a smile as the elevator descended to the ground floor and the men escorted her through the lobby. A cordon of police cars blocked the street and a plain clothes man met them at the door.

"Inspector Mitchell," he said and flashed his badge. "I'll take her from here. RCMP," he said when the ETF officers frowned at him.

"We have our orders," said the senior officer.

"And so do I," Mitchell said. "Now, we can wait for your team leader if you want, and then *he* can explain to the Danish Consular General why ETF has a Danish national in custody. Or," he said and slipped his badge into his pocket, "I can get the ball rolling and let your team leader deal with the other pressing matter – the death of a prominent Canadian lawyer on his watch." Fenna felt the officers relax their grip on her arms. "It's all over the radio," Mitchell said.

"Take her then," the senior officer said and shoved Fenna towards Mitchell.

"Wise choice," he said and pulled Fenna down the steps of the building towards a black SUV parked on the curb. He opened the passenger door and pushed Fenna inside. She watched as he jogged around the hood of the SUV, opened the door and climbed behind the wheel.

"RCMP?" Fenna said, as Mitchell pulled away from the curb and drove around the police cordon. She realised the motor had been running the whole time.

"Not exactly," he said and manoeuvred into traffic. He leaned across Fenna and opened the glove compartment. "There's some keys to your cuffs in there."

Fenna lifted the user's manual. She found the keys next to a phial of morphine. Fenna smiled as she slipped the keys into her hand. She fiddled with the cuffs as Mitchell stopped at a red light.

"There's a phial of morphine in the glove compartment," she said.

Mitchell glanced at her and then turned back to study the road ahead. He shrugged. "A mutual friend sends his regards," he said, "and requests that you get the fuck back to Denmark as soon as possible."

"Jarnvig," Fenna said and unlocked the cuffs. She tossed them into the glove compartment, took one last look at the morphine and closed the lid. "I should have guessed."

"Yes, and you should have maybe thought too."

"Meaning?"

"We've had our eye on Humble for a while. Did you really think he would let you live considering everything you know?"

"You mean the video?"

"Fuck, Brongaard," Mitchell said and accelerated as the light changed. "The video? Really? How about espionage and government-sanctioned acts of terror." Mitchell sighed as he turned, following the signs for the airport. "Humble had to go, one way or the other. But you tipped our hand, and we had to act. Hell, my cover is blown, that's for sure. I'll be recalled to Denmark any day now." Mitchell paused to glance at Fenna. He stuck out his hand. "Nicklas Fischer," he said.

"Is that your real name?"

"For the moment, yes."

"And you work for Jarnvig?"

"Let's just say we know each other and leave it at that."

The traffic on the highway was steady all the way to the airport. Jarnvig's man escorted Fenna through security and all the way to the boarding gate.

"Good luck, Konstabel," he said and walked away. Fenna watched him leave.

She found a seat close to the gate and waited, replaying the scene of Humble's death. The beginnings of a smile tickled the corners of her mouth. Fenna bit her lip to suppress a giggle. It was done. No more games. He was dead. The bastard was dead.

The Beach

BLÅVAND, DENMARK

Chapter 34

BLÅVAND BEACH, DENMARK

The sand dusted across the beach, settling on Fenna's jeans and filling her pockets. She picked up the dismembered pincer of a crab, pressed the tips of her fingers against the spines and lifted it to her nose to sniff at the meat rotting inside the claw. It smelled of the sea. It took her back to the summer ice-free waters of Greenland, on a rocky beach just down from the dog yard at Daneborg. A Labrador splashed into the surf in front of her, its owner apologising as Fenna brushed at the spots of salt water staining her jeans.

"It's not a problem," she said and wished the man a good day as she watched him hurl a tennis ball into the sea. The Labrador splashed after it, and Fenna smiled; her first of the day.

Once the dog and its owner had retreated along the beach and out of sight, she dug her hands into the sand and hid them there, feeling the cool sand beneath her palms, and the brush of the grains on the backs of her hands. She wriggled her toes into the sand and closed her eyes. She filtered out the chatter of the tourists on the beach, the flap and flutter of kites, focusing instead on the crash of the waves as they spilled onto the long, broad beach of Denmark's west coast.

She felt the soft tremor of city shoes in the sand before she heard the man's approach. Fenna had an idea of who it might be and opened her eyes, blinking at Per Jarnvig's face as he stared down at her.

"Konstabel," he said. "All well?"

"Yes," Fenna said and dug her fingers and toes

deeper into the sand, like tiny anchors.

"Still wearing the policeman's jacket, I see," he said. "Having difficulty letting go?"

"Yes."

"Good."

Jarnvig made a show of enjoying the sea air, smiling at a group of Germans as they walked past, the tiny dog at their heels paused to investigate what Fenna had buried in the sand. It scurried away as the children in the group called to the puppy.

"How's the house?" Jarnvig said when they were alone.

"It's nice," Fenna said and glanced over her shoulder at the beach house tucked behind the dunes. The tiles of the roof glittered in the sun. "Bit posh for a Sirius girl," she said.

"Hmm. About that." Jarnvig turned his head in the direction of the lighthouse to the north of where Fenna sat. "Walk with me," he said.

Fenna dusted the sand from her hands. She curled her fingers into the ankle loops of her boots and carried them, one in each hand, as she walked alongside Jarnvig.

"You've stopped limping then. How are your ribs?"

"They're fine. I'm fine."

"Physically, yes, I'm sure you are. But how are you really doing?"

"Do you care?" Fenna asked and double-stepped to avoid a sharp swathe of shells beneath her feet.

"Actually," Jarnvig said and lifted the manila folder he carried in his left hand. Fenna hadn't noticed it. "Your mental well-being is more important to me than the shape your body is in." Fenna laughed.

"You stirred the pot in Canada, Fenna," he continued. "But you also sent a message. The Canadian Security Intelligence Service will never recognise any association with Richard Humble, nor will they admit to knowing anything about covert operations in Greenland. You understand this, don't you?"

Fenna nodded, biting her lip at the mention of Humble.

"What happened in Toronto," he said and paused. "Let's just say we gained some ground and lost some. Fischer has been recalled, but Humble has been neutralised. I mention this freely as you and I have an agreement, Konstabel. You work for me now." Jarnvig lifted the folder in his hand and used it to point to the path between the dunes that led to the beach house.

Fenna followed his lead and felt the itch of the straw and grass beneath her feet, laid along the surface of the path to protect the dunes. They didn't speak until they reached the house. Jarnvig waited for Fenna to unlock the door, brush her feet on the mat and invite him inside. He placed the folder on the table as Fenna filled the coffee machine with water.

"What about my rank?" she asked as she heaped coffee grounds into the filter paper. The machine beeped as she turned it on.

"You'll keep your rank," Jarnvig said and sat down at the table. "But it will be more of a codename, than a title," he said.

"A bit like *The Magician*," she said.

"He's not your concern, Konstabel."

"No?"

"No," Jarnvig said and gestured for Fenna to sit

at the table. The chair legs squeaked across the tiles as she pulled it out and sat down.

"Whose *concern* will he be?" she said and tried to look Jarnvig in the eye. He was good at avoiding eye contact, she realised and gave up.

"We will deal with him if and when he turns up, not before."

"Then what do I do in the meantime?" Fenna said and reached for the folder.

"You," Jarnvig said and pushed the folder towards her, "are going back to school."

"University?" she said and frowned.

"Not that kind of school."

Fenna opened the folder and skimmed the first page.

"Tradecraft?" she said and looked up.

"It's jargon for communication skills and the practical application of..."

"Explosives?" Fenna said and tapped her finger on the page.

"That too. Yes."

"I thought I was going to be trained as an investigator?"

"You are," Jarnvig said and smiled. "But I like my investigators to be able to act, when the occasion calls for it." He let Fenna read and stood up to get two mugs from the kitchen. He poured them both a coffee and returned to the table.

"Your Arctic skills and knowledge of Greenland are invaluable, Fenna. That will be your area of operations, and your focus. But your training," he said and paused to take a sip of coffee. "Let's just say, there are things you can get away with in the desert that we just can't do here in Denmark."

"You're sending me to the Middle East?" Fenna said and looked up.

"Almost," he said. "Konstabel, I am sending you to Arizona."

Fenna closed the folder and leaned back in her chair. The sun glittered through the blinds and she squinted in the glare. *Arizona? That's a long way from Greenland.*

"One more thing," Jarnvig said. "Do you speak Chinese?"

"No," Fenna said and laughed. She studied Jarnvig's face and stopped laughing. "Not yet, I guess."

"Good," he said and stood up. Jarnvig picked up the folder, tapped it once on the table to settle the papers and slipped it under his arm. "You leave on Tuesday. I'll have someone pick you up and bring you some more suitable clothing."

"So there's a mission or an assignment?" she said and looked up at Jarnvig.

"Your assignment is to get top marks at school. Your mission, well," he paused, "there's something I want you to investigate."

"Where?"

Jarnvig smiled and said, "Somewhere north. In the shadow of a mountain."

A GREENLANDIC GLOSSARY

The characters of Maratse, Kula, and Dina in *The Ice Star* are from the east coast of Greenland. East Greenlandic is a dialect of Greenlandic. There is, to date, no real written record of the language and children in East Greenland are required to learn West Greenlandic. For Dina to learn English, she would have had to learn West Greenlandic, then Danish and English as her fourth language. There are no foreign language dictionaries translating East Greenlandic words to English. English is predominantly taught through Danish, with all explanations and points of grammar written in Danish. Dina, however, is unremarkable in the sense that many East Greenlanders learn English, and work in the tourist industry. But it is far from easy.

Here is a very brief glossary of the few East Greenlandic words used in *The Ice Star*, and the English equivalents.

East Greenlandic/English

iiji / yes

eeqqi / no

qujanaq/ qujanaraali / thank you

iserniaa / come in

ACKNOWLEDGEMENTS

The Ice Star has had a lot of help over the years since I first started writing it. It began life in 2013 as a project for my Master of Arts in Professional Writing at Falmouth University, England. A number of my peers critiqued the first few incarnations of the manuscript, and I would like to thank Ramon James and Erik Poirier for their "gloves off" feedback. Sarah Acton knows more about *The Ice Star* than I do, and has contributed to the development of many aspects, not least the main character. Isabel Dennis-Muir, also from the MA, has provided invaluable editing skills and feedback on the later drafts of the manuscript. Of the different supervisors involved in the project, I would like to thank Tom Bromley who saw the project through to its completion, with lots of valuable feedback and plot revisions along the way.

Research was a vital part of the project, and I would like to thank SIRIUS Sledge Patrolman Per Jessen, and Anders Kjærgaard, leader of the SIRIUS Sledge Patrol (2015-16), for their patience and insight. Both Per and Anders helped give the manuscript the authenticity I was looking for. However, I take full responsibility for all deviations from standard operating procedure and the dramatic license I have taken with the story. It is a thriller after all.

I spent seven years in Greenland – four on the island of Uummannaq, and my seventh year in the capital of Nuuk. I met many exceptional Greenlanders, professionals, and friends, but I would particularly like to thank Akisooq Vestergaard-Jessen for year six in Qaanaaq, and Stephen Pax Leonard, a Brit from the Scott Polar Research Institute, studying the Qaanaaq dialect, for year five. I must also thank Jes Lynning Harfeld for introducing me to a whole new world aboard a very special ship.

I had a sledge team of my own while living in Uummannaq, much to the amusement of my Greenlandic neighbours. While they will never know, it makes sense to thank the members of my own dog team: Kassassuk, Vitus, Trip, Piska, Simba, Hidalgo, Balto, Ninja, and Nansen. They taught me more than I could ever learn from a book, and I would like to think that by year three, we could finally call ourselves a team.

And to my wife, Jane Petersen – thank you.

A lot of people contributed to *The Ice Star*, but the mistakes and inaccuracies are all my own.

Chris

January 2017
Denmark

ABOUT THE AUTHOR

Christoffer Petersen is the pen name for an author living in Denmark. Chris started writing *The Greenland Trilogy* while teaching in Qaanaaq, the largest village in the very north of Greenland - the population peaked at 600 during the two years he lived there. He spent a total of seven years in Greenland. Chris continues to be inspired by the vast icy wilderness of Arctic and his books have a common setting in the region, with a Scandinavian influence. He has also watched enough Bourne movies to no longer be surprised by the plot, but not enough to get bored.

You can find Chris in Denmark or online here:

www.christoffer-petersen.com

BY THE SAME AUTHOR

THE GREENLAND TRILOGY
featuring Konstabel Fenna Brongaard

THE ICE STAR
IN THE SHADOW OF THE MOUNTAIN
THE SHAMAN'S HOUSE

GREENLAND CRIME BOOKS
featuring Constable David Maratse
and Sergeant Petra "Piitalaat" Jensen

SEVEN GRAVES, ONE WINTER
BLOOD FLOE
FERAL

GREENLAND CRIME STORIES
featuring Constable David Maratse

Series I
KATABATIC
CONTAINER
TUPILAQ
THE LAST FLIGHT
collected as
GREENLAND CRIME STORIES

Series II
THE HEART THAT WAS A WILD GARDEN
QIVITTOQ
THE THUNDER SPIRITS
ILULIAQ

THE GREENLAND TRAGEDIES

BLACK CROWBERRY

THE SIRIUS SLEDGE PATROL
featuring Oversergent Mikael Gregersen

PITERAQ

POLARPOL
featuring Constable Hákon Sigurdsson

NORTHERN LIGHT
MOUNTAIN GHOST
WINTER BOUNTY